Conjoined at the Soul

Seasons of Chadham High, Book Two

Huston Piner

Randy Clark has just looked in the mirror and figured out he's gay. So now, all he needs is a boyfriend, and finding one should be easy enough, right? The trouble is Randy has a knack for being attracted to the wrong kind of guy, like the one who hasn't spoken to him since he told him he had pretty eyes. Then there's that locker-room jock who's always putting him down. And new student Kerry Sawyer would be perfect—except for that girlfriend he left behind.

Obviously, when it comes to finding a boyfriend, Randy's got a lot to learn. So for dating tips, he turns to friends Jeremy Smith and Annie Brock. But although Annie's more than willing to help him find the right guy, between his own bad luck and her less than helpful advice (date a girl?), things are getting out of control fast. And while Randy struggles with bullies, bigotry, and his own self-doubts, he quickly finds that searching for love can be pitted with embarrassing misunderstandings, humiliating encounters, and hilarious missteps.

All in all, Randy's sophomore year is shaping up to be one to remember—if he can just live through it.

A NineStar Press Publication

Published by NineStar Press
P.O. Box 91792,
Albuquerque, New Mexico, 87199 USA.
www.ninestarpress.com

Conjoined at the Soul

Edited by Elizabetta McKay

Printed in the USA
SunFire Imprint
First Edition
February, 2018

Print ISBN: 978-1-948608-03-9

Also available in eBook, ISBN: 978-1-948608-02-2

Warning: This book contains sexually explicit content, which may only be suitable for mature readers, and depictions of bullying, homophobia, bigotry, and hate crimes.

To friends new and old, near and far, gone and yet to be revealed, and to the other one who stood at the corner of Gay and Mayo.

Acknowledgements

Thanks to Raevyn, Elizabetta, and Natasha, three of the most wonderful people I've ever encountered, whose encouragement and conviction are inspirational.

What is a friend? A single soul dwelling in two bodies.

~Aristotle

Chapter 1: Of Mirrors and Locker Rooms

SEPTEMBER 17, 1979

Today is a day of historic importance. See, I woke up this morning and discovered I'm gay.

I was brushing my teeth, and when I spit out and looked in the mirror, a pointy-nosed, sixteen-year-old with unruly blond hair stared back at me and said, "You, young man, are gay."

I know I know I know, it's not quite that simple. I didn't just go to bed last night as the straight Randy Clark only to have the gay pixie come and sprinkle fairy dust all over me in my sleep. The truth is, it's something I've kind of seen coming for a couple of years now. It's like a process: one day you start adding up all the times you've caught yourself looking at guys or couldn't stop thinking about a particular boy, and it just hits you—you're gay.

It's a lot to take in.

Luckily, I have the ride to school to think about it. When the bus stops, I check the time, and it's running late...again. *Three minutes* late.

I hate being late.

My best friend, Blake, stumbles on board like a zombie. His head's drooping, and his shoulders are slumped forward. Yup, it was obviously another late night for Blake Rogers.

I flash him my most saccharine smile and say "Good morning" with my most sarcastic cheeriness.

"Mumm-ning, Randy." He yawns and is already dozing before his butt even hits the seat next to me. And with that, it's guaranteed to be a quiet, peaceful ride the rest of the way.

It's funny, but now that I've admitted I'm gay, I'm more at peace with myself than I've ever been in my whole life. It feels natural. But it's kind of scary too. I mean, being gay isn't exactly the kind of thing you can just announce to the world. Some people would instantly hate you and tell you so, while others would express their opinion with a few well-chosen punches—and I get more than my share of those already. It's enough to make a guy a little nervous.

And then there's the problem—the real problem. Something's missing in my life—something important, something *very* important. See, a straight guy can look forward to the possibility of getting married, but what about me? Is there someone out there waiting for me? I mean, sure, friends are important in life, but they're not enough. What I need is a boyfriend, *my own special someone* to turn me on and send me into sexual orbit. That's what it's all about, right?

Blake starts snoring. I elbow him in the side and shake my head. He grumbles, but at least he stops snoring. The guy sitting across the aisle from us snickers.

Blake may be my best friend, but he won't be the first person I tell I'm gay. It's not that he'd stop being my friend or anything, it's just that it's more urgent for me to find someone I can go to for advice about guys first. Blake likes girls way too much to be of any help on that issue.

For that job, I know exactly who I need: Annie Brock and Jeremy Smith. They're in my art class. If there are any two people on earth who will be able to help me find a boyfriend, it's Annie and Jeremy.

I'VE FINALLY MADE it to fifth period after surviving a typically boring morning, and whatever it was they served for lunch. (They called it spaghetti, but I swear it was wiggling.)

Art. It's my favorite class, and unlike some of my others, I'm very good at it. I've got artistic flair. Our teacher, Mrs. Pilt, is the stereotypical art teacher. She wears smocks of various patterns and colors, and they're always stained with smears of paint.

The art room reeks of pottery clay, glue, and God knows what else. The walls are lined with shelves and paintings, and there are weird mobiles hanging like Picasso spiders from the ceiling. It's always noisy, and the radio constantly blasts out the Bee Gees, Dire Straits, and The B-52's, with a little Chic thrown in for good measure. There are a number of rectangular tables here and there with up to six people at each. Annie, Jeremy, and I sit at the table closest to Mrs. Pilt's desk. We're her favorite students.

The great thing about art class is, as long as you stay on task, Mrs. Pilt lets you chat with the people around you. At our table, Annie does most of the talking. I get in a few words every now and then, and Jeremy rarely speaks at all.

We're starting a new project, and for the moment, even Annie's quiet while we all consider the charcoal and paper before us. If I'm going to tell them I'm gay and enlist their help, now is my best chance. I'd better act fast.

I open my mouth, but suddenly a lump forms in my throat. I take a deep breath and try again, but my stomach flutters.

What's wrong with me? Why am I so nervous all of a sudden? Maybe if I ease into the subject?

I clear my throat. "Did you see Andy Gibb on TV this weekend? He's good-looking." I manage to say it without stammering.

Annie pulls at a lock of wiry black hair and grunts out one of her peculiar snickers. "Honey, *good-looking* doesn't even *begin* to describe Andy Gibb."

Annie's laugh is kind of a cross between a giggle and the sound some people make when they're blowing their noses. Like Annie herself, it's unique. She's outspoken and outlandish, and she doesn't care who knows it. And she's definitely got more than her quota of artistic flair. It extends right down to the clothes she wears. For example, today she has on a tangerine and lime-colored disco party dress with three-inch-high clogs.

"Yeah, I really like Andy Gibb," I say.

Without looking up, Jeremy says, "He's okay. What other singers do you like, Randy?"

One of the nice things about Jeremy is he's not only quiet, he gets along with everybody—except for that low-rumble, love-hate thing he and Annie have going on. It's okay though, because in the three years I've known them, they always sit together, and they look out for each other, despite constantly bickering.

"Well, on the male side, I guess I'd have to say Rod Stewart. That Georgie song was just so moving."

"The one about the gay guy?" Jeremy mumbles, and Annie starts to snicker.

"Yeah, I'm gay."

So much for easing into the subject.

Annie freezes in mid-snort. Jeremy looks up without raising his head.

"Of course you're gay, sugar," Annie says with a chuckle. "But you don't have to say it so loud."

I quickly look around, my cheeks burning, but none of the other students are paying us any attention.

Annie's smile softens. "Now, don't be embarrassed. I just mean I've had my suspicions about you for a while. You dress too well, and you're always combing your hair. And you even like the Village People."

"So what? Lots of people like the Village People. What's that got to do with anything?"

Annie stares at me. "Randy, you do know they're all gay, don't you? I mean, you do know what "Y.M.C.A." is all about?"

"It's about working out at the Y.M.C.A., of course."

"It's about *hanging out* with all the *boys*. You get it now?"

Jeremy slowly shakes his head and rolls his eyes.

It's painfully obvious that Annie knows a lot more about the gay world than I do. I've got a lot to learn. And being the generous, take-charge person she is, Annie's more than ready to take on the mission of teaching me, as well as helping me find a boyfriend. She immediately launches into what promises to be the first of several lessons, beginning with how to spot a gay guy.

"Now there are some basic things you need to look for. Like if he talks kind of girly, or sort of walks like a girl, it might mean he's gay."

"I don't talk girly, do I?" I squeak in alarm.

"No, sugar, you don't talk girly," she says and preemptively adds, "*and* you don't walk girly either."

"And that doesn't prove anything anyway," Jeremy mutters, scratching his nose and leaving a dark charcoal smudge. (He's always talked kind of girly himself.)

"I said it *might* mean he's gay, not *proves* it," Annie snaps. She looks at Jeremy, points to her nose, and he tries to wipe the smudge off his own.

"I don't get it," I say.

"It's part of the overall assessment you need to make before you stick your...uh...neck out."

Jeremy sighs. "About as subtle as a wet tongue in the ear."

Annie continues, totally ignoring him, "Another important thing is the look."

"You mean, is he good-looking?"

"No, sugar. How he *looks* at you. Like, do his eyes linger on you? Haven't you ever been in a room full of people and seen somebody you thought was really attractive?"

"Yeah."

"Okay, well, I bet you looked at him a bit longer than you did the other people in the room. Maybe you even kept coming back to look at him again."

"Yeah, I guess so."

"So if a guy looks at you like that, it may mean he thinks you're attractive. Which would mean...?"

"He's gay," I reply like a first grader just realizing two plus two equals four.

By the end of class, we've covered a lot of ground, but I'm pretty sure I've got the main point. It's all in the eyes. *Eye contact and a lingering glance are the keys to identifying a gay guy.*

No problem.

This is going to be so easy.

BUT AFTER ART, I go to the one place where eye contact means something completely different than finding a guy attractive. A high school locker room.

In a locker room, guys *always* look each other straight in the eye, or try to. See, in any group of teenage males, the first one caught looking at another guy *down there* automatically becomes the target for putdowns, threats, insults, and the occasional punch. It's like a tradition, and believe me, it's something you want to avoid. And avoiding it is not always easy—for me, anyway. I guess it comes with the territory when you're gay, but towels provocatively rubbing against firm flesh are just hard to ignore. No matter which way I turn, a parade of legs, butts, and crotches all flex, wiggle, and bounce in front of me. The musty, sweaty boy-smell doesn't help matters much either.

It's not fair. And it's not like I'm the only guy in history to ever get a hard-on in a high school locker room. For a lot of guys it's a natural reaction to the cool moist air. But the trouble is, around certain guys, I'm *radically* reactionary. Like my eyes drift over to Rick Payton, and while I'm admiring his silky black hair, my body just reacts. Billy Mason and Jeff Gray also make my skin tingle. And whenever I see Jamie Becker changing—Oh God.

Don't get me wrong. It's not like I drool or anything. And over time, I've learned to focus my thoughts elsewhere with Buddha-like concentration. But back in August, on that first day of gym class, before I could get focused, too many guys noticed my natural reaction.

It's a month later, and I'm still working to live it down.

"Hey, faggot," Bradley Romero says with a smirk, "like what you see?" He shakes himself at me to a chorus of snickers.

Jamie chuckles. "Now don't be so *hard* on him, Brad. You don't want him to jump you. Remember, his name *is* Randy."

I throw my clothes into my locker and turn back to face them.

"Jamie, it always amazes me how you can talk so clearly with Brad's dick in your mouth."

Without running—that would look too much like defeat—I dash out the door while shouted threats, insults, and laughter echo behind me.

Brad and Jamie call me a faggot nearly every day. I'm used to it. They're just frustrated because they want the girls to think they're jocks, and I'm better at a lot of things in PE than they are—which isn't really saying that much. But if they knew I really am gay, they'd make my life a living hell. As it is, I'm on safe ground as long as I keep making crude comebacks.

By the way, I always direct my comebacks at Jamie. It appeals to Brad's sense of superiority, and it embarrasses Jamie. And he just looks so cute when he's blushing.

Ah, Jamie—if only he could be my special someone. Back in the seventh grade, we were playing kickball one day, and I remember watching Jamie sliding into home. Even then, he was tall for his age. He was tanned, and something about his legs gave me a tingly sensation that just did it for me. At the time, I didn't really know what *it* was, but I couldn't stop looking at him and just wanted to be near him.

Today, when we all get inside the gym, Coach Horne announces we're going to play dodge ball, which he says will help us hone our reflexes. In reality, it just confirms my theory that he's a sadist. I mean, it's bad enough that I have to be careful in the locker room every day. It's worse when I have to watch out for both Brad *and* Roderick "Ramrod" Fuller aiming a ball at me as well.

Of course, I'm the first one to get hit. Billy Mason's long, muscular legs distract me. Ramrod notices I'm not looking in his direction, and the next thing I know, I'm limping off the court, doubled over in nut-crunching pain. The coach gives Ramrod a five-minute timeout and tells me to hit the showers while I recover.

Actually, by the time I get to the locker room, the pain in my groin isn't that bad anymore. But there's absolutely no way I'm going back in that gym when I've got a great excuse to shower off in peace.

After stripping down, I walk into the shower room and freeze. There before me is the hottest body to ever stand only five foot six. It's Gene Murphy, a senior with big, light brown eyes and long sexy lashes. Shampoo is streaming over his broad shoulders and sliding down a muscular but not chiseled chest. My gaze involuntarily slides down with it, and *Oh my God.* My jaw drops.

In less than five seconds, I go from still being in pain, to tingling all over, to rock hard. It's like I've just been turned to stone.

I've had a thing for Gene since last year. One day, an upperclassman called me a faggot while shoving me out of his way, and as I stumbled into a wall, I came face-to-face with Gene. He grinned at me, while I turned so red I must have looked sunburned. It was a case of pure lust at first sight. I didn't even know his name until I spent a half hour looking him up in my yearbook. From then on, my eyes have been glued to him every time I see him.

"Hi," he says, bringing me out of my trance.

Oh God. I've been standing there staring at him—well, *it* really—for God knows how long, with only a bar of soap to cover me.

I quickly look away and turn on the water.

"I said hi."

"Hey," I say, desperately trying to will down my hard-on.

But when I finally get up the nerve to look back at him, I catch sight of those big, pretty eyes staring right at me, and it's like being charmed by a cobra.

"What's your name?"

"Uh, Randy. Randy Clark."

"Hi, Randy. I'm Gene Murphy. What grade are you in?"

It takes me a second to remember.

"Uh, t-tenth grade."

"Got your license yet?"

"I, uh, no. Not yet. I'll be going in for try number three next week."

He tilts his head to one side and says, "Don't feel so bad. I was surprised I passed on my second try. I'm sure you'll do fine this time."

My other natural reaction is blushing. Even the littlest thing can bring it on. And what again draws my attention before I can look away isn't very little at all.

Gene breaks into a devilish grin. "You're looking at me, and I think we both know why."

I couldn't blush any harder. Here I am, naked, with a hard-on that could break rocks, staring at him, and he's not only caught me looking *down there*, he's calling me out about it.

Without warning, he tosses his shampoo my way. Somehow, I catch it, dropping my bar of soap in the process.

"Go ahead," he says. "Use as much as you need. You'll like it."

Almost unconsciously, I pour some in my hand, and toss the bottle back to him. The shampoo has a light, enticing aroma. I rub it into my hair, and it lathers instantly. At last, I'm able to take my eyes off him. But the shampoo is sliding down my back and around my butt, and it just makes me more aware of being naked in front of him.

I do my best to invoke my Buddha focus, and by the time I rinse off, I'm partly successful. Of course, it helps that by then, Gene has already left the shower. But when I walk into the locker room and find him still there, dressing, it's like I haven't even been trying. Mercifully, he either doesn't notice my condition or pretends not to.

He keeps the conversation going while I stumble around trying to dry off. It turns out we don't have a lot in common, but I pretend to like a few of the things he mentions—anything to keep those eyes aimed my way. I'm so mesmerized by them I end up just sitting there with the towel draped over my lap, hoping he won't notice the tent.

"So, are you dating anybody?"

"No," I say, and hesitate before adding, "not at the moment. You?"

"Me? No, my girlfriend broke up with me."

"She didn't deserve you," I mumble in spite of myself. He breaks into a soft smile and keeps me locked in eye contact while my cheeks burn and I become even more conscious of the tent in my lap.

After he's finished getting dressed, he sits down close to me to tie his shoes. The more he shines those beautiful eyes on me, the more I'm attracted to him. And even though he's just mentioned a girlfriend—well, ex-girlfriend—I get the feeling he might be attracted to me.

I keep telling myself *It's just my imagination*. But I don't believe it.

"Well," he says, "it was nice talking to you, Randy. I hope we get a chance to do it again. You seem like a real cool guy."

Then he reaches over and gives my knee a squeeze before standing up to leave. It's nothing more than a friendly gesture, but it goes all over me. He walks out, leaving me blushing, and dripping.

When the guys come back in, I've only just barely calmed myself down. While they shower and change, I wait for the bell in the hallway. The lingering smell of Gene's shampoo flirts with my nose, and I keep reliving the memory of the two of us naked in the shower room.

Gene Murphy is now at the top of my boyfriend wish list.

THE BUS STOPS, and Blake disappears out the door. Time to stretch out again. I'm on my own for the rest of the ride.

My eyes drift over to Theo Hayes. I can't help it. He's on the baseball team this year, and he's really developing that hot, young athlete look—you know, super fit with an air of innocent cuteness.

I've only been looking at him for a second or two when he sees me and scowls. I quickly look away.

Theo hates me, and I've got no one to blame but myself. See, I've got this bad habit of letting my imagination run away with me. I start daydreaming, and the next thing I know, I've said or done something stupid.

Theo's the perfect example.

One day last spring, we were chatting in the courtyard outside the lunchroom, and I slipped up and made a fool of myself.

I found myself staring at him, and I said, "You're lucky."

"Yeah? Why am I lucky?"

"Because you've got good skin and the most beautiful dark green eyes I've ever seen in my life."

Let's just say we're not on speaking terms anymore. It's a shame, because not only is Theo hot, but up until then, we'd been getting to be good friends.

The bus stops, and I walk the half block to my house. Home sweet home. The Clark family is a by-the-book picture of domestic bliss. There's me, my parents, and my little brother. But don't expect a lot of hugs and kisses in this house.

My mom's happy enough—as long as I fit in and don't do anything weird to embarrass her socially. Dad, on the other hand, is never happy. And he's never forgiven me for that time in seventh grade when I slipped up and said I thought Jamie was cute. Around the house, he's like a drill sergeant, and as far as he's concerned, I'm Private Snafu. Sometimes, I think he goes out of his way looking for opportunities to humiliate me. And when he's not railing about the Blacks, it's the Mexicans, or it's the Asians, you name it. And the worst part is he's even been known to do it in public. Really, it's so embarrassing.

And then there's my brother Wally. He's four years younger than me, and he's the classic younger brother—you know, a turd. "The Turd" is kind of like that old nursery rhyme about snails and puppy dog tails. He's got the intelligence of a slug, and he's about as well house-broken as a Chihuahua. Unfortunately, he's also following right in Dad's footsteps, and he's so prejudiced he makes Archie Bunker look like Iggy Pop.

As soon as I get inside, I sneak upstairs to my room, close the door behind me, and hear that satisfying *click* when I turn the lock. My room is my private sanctuary from the world and all its troubles. I used to have to share a room with The Turd. But when I turned fourteen, my parents gave in and let me have the guest bedroom. It was either do that or face the fact that sooner or later one of their children was going to kill the other.

I drop my book bag, flop onto the bed, and switch on the record player. The sound of Kansas kicking out "People of the South Wind" fills the room, and I start daydreaming. It's time to choose an object for my daily exercise in adolescent lust.

Ah, memories. I've got like a mental catalogue of images to choose from. Okay, even though I always use my Buddha focus in the locker room and showers, I *am* an artist, and appreciating the human form is a sign of the artistic temperament. I mean, Michelangelo had to have *some* familiarity with the human form to sculpt his *David*. And let's face it—*David* is one good-looking statue.

Today, I don't even need to open my mental catalogue. After that shower in PE, Gene is the perfect choice to inspire my artistic temperament. I see myself rubbing my hands all over him and imagine him kissing me. It's amazing what a little inspiration can stimulate in a guy. I bet he'd make the perfect boyfriend.

Twenty-three minutes and some minor clean up later, I'm again ready to face anything the world can throw at me—even Wally The Turd.

Chapter 2: Blake versus Gene

OVER THE LAST week and a half, I've spent a lot of time checking out guys for signs of that eye contact thing Annie taught me about. But so far, the only one who's given me any significant eye contact has been Gene—which, mind you, isn't necessarily a bad thing. Since our little locker room encounter, I keep running into him in the hall, and whenever he sees me, he goes out of his way to say hello. A couple of times, he's even stopped to chat.

It's kind of confusing though; he talks about girls a lot, but I've caught him checking me out *down there* a couple of times. Of course, he's caught me checking *him* out too, and my glowing cheeks left little doubt why I was doing it. The thing is, every time he catches me, he just grins. There's definitely something going on between us, but I'm not sure what. When I'm with him, it's like he hypnotizes me until all I can do is blush—well, blush and...you know.

In art class today, we're continuing work on our charcoal projects. Annie's chattering on about Gwen and Jacob. Gwen is a friend of hers, and Jake's the guy Gwen's just started dating. Annie hasn't liked him since he said something about the Klan in her history class. I never quite found out what he said, but apparently, Annie really lost it. I did ask her about it, but she just grumbled something about her uncle, and wouldn't say anything more.

"Jacob Wilson." She spits out the name like it reminds her of cod-liver oil. "I said, 'Girl, you can do so much better. He's an asshole, and if his snotty, preppy friends don't approve of you, he'll drop you like a hot potato.' I'm telling you, that boy is just plain ugly."

She pauses to stare down Mike Kowalski, who's getting a new charcoal from Mrs. Pilt.

"Oh, I don't know," I interject, "Jake's okay. At least I haven't seen too many mirrors crack when he passes them."

"Well, he may not look it," she counters, "but trust me, he's ugly, *and* he's an asshole. He dumped Stephanie Brigham with no more thought than stepping on a cockroach. If Gwen had any self-esteem at all, she'd set her sights higher. I mean, Christ Oh-Mighty! Even *Ramrod*'s got more class than that boy."

"I'm not so sure about that," I say. "Ramrod takes being an asshole to a whole other dimension. In some universes, he'd be the ideal asshole all the other assholes study to learn how."

Annie snorts out a snicker and continues rubbing the charcoal on her paper into delicate shades and shadows. For a rare few seconds, our table falls silent. Jeremy sighs and makes graceful marks on his page. He's got a charcoal smudge on his nose again, and there's another one on his ear, but I'm too busy thinking about that last encounter I had with Gene just before class to point them out.

Suddenly, Annie's head jerks up. Mike is staring at her again from his table across the room. She sticks out her tongue. He blushes and ducks back down to his project.

It's been obvious for a few weeks now that Mike likes Annie. It could even be that Annie likes Mike, but every time he tries to speak to her, she cuts him off. And then there are those little public displays of affection she always sends his way, like that last one. If it's a courtship, it's definitely a strange one. But then again, this *is* Annie Brock we're talking about.

While she's busy giving Mike the evil eye, I take advantage of the break.

"Hey, what do you guys know about Gene Murphy?"

Annie's vacuum cleaner laughter comes to life. "Gene Murphy? Honey, you're barking up the wrong tree if you've got a thing for Gene Murphy. He's going with Becky Worthingham."

"*Was* going with her," I say. "He told me they broke up."

Annie dismisses the notion with a wave of her hand. "If they broke up, it's because he's an asshole."

Without looking up, Jeremy asks, "Was he giving you the eye?"

"Yeah, I mean, maybe. We...uh...we kind of got to know each other last week, and ever since then, he's been acting real friendly every time he sees me. And when we're talking, he always stares me right in the eye."

Annie shakes her head. “If it was anybody else, I might say you were onto something. But not Gene Murphy. He’s not gay; he’s just intense—an intense asshole.”

Jeremy glances up from his work and scratches his nose, adding a second smudge before adding another line to his paper. Annie resumes her tirade about Jacob Wilson, and I go back to work on my portrait.

I still think something is going on between Gene and me irregardless of what Annie says. Or is it “regardless”?

Whatever.

BLAKE FINALLY BLOWS into study hall, eleven minutes after the bell. He gives Mr. Warren a note and plops down next to me. I make a point of looking at my watch.

“Hmm, eleven minutes. That’s a new record. Why were you late *this* time?”

“Would you please quit obsessing about time? Jeez, I bet you’d have a stroke if your watch ever stopped.”

“I don’t obsess about time. I just believe punctuality is a virtue. So where were you?”

“Well, if you must know, Mr. Szinhely wanted me to drop off a report to the principal’s office, and I kind of took my time about it.”

He pauses and looks around melodramatically, and then he leans over and whispers, “We’re getting a new student. I overheard Mr. Allen talking with the guy’s father. He starts Tuesday, and he’ll be in your homeroom. His name is Kerry Sawyer. You’ll have to tell me all about him.”

“I promise. I’ll give you an exclusive report.”

“That’s my boy.” He leans back in his chair, happy that he’ll have the inside scoop before anyone else.

Blake’s big ears are no lie. He’s Chadham High’s resident Rona Barrett. He likes to stay “in the know.” It’s like his hobby. So far, though, it hasn’t helped him find a girlfriend.

But since he knows practically everything about everybody, I decide to try to get some gay info from him, starting with the Drama Department. He’s been interested in theater since sixth grade, and he’s been in the drama club since last year.

"So, how's Theater going?"

"It's great, we're looking at musicals for this year's project—you know, the band and chorus will all be involved too. It's going to be exciting. This is your chance, Randy-man."

He's also been trying to get me to join the drama club since last spring.

"So, I guess you get a lot of different kinds of people in Theater, huh?"

"Yup, all kinds of people. So don't worry. You'll fit right in with no problem."

"Do many of them like the...uh...Village People?"

"Practically everybody, especially the girls."

"Oh, cool."

I'm getting nowhere.

"That reminds me," he says. "When are you taking your driving test again?"

"Friday afternoon. Mom's taking me as soon as I get home."

"Well, remember, as soon as you've got wheels, we can start hitting on the chicks for dates."

Blake wants nothing more in the world than the warm caress of a girl's ass, and believe me, it's something he loves to talk about. But so far, all his girl-talk has been purely hypothetical. He'd probably faint if he actually had to ask a girl out, much less reach out and touch one. And the funny thing is, with his Luke Skywalker hair and those disco bell-bottoms he wears, he should have girls dripping all over him. I guess it's some kind of a psychological thing. Nerves maybe.

THE NEXT DAY, I'm on my way to first lunch. It's six minutes since the bell rang, and I'm starving. Mrs. Dawson was generous and gave me extra time to finish that last geometry test problem. The extra time took some of the stress off, but I doubt it helped my grade any. Having artistic flair doesn't translate over to my other classes.

I've just passed the library when I hear a voice behind me.

"Psst, Randy."

I turn around to see Gene tiptoeing towards me. Those eyes immediately cause something to rumble inside me, but it's not my stomach.

"Hey," he says in a hushed voice.

"Hi, Gene."

He stands close, and his cologne flirts with my senses.

"You want a ride home today?"

"A ride? Sure. What's the occasion?"

"I usually carpool, but I had a doctor's appointment this morning, so my mom let me drive. Wait for me outside after school."

"Okay," I say, blushing like he's just asked me for a date.

By the time I get to the lunchroom, I've forgotten how hungry I am, and decide to go sit with Annie and Jeremy instead. I don't say a word about Gene though. Once a man gets on Annie's asshole list, he never gets pardoned.

The rest of the school day is a blur. I totally ignore Brad and Ramrod's insults in PE, and I don't even remember going to Chemistry. Blake's staying after school for something to do with the Drama Department, so I spend study hall just counting the seconds.

When the last bell rings, it's all I can do to contain my excitement as I battle the crowds. Once outside, I find a safe spot on the steps and settle down to wait for Gene. People pass me, a few say goodbye, and the parking lot slowly empties.

After sitting there for twelve minutes, I begin to worry that maybe Gene forgot me.

"Sorry to keep you waiting," a voice says over my shoulder.

I turn to find Gene behind me, grinning.

"No problem," I say, standing up. I don't tell him he only barely surprised me. One more second, and his cologne's captivating aroma would have given him away.

By the time we've walked across the parking lot, I've already completely stiffened up. I blush hard when he rubs against me while unlocking the passenger-side door. He gets in behind the wheel and smiles broadly before starting the car.

"This morning, I saw Amanda Worthingham outside," he says, glancing my way. "You should have seen the skirt she was wearing. The light was shining right through it, and man, was she hot."

He goes on to describe what the sunlight revealed she was, and wasn't, wearing. He's getting aroused by his own story, and the sight finishes the job of turning me on. He adjusts himself and catches me staring.

"Yeah, you like that, don't you?"

He grins, I blush, and he winks. I'm totally under his spell, and he knows it. No matter what Annie and Jeremy say, there's definitely something going on between us.

The ride home is a casebook example of gay teenage horniness. Gene talks. I blush and stare. He catches me staring and grins. I get even more turned on and blush harder.

When we get to my house, he pulls into the driveway, and just as I'm about to get out, he surprises me by giving my knee a squeeze.

"Randy, give me your number."

I scribble it out and hand it to him.

He flashes me a smile that's almost a smirk. "I'll call you sometime."

God, he's so sexy.

Once I get to my room, I plop on the bed, lost in a haze of excitement. *Gene's a senior. He's so hot, and he likes me, and he wanted my number so he can call me.*

Then, just as I'm ready to drift off into a pleasant sexual daydream, it hits me: *Damn it. Why didn't I get his number?*

OSCAR WARREN CAN be quite generous on a warm, sunny Friday afternoon. He's not like most of the teachers. He's one of those post-hippie types—you know, weedy, with a moustache. The other thing that sets him apart from all the other teachers is music. His zeal for teaching biology is only matched by his love for jazz. Rumor has it, he and his wife spend most of their weekends visiting jazz clubs around the region. Different strokes, I guess. Anyway, he's very casual and doesn't even grouse when some of the students call him Oscar instead of "Mr. Warren." Today, he's decided to let us spend the last hour of our school week outside and releases us early from study hall.

Blake and I are making a quick run to drop off a book at the library before joining the others in the quadrangle. It should be a quick stop, but as soon as we walk in, Blake spies a girl on the other side of the room.

"Hey, can you give me a minute?"

He wanders over, and they share a lively—but by no means brief—chat. It's funny. Blake doesn't look nervous at all, and she's the kind of girl he'd usually be drooling over. But there he is, casually leaning on one foot, like he hasn't got a care in the world.

Most of the period slips by before one of the librarians shushes them. He smiles at the girl, and even winks at her, before walking back my way. I'm amazed. Once we're outside soaking up the sunshine, my curiosity can wait no longer.

"Who was that girl you were talking to in the library?"

"Oh, her? That's just Mary Beth. I'm trying to get her interested in this year's show."

I raise an eyebrow and grin. "And is that the *only* thing you're trying to get her interested in?"

"What? You mean me and her? Naw, she's nice enough, but we're just friends. She sings in my church choir."

It's mind-boggling. Blake can be perfectly at ease with girls. He can talk to them and spend time with them. And he can even be friends with them. But as soon as he thinks about asking one out, he turns into a stuttering stick of stupidity. And this from a guy who otherwise struts around like John Travolta in *Saturday Night Fever*.

"Now if you're interested, Randy-man," he continues, "I could put in a good word for you, maybe even introduce the two of you."

"Blake, I've got something to tell you. I'm—"

Just then, the bell rings, everyone starts packing up, and streams of people come flowing outside.

Sixteen minutes later, we're rumbling down the road. At first, the noise of the ride keeps Blake distracted, and we sit quietly. But halfway to his stop, he looks over at me.

"Hey, what was it you were going to tell me?"

I shrug a shoulder and turn away to look out the window. "Oh, I don't remember."

It would be one thing to tell Blake I'm gay, outside in the quadrangle, where nobody could hear us. But there's absolutely no way in hell I'm going to tell him on the bus. It would be just my luck for everyone to stop talking just in time to hear me.

"Good luck on the driver's test," he says when we pull up at his stop.

My driver's test! I've been so preoccupied dreaming about Gene that I've completely forgotten to worry about my driver's test. And Gene is so sweet. He said he knows I'll pass this time, so I'm going to try really hard. I want to show him I'm worthy of his confidence and maybe even make him proud of me.

But as I walk up the block and spy my house, the specter of Dad's car in the driveway greets me, and I cringe.

Oh no.

Dad's car home at this hour can only mean one thing: *He's* taking me to the license bureau this time instead of Mom. It's a recipe for absolute failure.

Fourteen minutes later, I'm behind the wheel trying to focus on the road while Dad criticizes everything about my driving. And I do mean everything. Jeez, the way he's going on, you'd think *I* was the one who put the potholes in the street.

"Watch where you're going."

I'm driving straight ahead on a straight street.

"Did you even look before you changed lanes?"

There's not another car within three blocks of us.

"You try running a yellow light like that with the officer, and you'll be coming back a fourth time."

I was already in the intersection before the light changed.

"Do you have any idea what the damn speed limit is here?"

Okay, I guess I'm driving too fast.

"Christ. You drive like a little old lady."

Or is it too slow?

By the time we pull into the DMV lot, I'm a nervous wreck.

Luckily, there are a few kids ahead of us, so I have a little time to try and calm down. At least I'm not the only one stressed-out here. The other kids look to be about as nervous as I am. One guy is bobbing his foot. Another is biting his nails. He's kind of cute.

Just ahead of us, a black girl is waiting to sign in. Her father is with her, and from the expression on her face, she looks thoroughly demoralized. She glances over at me, and for a second, we share a kind of silent camaraderie. After we sign in, Dad maneuvers me to a seat as far away from her and her father as possible.

A kid comes back in with the driving-test officer. It's not exactly a morale-boosting scene. The kid looks embarrassed, and the officer looks traumatized. Of course, the officer is black, so Dad looks over at me and raises an eyebrow. What little confidence I have left oozes out of my shoes into a pathetic puddle on the floor.

The kid gets his failure notice and leaves with his mother. Before calling the next name, the officer takes a gulp from a glass, and I wonder what he's drinking. The boy who's been biting his nails stands up. When they go out, he and the officer both look like they're praying.

While people take their turns passing or failing the driving test, I go into my Buddha trance and eventually find my happy place. My consciousness closes in on itself until I can ignore the people around me, especially Dad. Slowly, confidence oozes back into my shoes, and an ocean of calmness wells up inside me. I'm at peace.

That is, until Dad elbows me. The man is calling my name. This is it.

Dad's ever-confident words of encouragement follow me outside. "Try not to embarrass yourself *too* much."

The officer glances at me with apprehensive eyes.

THIRTY-SEVEN MINUTES LATER.

I can't believe it. I actually passed the test. I'm a free man—well, as free as you *can* be when you've got to get permission to use the car.

But what am I worried about? That won't even be an issue for me. A hot new license in the hand doesn't impress Dad. He *still* doubts my ability to drive safely.

"The only reason you 'passed' was that black guy was too stupid to fail you. I'll bet he can't even drive worth a damn himself."

I try to ignore him and focus on a man walking along the side of the road up ahead.

"Watch out for that Mexican."

Dad's also convinced I'm legally blind.

"I see him."

The guy is only like about a *mile* away from us.

"You better slow down. You never know what a wetback's going to do. He's probably drunk."

We're now a quarter of a mile closer.

"I said you better slow down."

A half mile still separates us from Señor Pedestrian.

Suddenly, Dad screams like he's just been stung on the nut by a hornet. "GODDAMN IT, SLOW DOWN!"

I jump and slam on the brakes. Dad flies forward and smashes against the front window—wearing a seatbelt *is* important. He falls back into the seat and quickly buckles up. I start driving so slow little old ladies are passing me.

He doesn't say another word until we get home. When we get out of the car, he just holds out his hand, takes the keys, and walks away rubbing his forehead.

SUPPER IS ONE long lecture about responsibility and priorities. Dad pours on the humiliation about my driver's test, convinced that I only passed because the officer was obviously incompetent—because he was black, of course. He even tells Mom and my super-smug brat of a brother how I nearly got him and Señor Pedestrian killed. God. He goes on and on, and he pounds it into me over and over that driving is a privilege, not a right.

The Turd just snickers. He's eating this up.

By the time I leave the table, I feel like I've been beaten over the head with the driver's handbook.

But I've only been in my room for three minutes when the phone rings. It's Blake. He's dying to hear the good news.

"So, did you pass this time?"

"Yeah, I passed."

"Hot damn. When do you get here?"

"Probably sometime around June."

I go on to tell him about the whole ordeal, including Señor Pedestrian, and he laughs hysterically. Actually, the more I think about it, it does sound kind of funny. That's the good thing about best friends. They can make you laugh at life's little tragedies.

Chapter 3: Kerry Sawyer

NEEDLESS TO SAY, driving around with Blake over the weekend never happened. Any hope I had that Dad would let me use the car vanished Saturday morning as soon as I spied that beaut of a bruise on his forehead right where it had hit the windshield. Between the obvious pain, and the visual reminder every time he looks in the mirror, I'd guess the next chance I'll get to drive will be the turn of the century.

After such a miserable weekend, another week of school was the last thing I wanted. But yesterday wasn't too bad, and Tuesdays are always easier than Mondays. It also helps that I've got homeroom to invoke my Buddha focus and build up the spiritual energy needed to survive the day.

Ah, homeroom. A chance to center yourself and reflect on the deeper meaning of life.

A time to contemplate the many lessons we learn inside—and outside—the classroom.

An opportunity to—

"Hey, Clark. Did you get a good enough look at my ass in PE yesterday?"

I look Ramrod squarely in the eye. "Not half as good a look as the one I'm getting right now."

What kind of god would create a disease like Roderick "Ramrod" Fuller without providing a cure? Ramrod should try out for the All-American Asshole award. He'd have better than even odds of winning.

The constant insults and putdowns used to get to me, but then I noticed that he does it to every guy who's not the same kind of foul-mouthed, girl-grabbing, muscle-bound jockstrap he is. And to Ramrod, girls exist only to satisfy his sexual pleasure—or would if he could actually convince one to date him.

Mrs. Beach clears her throat and effectively silences Ramrod from responding to my insult. I wait my chance, and when she's not looking,

I'm about to whisper a follow-up putdown just to irritate him even more, when our principal Mr. Allen enters.

Oh yeah. The new student.

Thanks to Blake, I'm ready for this.

What I'm *not* ready for is the guy who follows Mr. Allen in.

My jaw drops open, my heart skips a beat, and the blood rushes to my face—and somewhere else.

That's the new kid?

"Mrs. Beach, I'd like to introduce our newest student to you. This is Kerry Sawyer. Kerry's family has just moved in from Petersburg, and he'll be joining our sophomore class. I know you and the students will make him feel welcomed at Chadham High."

While Mrs. Beach takes down Kerry's vital information and goes over difficult things, like the correct spelling of "Sawyer," I check him out.

He's a bit taller than me, but while I'm scrawny as a twig, he's as solid as a rock, and those tight new-wave-style jeans are covering legs even more muscular than Billy Mason's. He has coarse brown hair, a sturdy chin, and the kind of hazel eyes that seem to change color every time you look at them.

In short, he's the very definition of beautiful.

Mrs. Beach looks around. "Who has Literature first period?"

My hand shoots up. "I do."

Kerry smiles and takes the seat next to mine. He's even better looking up close.

"Hi."

"Hi, Kerry. I'm Randy. Randy Clark. Let me see your schedule."

The whole time I examine the paper, I feel his eyes on me. It's hard to concentrate. All I want is to spend the next hour staring into them.

Besides homeroom, Kerry and I are in a total of three classes together, plus first lunch and study hall. I'll be indispensable—and available—to him all day, starting with first period.

The bell rings, and we make our way to the English Department.

"How come you didn't start yesterday?"

"We're Jewish. We spent all morning yesterday in the synagogue. My family's not really very religious, but my parents do like to hit the big holy days."

"Cool."

I don't really know much about Jews, other than they're one of the many groups of people my father doesn't like. I, on the other hand, definitely like *this* boy.

"So, what's your dad do?"

"He's a lawyer. He's joining Frank Brady's law firm downtown."

"Mr. Sawyer, the lawyer?"

He smiles. "Yeah, I guess it *is* kind of funny sounding, isn't it?"

During the next two periods, I manage to glean some additional information from Kerry. Besides the usual Government-Issued parents, he has both an older and a younger sister. The younger one is in the same grade as Wally. I make a mental note to find out if Kerry likes her. If so, I'll have him warn her about The Turd.

After History, I drop Kerry off for French and join Blake next door in Mrs. Burnett's Spanish class. At Chadham High, French is for those who want to learn a second language; Spanish is for those who want to earn a second language credit. We've been in school four weeks and we're still struggling with "Hola."

As soon as I sit down, Blake leans over. "So, what's the new guy like?"

"He's okay." I try not to sound *too* enthusiastic. "I like him. He's got two sisters, older and younger. And—get this—he's already taking Algebra II."

"I hear the girls saying he's good-looking."

"Like I said, he's okay."

There's no way I can even begin to describe how handsome Kerry really is. "Don't worry. You'll meet him in study hall."

When the bell rings, I guide Kerry to Algebra II with Miss Patterson, and then suffer through an hour of Geometry torture with Mrs. Dawson. In the lunchroom, I warn him off several of the more nauseating options. While we're eating, we chat, and I'm captivated by the sparkle in his eyes. They're even more beautiful than Theo's.

After lunch, he stands close while I point him in the direction of his business class. He smells nice. Then I stand there watching him disappear into the crowd before I drift along to Art, still blushing like an idiot.

Damn. That guy is so attractive.

"AND I TOLD Gwen she was crazy to think Jacob was even worth spitting at. But, did she listen to me? Oh no. And she says she *still* loves him."

Annie's been talking nonstop for twenty-one minutes.

"I told her. I said, 'Girl, just forget him.' The boy is just ugly, and the sooner she realizes she's better off without him, the better off she's gonna be."

When Annie declares a guy "ugly," it's the kiss of death. She's like the guardian of the Chadham High Asshole Registry.

Jeremy pushes a fringe of stringy auburn hair behind his ear.

"Tell us about the new boy, Randy," he says without looking up.

"His name is Kerry Sawyer. He's very nice, and he's smart, real smart. He's taking Algebra II, and he's only a sophomore. And get this—he's got Business *and* Advanced Placement Physics. Can you believe it? AP Physics."

Annie sneezes out a chuckle. "You forgot to say he's also got AP *Gorgeous*. I've seen him."

Jeremy sighs and leans down to concentrate on his project.

I shrug my shoulder. "He's okay, I guess."

"Oh hush," Annie says, with a snicker. "You know you're just trying to keep him all to yourself."

"No. I mean, I guess he's all right—if you're into that *tall, dark, and handsome* kind of thing—but why anyone would even look at him twice when he's standing next to me is a mystery."

Annie erupts in a fit of laughter so violent I expect to see a lung fly out her nose.

"Randall Clark, you may not be *that* hard on the eyes, but, honey, you're not even in the same league as *ole Hot Body* Sawyer. All he needs is a tall, ebony beauty like me on his arm."

"Sorry, doll, you'll have to take a number."

"Who's he hooked up with?"

"Annie, he's only been here, like, five hours. Let's just say he's still playing the field."

"Honey," she purrs, "He can play in my field any time he wants."

I sigh, and Jeremy slowly shakes his head without looking up.

I FIND KERRY leaning against a wall waiting for me. He could have easily found his way to the locker room from here, but he's actually waiting for me. Just seeing him makes me smile, and he rewards me with a lopsided grin.

In the locker room, while I get my daily insults from Brad and Ramrod (Jamie is too distracted by the new kid to contribute today), the other guys introduce themselves to Kerry. Several guys try to latch on to new-buddy status with him, but as we file out to the gym, he gives me a reassuring wink.

The period is spent playing basketball. I'm not very good at it, so I just keep moving around and try to block members of the other team. Kerry, on the other hand, is *very* good, and it's thrilling to watch the way he moves. Sweat glistens on his face and arms. He's got a runner's physique with powerful legs, and he jumps higher than you'd think is humanly possible. By the time Coach Horne whistles to end the game, Kerry has scored once and assisted twice.

The post-PE locker-room experience is worse than the pre-PE one. It not only features naked teenage males, but wet ones as well. By the time I get there, the showers are all running, and any guy not already soaping up is stripping down. I'm on full Buddha autopilot as I wash the sweat off and try to ignore the scent of the twenty-nine hot young male bodies around me.

It works, until I walk back into the locker room, wiping the water out of my eyes. Kerry's still drying himself off, toweling his hair. I take one look at him and my Buddha trance totally collapses. We're both naked, but his nakedness is like a work of art. That stunning face is attached to a body that makes Michelangelo's *David* look like a gargoyle.

How can one guy be so nice and so totally hot at the same time?

As quick as I can, I throw my clothes on and bolt to the hallway. When he comes out, he finds me standing by the water fountain, still dripping. My hair is still wet too.

After dropping him off for Physics, I go to Chemistry, and after that escort him to Mr. Warren's room for study hall. Blake and Kerry hit it off. Of course, Blake wants to know all about the girls in Petersburg, and Kerry says they're nice. When Blake asks about girlfriends, he just mentions having had a special someone.

I bet he has. He's so handsome.

Blake and I exchange phone numbers with Kerry just before the bell rings. When I hand Kerry my number, I feel shy. I watch him as he heads off to the "townie" bus before catching up with Blake.

As we rumble along, Blake talks about something to do with the drama department, but I'm not listening. I'm reliving every minute since homeroom. I've been the new kid's best friend and personal tour guide all day. It's been exciting and a bit surreal, like having the hottest date at the dance. Heads have turned, and people have stared at us everywhere we went.

And speaking of people staring, if jealousy was knives, I'd be Julius Caesar right now. The eyes of every girl at Chadham High burned holes in my head all day. They're all attracted to Kerry, and I can't blame them. Spending time with him is intoxicating. He's friendly and easygoing, and I'm so drawn in by his good looks. I'm sure it won't be long before he hooks up with some lucky girl; it's just a matter of time.

And believe me, he's the kind of guy who will have his pick of the litter—if Annie Brock doesn't kidnap him first.

Chapter 4: Complications

IT'S BEEN THREE weeks since I looked in the mirror and discovered I'm gay, and my life seems to be getting more and more complicated. It used to be that if I was attracted to a guy, I could at least keep it to myself emotion-wise. The closest I ever really came to slipping up was the disastrous *Incident of Theo's Beautiful Eyes* last year. But nowadays, crushes seem to take on lives of their own. It's like I see a cute guy, and I nearly lose it.

Since Tuesday, things have really gotten out of hand. See, the thing is, I've now got crushes on two different guys.

First, there's Kerry Sawyer. My crush on him has been growing all week. We're together four periods a day, and he's so lust-worthy it's all I can do to keep my hands off him. Believe me, it ain't easy. Those hazel eyes of his are so hypnotic I could stare into them forever. And I could chew on those full sexy lips all day.

Then, there's my other crush—Gene Murphy. With those beautiful, long lashes and those broad shoulders, he's like a little lust-sicle I want to lick all over.

I've never come across anyone quite like Gene. It's weird. He talks about girls even more than Blake does. But the way he pulls me aside in the hall, and the way he gets up close so only I can hear him...it's like being emotionally felt up, or taking a lust vitamin strong enough to last the whole day. And the way he looks at me—*Oh God.*

Before I realized I was gay, I'd have the same kind of feelings I do now for guys like Gene and Kerry, but back then, the gate on my lust gland was shut tight, and I could sort of keep things under control. But now that I know I'm gay, it's like that gate is wide open. I manage okay in the morning, but between classes with Kerry, and occasionally running into Gene, my afternoons are getting really hard. (Pun intended.)

Today is the perfect example. We're in the locker room changing, and Kerry's pulling his pants off. As soon as I hear the sound of his belt buckle, my Buddha focus evaporates, and my body starts reacting. I try to distract myself by bending down to tie my shoe, but as I sit back up, my eyes are drawn to the curve of his leg, from his ankle all the way up.

Oh damn, I need a distraction fast.

"Hey, Clark. Can I borrow your tweezers when you finish jerking off with them?"

Right on time.

"Jamie, it must be so sad knowing you'll never be the man your mother is."

Even Jamie himself laughs at that one. For a second, my lust gland relaxes, and I'm back to normal. But then I glance over at Kerry, and when I see those stunning hazel eyes and that cute lopsided smile, I can barely manage to keep from drooling. So I change as fast as I can without drawing attention to myself, and get out of there.

Thankfully, Coach Horne has us running sprints today, which helps me burn off some energy and temporarily takes my mind off Kerry and a few of the other guys.

By the end of the period, we're all worn out, and I've got everything fully back under control. But of course, I see Kerry in the shower, and before I can get out, I'm totally turned on again.

Then, I have to use the restroom during Chemistry, and as soon as I come out and stop at the water fountain, Gene walks up. The second I lay eyes on him, my body reacts, and of course, as soon as he sees me, he breaks into a grin and pulls me back into the restroom.

The touch of his hand on my arm is sending my lust gland into overdrive, and his eyes are boring into me. His cologne is making me feel so drunk I have to bite my lip to keep from saying something embarrassing. Seriously, it's all I can do to focus on what he's saying, which isn't helping.

"Have you seen Billie Jo Jackson today?" he says, rubbing his crotch. "Damn, she's hot. That dress is so short I got a major view at lunch."

I just stare, mesmerized by what he's doing, and what it's doing to me.

He sees me staring and grins. "I bet you'd like to get a hold of that, wouldn't you?"

"Uh...uh-huh," I stammer.

"You and I should get together sometime," he says, and I twitch at the very thought. "Who knows? Maybe we could find us two other girls and do a foursome. I'll call you this weekend."

I wander back to class in a fog of teenage horniness. And of course, I've still got study hall to look forward to, and that's one more period with Kerry. Is it any wonder the only class I'm doing well in is Art?

Oh, and if Gene and I do get together this weekend, I hope it's just the two of us. Having two girls along would only work if Gene wanted the pleasure of *three* people competing for him.

I spend the rest of the period with Ann Wilson's voice in my head singing "Crazy On You."

BLAKE, KERRY, AND I are waiting for our library passes when a girl leans against the classroom door, her weight on one foot, ankles crossed.

"Mr. Warren, Mr. Szinhely asks if it's okay can we borrow Blake?"

He glances at Blake and cocks his head towards the door. Blake turns to Kerry and me. We fake tearful goodbyes. He makes a face and follows the girl out. Kerry and I leave for the library.

"Looks like it's just the two of us."

"Ah yes, alone at last," Kerry says. Then he winks at me and whispers, "Hey, don't you think it's too nice a day to spend our last hour inside?"

The more I get to know Kerry, the more I like him. Besides being so drop-dead gorgeous, he's just a lot of fun to be around. Sometimes when I'm with him, I can almost forget how attractive he is.

We look around and turn up the back hallway. The only tricky part about skipping is that to get to the best place to hide out, you've got to go right past the Office. We approach from behind and quietly make our way to the hall next to the lunchroom.

Peeping around the corner, I survey the open area and glass wall that's the only thing separating us from the Office, take a step back, and turn to Kerry.

"What do you think's the best way to handle this?"

"Sherlock Holmes once told Doctor Watson about a burglar who was bold enough to call in a locksmith to get him inside a house he wanted to rob. So I say we just boldly walk out."

I nod, and we do just that.

Once outside, we wander past the kitchen and perch ourselves on the loading dock wall, relishing our successful truancy. The sun is warm, and a breeze helps drive away the lunchroom garbage smell. Kerry's eyes take on a special sparkle in the afternoon light. The way his pullover clings to his chest and the curve of his jeans around his...

Well, like I said, *sometimes* I can almost forget how beautiful Kerry is. Other times, *like now*, just catching a glimpse of him drives me wild.

Speaking of now, I've got to make a decision. Either I sit here until it becomes blatantly obvious I've totally got the hots for him—I've already got a hard-on—or I find something to talk about quick, and hope it distracts me. I cast around for a topic, but all I can come up with is the lamest conversation starter in history.

"So, how does Chadham County compare to Petersburg?"

"It's not bad. There are fewer people here than in Petersburg, but that's okay."

"Do you miss it?"

"No, not really. I mean, I miss it sometimes, but it helps that I've met some really nice people here. What about you? Have you lived here all your life?"

"Unfortunately, yes, my family goes way back. They were some of the first hick settlers."

"Really? So how did you manage to avoid becoming a hick yourself?"

"What do you mean *avoid* becoming a hick?" I say, rolling my eyes. "I *am* one."

"Naw, man. You're no hick. You're different; you're cool, major cool."

"Thanks. You're major cool yourself. I really like you."

"I really like you too."

For a second, we just look at each other. His cheeks seem to glow in the sunlight. The desire to touch them has my own cheeks burning. I'm suddenly longing to taste his lips. The breeze blows a lock of coarse brown hair across his forehead. I imagine leaning over, brushing it aside, and kissing him. I move forward, if only a fraction of an inch.

Stop it. This is exactly how you ruined things with Theo, letting your imagination run away with you. The quickest way to lose a friend is to fall in love with him, especially if you're gay and he's straight. You've got to come up with something to talk about. Come on, think. Think.

"So," I say, clearing my throat. "What do you think of that Gaspard guy in *A Tale of Two Cities*?"

BACK IN MY room after school, the door locked and The Turd safely outside, I lie on the bed and sigh.

The sunlight on Kerry's hair this afternoon was dazzling. God, he's so sexy. And he likes me, and he thinks I'm cool.

Okay, I know he only *just* likes me, but that doesn't mean I can't at least fantasize about him. The radio starts playing a Starland Vocal Band song.

Perfect timing for a little afterschool delight.

I walk into the locker room. Kerry is lying on one of the benches. We're both naked. I kneel down and run my hands all over him. His skin is smooth and hard, and he's aroused. I stroke his hair and kiss him. The bench turns into a bed. We kiss. His body rubs against me, and we both shiver as the passion builds. He caresses me until I'm right on the edge.

The phone rings, and The Turd yells that it's for me.

Damn it.

Blake's overly excited voice blasts from the receiver. "Randy-man, I'm about to let you in on the scoop of the century."

"Jimmy Carter's cornered the market on toothpaste?"

"No, dummy. The Drama Department is putting on *South Pacific.*"

"Okay, so?"

"So? So you can get a part. You're a natural. I bet you could get the Billis part. We'll even have a song together."

"Blake."

"We'll have a ball, and the chicks will drool all over us."

"Blake!"

"And next year, we'll talk them into doing *The Music Man*. Oh man, you'd be perfect as Harold Hill."

"Blake, will you shut up. What in hell makes you think I can even sing?"

"Anyone can sing," he scoffs.

"Blake, I don't want to be in *any* show, musical or not."

"Come on; you know deep down you'd like it."

Twenty-six minutes later, I finally convince him that I'm serious and don't want to be in a show. Four and a half minutes after that, he accepts the fact that I won't do it just because he wants me to either. And after eleven more minutes, I've fully persuaded him that me not being in the show is all for the best because the two of us on stage together would obviously be more than any female could handle.

I've got to go ahead and tell him I'm gay so he'll stop trying to use girls as bait to get me to join the drama club. I mean, I love him, but there's absolutely no way he's ever going to talk me into having anything to do with a show, even taking tickets. It's just not going to happen.

But I guess there is at least one good thing about *South Pacific*. Blake will undoubtedly get a part, and he'll talk about that instead of girls—at least for a while.

Chapter 5: The Murphy House

SUNDAY AFTERNOON, 12:08. It's cool but not too cold for a pullover and shorts. I'm biking into town.

Yesterday, I got a surprise call from Gene. He asked me if I'd like to go see *The Prisoner of Zenda* with him. Overjoyed, I told him I was ready to go any time he was. But then he explained that he meant to go today and asked me if I was still interested. Of course, I said yes and wrote down his address. Consequently, I spent all day yesterday fantasizing about things like walking in on him while he's getting dressed, and last night, all I did was dream about him.

The Murphy house is located near the end of a block in a modest neighborhood. I leave my bike on the lawn, walk up to the porch, and knock on the door. Mrs. Murphy greets me. She's about the same height as Gene, with the same long lashes, but her hair is jet and wavy.

"You must be Randy," she says.

"Yes, ma'am."

"Come on in. I'm afraid Gene's still in bed. Maybe *you* can get him moving. His room is upstairs, last door on the left."

She shows me to the stairs, and I thank her and start up. The house is old but well maintained. Family pictures line the wall. I pause to look at a photo of Gene that looks like it was taken a few years ago. He's outside somewhere, and he's wearing swim trunks. He looked hot even then.

When I reach his room, the door is closed.

I knock.

His voice drifts out lazily. "Yeah?"

"Hey, Gene. It's me, Randy."

After a couple of seconds, he tells me to come in.

Closing the door behind me, I find a moderate bedroom with a dresser, a twin bed, and a night table. The walls have a couple of posters—the usual cheesecake ones that adorn teenage boys' rooms everywhere—and a stereo turned on low in the corner. Old issues of *Rolling Stone* and *CREEM* magazines, clothes, and record albums of various bands—Bad Company, The Allman Brothers, and Boston—litter the floor. Even with the open window, the room is warm and smells sexy with Gene's cologne.

Gene is stretched out in his bed. He's lying on his side, propped up on one elbow. The covers are pulled up to just below his bare shoulder, and one of his arms is on top. It's a seductive pose, and I feel a hard-on starting.

"Hey, Randy." He motions for me to sit on the edge of the bed. "Sorry, I haven't got dressed yet. You know how hard it can get on weekends."

I'm suddenly aware of everything around me, especially the light breeze tickling my legs.

Sitting inches away from a cute guy lying in bed is getting to me. I'm blushing and very conscious of the fact that I'm only wearing shorts and a pullover. And he can't have on much more than pajama bottoms under those covers.

"Yup," he says, stretching out. "Some days, it just takes a good pull to get me motivated. So, uh, shall we get to it?"

He's staring directly into my eyes.

"Whenever you're ready," I mumble, hypnotized.

"Yeah, I guess I *have* kept you waiting long enough."

Without warning, he grabs the covers and with one swing pulls them back.

There he is, completely naked, reclining on his side.

My gaze involuntarily moves down, and all I can do is gasp. *Oh my God.* He's aroused, and as I stare, frozen, he wiggles a little, and my jaw drops open stupidly. It's something I've literally dreamed about, but the reality is hotter than I ever imagined.

"Why don't you come over here and give me a hand," he whispers. It's not a question.

He just lies there. He doesn't move—except in that one place. I squirm a bit and feel my hard-on flex against my leg. My mind is slowing to a halt.

"Come on," he whispers. "We both know you want it."

In a trance, I lean forward. He's hard and hot in my hand. He smells clean with a hint of something else that captivates me. It's intoxicating.

The clothes I'm wearing suddenly feel obscene and oppressive. I want to tear them off and feel his skin against mine. He tugs at my shirt and rolls onto his back, and I act on impulse. I lie down and take him in. He hums and runs his fingers through my hair.

This is reckless, and I shouldn't be doing it. The door is unlocked. His mother could walk in any second. But Gene is so beautiful, and touching him, tasting him, is such a turn on that I can't think about anything else. He's perfect, and I'm holding him, and right now, he's mine. And he's whispering things and making little sounds that drive me on, making me almost desperate.

We sway together. My hand slides along his thigh and up his chest. I taste hints of something exquisite and addictive. Everything else vanishes. His leg, with its light coating of soft hair, is sturdy and lean. It brushes up against me and finds its way.

He begins to squirm, and words give way to soft moaning. He arches his back, and suddenly, I'm drowning in something exotic. But I can't stop. His leg slides between mine, sending me into overdrive.

We both collapse. I lie on top of him exhausted, my cheek resting on his abdomen, rubbing my fingers over his chest.

After a few seconds, he rolls me off him. I watch him pick up a towel and go to his dresser. He pulls out a pair of boxers and throws me a T-shirt. I just lie there, my mind overthrown by what just happened.

"That was nice," he whispers, looking down on me. "We'll certainly have to do that again soon."

He goes out and closes the door. I listen to his footsteps and the sound of another door closing. I'm still staring at the ceiling when he comes back in, drying his hair. He pulls on a shirt and shorts and sits down next to me. His leg rubs against mine, and I react.

"Come on," he says with a grin. "I'm hungry. Let's grab a bite to eat and get to the movie."

THE REST OF the day, I guess I'm kind of in shock about what we did—what *I* did. When we stop at a fast-food place, Gene says he'll order for me. He comes back with a hamburger for himself and smirks as he passes me a hot dog. We don't say a word about what happened in his room. Instead, he talks about the females coming and going around us. I listen, wanting him to do the same things to me he says he'd like to do to them.

But I begin to understand. Despite what we did—or what he let me do to him—Gene likes girls, and he wants to make sure I know it. During the movie, he continues to make sure I get the message. He tells me several times how sexy Elke Sommer is, leering at her and saying things like, "I'd do her in a minute."

When we get back to his house, I'm hoping against hope he'll invite me up to his room. But he stops on the porch and says he's glad we got together.

"Me too. I'd like to do it again sometime."

"Yeah, I know." He smirks and rearranges himself. "And I have some ideas for next time that I know you'll just love."

He gives me a wink before going to the door. I push my bike to the street and start off. The wind tickles my legs and arms. Gene's image dominates my mind the whole way home. When I get there, I go upstairs to shower—and to relieve the tension. In my head, Linda Ronstadt is singing "Heatwave," and I dream about being in Gene's bedroom again. I remember every detail—the taste of him, his smell, the sounds, and the look of satisfaction on his face.

Annie and Jeremy were wrong about him—sort of. He may like girls, but what happened today was no accident. He wanted it, and he had it all planned out. Why else have me bike over to his house when he was going to drive us to the movie?

All those things he's been saying to me, the way he looks at me, those little touches— He's been testing me the whole time to be sure I wanted him. He may not have known exactly how I'd react once he got me into his bedroom, but he arranged things so he could get a chance to find out.

Well, he got his chance all right. And he sure gave me mine. He unleashed a hunger in me I never even dreamed was there. I mean, I knew I was gay, but being with him today, doing that to him, really got me off more than I ever could have imagined.

And now, he and I both know I'll go to him whenever he calls.

Lying on my bed, listening to Cheap Trick, I'm melancholy. I've joined the ranks of all those thousands of kids who've had sex in one form or another. It was amazing, but now that it's over, I sort of feel ashamed.

But I can't help wanting to do it again.

IT'S A COOL, windy mid-October day. Kerry and I step outside, more to get away from the stench in the lunchroom than to enjoy the great outdoors. He's telling me about some guy named Eno who works with the Talking Heads and does this really strange music.

Kerry's kind of an enigma. So far, he's not quite turned out to be the lady's man I thought he would be. It's not that he's shy around girls exactly; he just doesn't take the bait to play it up when a girl shows interest. Like the other day when Billie Jo Jackson tried to hint around about the dance next week he said, "I'm no good at dancing," and walked away. Nope. Like I said, this guy doesn't take the bait. Maybe he's still got a thing for that girl back in Petersburg he called his "special someone."

And he's not into going on and on about girls either. When Blake falls into one of his gotta-get-a-girl fits, Kerry goes along with it the same way I do. We nod politely and wait for him to talk it out of his system.

The two of us have just crossed the courtyard and rounded the corner to the quadrangle when I spy Jeremy walking by himself on the far side. As always, he's dressed in his trademark black shirt and jeans, and he's walking fast, clutching his books to his chest like he's afraid someone will steal them.

I'm about to yell over for him to join us when a couple of guys march up behind him. They're almost twice as big as Jeremy. At first, they separate like they're going to pass him by, but suddenly, one of them reaches over and knocks his books out of his hands. At the same time, the other one pushes him. Jeremy stumbles over his books and lands hard on the sidewalk. The two bullies laugh and keep walking.

I'm already halfway across the quadrangle, with Kerry right at my heels, when we see Brad Romero heading for Jeremy too. But he isn't running up to help him; he's sauntering over with an amused look on his face.

"Well, well, what happened?" he says and snickers. "Did little Jenny fall down and go boom?"

"What's going on here?" Kerry demands as we help Jeremy to his feet.

"What does it look like?" Brad says, walking away. "The little faggot tripped down."

I hand Jeremy his geometry book. "Are you all right?"

"I'm fine."

"I can't believe those jerks would do something like that," Kerry says.

Jeremy sighs. “Why not? They do it all the time.”

“All the time? But why?”

“Because they’re big, I’m little, and they can,” he says, examining the scrapes on his palm.

I shake my head. “You should go to Mr. Allen. He’d put a stop to it.”

“Don’t kid yourself,” he says, shaking his head. “Allen’s not going to lift a finger.”

“But Jeremy—”

“Look, just forget about it.”

Kerry and I stare in wonder as he brushes himself off and walks away like nothing ever happened. But his frown and the look in his eyes say it all.

FRIDAY AFTERNOON. THE bell rings, and I get up to leave for study hall. One more hour, and the weekend that I’ve been longing for since Monday morning will finally be here.

I’ve only just stepped out of the Chemistry room when I hear Gene calling me.

“Hey, Randy, wait up a second.”

This week, Gene and I haven’t run into each other as much as before. And the one or two times we did, he seemed standoffish. I had begun to worry that he was embarrassed about what happened Sunday, but this time, he looks happy to see me.

I step to one side, so a couple of girls can pass. He comes up close.

“If you’re free this afternoon, why don’t you stop by?”

He doesn’t have to say anything else; we both know what he’s inviting me over for.

“Well, I don’t know if I can.”

He casually runs a finger along my forearm. A spark of excitement ignites inside me, and my face begins to burn.

“Come on,” he whispers as a boy passes us. “You know, you could drop by for a while right after school. Hell, you could even ride in my carpool, and I’ll drive you home later. Please.”

He sounds so cute, and his eyes are flirting with me. But explaining to Blake why I rode home with a bunch of guys I don’t even know would just be too awkward.

"No, that's okay. I'll bike over. Is four o'clock too late?"

"No, that's perfect. See you then." He shoots me a wink and turns to go.

I'm in my own little world the rest of the way to study hall, reliving Sunday and thinking about what might come later. *Maybe this time Gene will tell me he loves me, or kiss me, or something.*

Somehow, I survive until final bell despite the temptation of having Kerry to look at the whole time. On the bus, Blake continues his campaign to get me to try out for *South Pacific*. He keeps harping on it, and I keep saying no. Usually, I don't have much trouble putting him off on this kind of thing, but thinking about what I'll soon be doing with Gene makes Blake's missionary zeal especially annoying today.

As soon as I get home, I race upstairs, check myself out, and try to comb my hair. A change of shirts, shorts, and a dab of cologne for good measure are all in order. I even brush my teeth in case Gene wants to kiss me this time. I know it's crazy, but I can't help it. I want Gene to find me attractive—which is ridiculous because why would he be inviting me over if he didn't?

One final glance in the mirror, and I run outside and jump on my bike.

FIVE FORTY-SIX.

I'm naked again. Steam covers the shower doors. I need this—I'm sweaty, I'm exhausted, and I'm kind of messy. As soon as I got home, I hid my boxers until I could throw them out. There's no way I can ever let Mom see them like that.

I'm lost in the confusion of a new reality. As of today, I'm a fully functioning homosexual. And my body may be in the shower, but my mind is still at the Murphy house. Everything that happened there today is seared in my memory.

"Lock the door and come here," he says, and I do.

I rub shampoo into my hair.

He pinches me and I moan.

The shampoo splashes from my hair and runs down my spine. I lean against the shower stall wall, my eyes closed, rinsing it away, and rub the soap over my body. My fingers feel foreign. My skin tingles.

Oh God! I'm holding him, and waves of the best sensation I've ever felt are flowing through me, getting stronger and stronger. But all too suddenly, it's over.

I turn off the water and lean against the wall. The water drips off me. I step out of the shower.

He and I stand by his bedroom door. I lean forward to kiss him, but he puts out a hand.

"Sorry, I don't do that. It may be okay for you, but I'm not queer. Only fags kiss guys."

My hand shakes as I unlock the door.

I dry off, still shaking, wrap a towel around me, and stand in front of the mirror.

What the hell was that? How did he make that happen to me? Am I the only one it happens to?

I'm not entirely over it. Hell, I may never get over it. One thing's sure though, I'll never forget it. I'll remember it until the day I die. I feel embarrassed, humiliated, and sort of compromised, like the whole world is watching me even though I'm alone. But I also feel strangely satisfied.

Gene's face flashes before my eyes, and I feel a tingle wash over me. Am I falling in love with him? I don't know, but I do know one thing; from now on, I'll do whatever he wants, anytime he wants—anything—if he'll just make that happen to me again.

As I walk back to my bedroom, I start to worry that I'm walking girly. Then I smile and wonder if the kind of thing Gene did to me is why girls walk like that in the first place.

Chapter 6: Rosa Martinez

IT'S BEEN NEARLY three weeks since Kerry came to Chadham, and since then we've become really good friends. Sometimes, it feels like I've known him all my life. Like something will happen, and I look at him, and he flashes me that lopsided grin of his, and we burst out laughing. Imagine meeting someone who's everything you ever dreamed of in the perfect friend. He's handsome, and he's really smart, and he likes being my friend as much as I like being his. We agree on just about everything—except for some of the so-called food in the lunchroom.

Wednesday is pizza day at Chadham High. The lunchroom smells like a cross between a sewer and a dead skunk. Chadham High pizza consists of a cardboard crust and sauce made of mud, topped with some kind of fungus that looks suspiciously like phlegm pretending to be cheese.

Despite my warnings, Kerry is game to test his immunity today, and he's chewing on the cardboard cuisine. I, on the other hand, am much more wary of the lunchroom staff's biological warfare and sip on a carton of milk.

"Hey, Ker, Rosa Martinez just winked at you."

"You never told me you wear glasses," Kerry says, tearing off another mouthful of *crapperoni* pie.

"I don't."

"Well then, you might want to have your eyes tested, because if you're talking about that dark-haired girl over there, you're the one she winked at."

"Get off."

"I'm serious, dude," he says between chews. "She's been staring at you since we sat down."

"And what makes you think it's *me* she's been staring at?"

"Well, when I went back for salt, I noticed she was keeping her eyes on *you*."

"Yeah. Right," I scoff.

He drops the remaining reeks-ah on his tray, gets up, and strolls over to the trash can.

I look back in Rosa's direction.

She's still smiling.

At *me.*

She nods a silent hello and winks.

My stomach lurches.

A girl can't *like me! People will start asking why I don't go out with her.*

In a panic, I rush to catch up with Kerry. My milk carton lands in the trash can before he even gets there. He disposes of his tray, and I follow him to the courtyard.

"She can't be attracted to me."

He winks and slaps me on the back. "I don't see why not. Come on, Randy. Why shouldn't she be attracted to you? You're certainly good-looking enough. And you *do* have that winning smile."

For a second, Rosa and everything else vanishes from my mind, and I start blushing. He gives me a light punch in the arm and leaves for business class.

Okay, I can't help it. I'm crushing on Kerry. To quote Annie, he's got *AP Gorgeous,* but he's also just plain fun to be around. I mean, Gene turns me on physically and all, but except for the hard-on factor, he's kind of boring. With Kerry, it's different. I look forward to every minute I'm together with him.

I bet sex with Kerry would be totally awesome...

There I go, setting myself up again. I've got to stop it. I don't want to blow my friendship with Kerry just because of what else I'd like to—well, you know. Until I ruined things with Theo Hayes, he and I had been becoming fairly good friends. I already like Kerry too much, *and* I'm way more attracted to him than I ever was to anyone else.

Suddenly, Rosa's smile flashes before me, and I feel sick. I rush to the nearest boys' room and hurl.

BY THE TIME I get to Art, I'm two minutes late. Mrs. Pilt gives me an appraising glance, corrects her attendance book, and goes to the back table. Chad Maddox, one of the less-artistically-inclined, is throwing bits of dried clay at a wooden palm tree, one of the props being painted for *South Pacific*. He's got a bad reputation, and I usually try to avoid him. Annie says he's an asshole, but I just think he does drugs.

Annie takes one look at my face, still green from having just thrown up, and frowns.

"Ooo, Randy. Tell me you didn't eat the pizza. That crap is deadly."

Jeremy nods in agreement.

"It's worse than that," I groan.

"You had *two* pieces?"

"A girl winked at me. Rosa Martinez. I think she wants me to ask her out."

"Sugar, that's no problem. If she wants to go out with you, just ask her out."

I lean forward and hiss, "Annie, I'm not joking about being gay. It's a *guy* I want to go out with, not a girl."

She rolls her eyes. "You're missing the point."

"What point?"

"Do you want *everyone* to know you're gay or just the people who will be cool about it?"

"What kind of stupid question is that? If Brad and Ramrod knew I was gay, they'd use my face for batting practice."

"Exactly. So, all you have to do is ask the girl out and show her a good—but not great—time, and that's that. You'll be on record as having dated a girl, and you won't have to worry about being beaten up by football players—that is, unless you're *into* that kind of thing."

Jeremy rolls his eyes.

"But I can't ask her out," I whine.

Annie waves a dismissive hand. "Don't be silly. Of course you can ask her out."

"But what if she wants to—uh—you know?"

"If you mean *kiss* you, just let it happen. Honey, how bad can it be? What are you afraid she's going to do, give you cooties?"

"Why even worry about it?" Jeremy asks. "Does anybody even know this girl winked at you?"

"Uh, yeah. Kerry does."

"Then that settles it," Annie says with a snicker. "You have to ask her out. It's either that or let *Mr. Hot Body* start wondering why you won't. Or are you planning to ask *him* out?"

"I wish," I grumble. "I told you, he's got a girl back home."

"Yeah, maybe," she says. "But even if he does, it hasn't stopped you from drooling all over him. So the real question is would he be cool if he knew you were gay?"

"I don't know. I think so. I mean, I hope so. I mean...I don't know, damn it."

"Then, honey, it's time you start deciding where you're going to take Rosa, and what you're going to wear."

Jeremy shakes his head, and Annie goes back to her project, triumphant that she's silenced all opposition. I look down at my paper as her giggle-snorts echo next to me.

TIME PASSES LIKE radio music in a car when you're thinking about something else.

In PE, I'm so distracted I don't even need my locker room Buddha focus, and I'm barely conscious of the time spent on the basketball court. In Chemistry, I don't have a clue what Mr. Ferguson is lecturing about.

Then, in study hall, Kerry spills the beans.

"Hey, Blake. Rosa Martinez winked at Randy today at lunch. She likes him."

Blake's eyes go wide. "Rosa Martinez? She's hot! Randy, you've got to ask her out."

Great. Now Blake knows. That was all *I needed.*

He's so overjoyed you'd think *he's* the one Rosa's interested in. He goes on and on, and demands that I ask her out—like *yesterday*—and when I protest that I don't have her number, he promises me he'll get it and call me tonight.

On the bus ride home, I'm on the verge of a full-blown panic attack. I'm terrified that if I don't ask Rosa out, Kerry will realize I'm gay and reject me.

But if I do ask her out, what about Gene? I couldn't stand it if I lost him. Okay, he doesn't really show a lot of affection—hell, he makes it perfectly clear sex is the only reason he gets together with me at all. And since we started doing that one thing on a regular basis, he's started calling me a fag and a cocksucker while we're doing it.

But despite all that, I can't help hoping he'll change, that he'll fall in love with me. And every time we do it, or he does it to me, I feel more and more bound to him. I need him, I need him to do it to me, and I want him to need it as much as I do. I can't jeopardize losing him because of Rosa.

AS SOON AS I get home, I clean up and race straight over to Gene's house. He's surprised but happy to see me, and I go all out to do everything I can to please him, all the things that drive him crazy.

In the end, we're both panting and moaning.

"How was that for a little midweek tension breaker?" I whisper.

"Not bad."

"Only not bad?"

He snickers. "Well, you're not a girl, but you're okay. You'd have to work a lot harder to compete with a couple of the other girls I've had. Now, I've got some things to do, so you better get out of here."

I'm humiliated, depressed, and jealous. *I'm not good enough? How could Gene not be satisfied by what I do to him? Why does he even want a girl when he's got me? Why can't I be everything he wants? I hate those girls, whoever they are. I've got to try harder next time.*

AFTER BIKING HOME, I take my now traditional post-sex shower and go to my room. By six o'clock, Blake's on the phone repeating Rosa's phone number over and over. I don't know how he was able to get it so fast. I mean, really, the guy should work for the intelligence community. When I finally get him to hang up, he's repeated the number so many times it's permanently burned into my memory.

While I pick at my plate, The Turd offers a disgusting assessment of tonight's supper and Dad yells. As soon as I possibly can, I sneak back to my room. At seven thirty-six, I'm still staring at Rosa's phone number and arguing with myself about whether to go through with this.

What if she figures out I'm gay and makes a scene in the lunchroom? Being gay is one thing; having everyone know it is something else. I'll be the official school punching bag. And oh my God, Gene won't want me around if everybody knows I'm gay.

But if I don't ask Rosa out, Blake will never let me hear the end of it. And if Kerry figures out that the reason I won't ask her out is because I'm gay, he'll reject me.

No, I've got to do it. It's the only way to shut Blake up and keep Kerry's friendship. And maybe it won't be that bad. Like Annie said, just give her a good—but not great—time, and get it over with.

So I hold the phone and sweat out three rings, hoping against hope Blake got the number wrong.

"Hello?"

"Uh...hello. Is this Rosa?"

"Yes?"

"Uh...hi, Rosa. This is Randy...Randy Clark."

"Hi, Randy. What's up?"

"I...uh...I'm...going to the movies Saturday afternoon and was wondering if you might like to...uh...maybe...you might want to see it too."

"Oh, I'm so sorry, Randy. I've got to go to my aunt Ginny's birthday party Saturday."

"Oh, that's okay—"

"But I *could* go with you Sunday."

I'm stunned, but stutter out that Sunday will be fine. We confirm a time, and she says she'll meet me there, and she's looking forward to it.

I breathe a sigh of relief when we say goodbye. It's done. I've made the call.

Then it hits me. *Oh crap! I've got a date—with a girl.*

Before the night is over, Blake calls, followed soon afterwards by Kerry. Blake is amazed at what he considers my smooth, quick thinking in getting the date Sunday—like I knew about Aunt Ginny's birthday party all along. Kerry is congratulatory but more low-key. He senses my nervousness and tells me I've got nothing to worry about. It's obvious he's had more than a few dates before. By the time we hang up, he's given me a great pep talk and eased my nerves, at least for tonight.

WAITING FOR SUNDAY is almost unbearable.

Wednesday night, I get really paranoid and start imagining things: All the girls are laughing at me. They all know I'm gay, and this date-thing is just an elaborate setup to humiliate me. The straight guys all crack their knuckles waiting for the announcement that it's open season on Randy Clark, and the gay guys—whoever they are—shake their heads and gossip about what a loser I am.

When I get up Thursday morning, I get this crazy idea to hide from Rosa, like if she doesn't see me, she'll forget about me and the date. No such luck. She stops me as soon as I get off the bus and tells me how much she's looking forward to Sunday. Then, every time she passes me in the hall, she makes a big deal out of smiling at me.

By fourth period, my nerves are completely shot. On my way to Geometry, I spy her walking my way, and I duck down like a wanted criminal and hide behind a trash can. As she disappears around the corner, a female voice startles me.

"Randy, what on earth are you doing?"

I nearly jump out of my skin and whirl around to find Annie looking at me like I've lost my mind.

"I...uh...that is... "

"You can't hide from her forever," she says. "What are you going to do at lunch?"

"I'm not going to lunch. I'm going to hide out behind the dumpster."

She rolls her eyes. "Randy, you're being ridiculous."

I shudder and she sighs. "Okay, meet me in the art room."

When the lunch bell rings, I race to Mrs. Pilt's room like I'm being chased by a pack of werewolves. Annie spends the whole period (and lunch the next day) calming my nerves, counseling me, and giving me pointers. She assures me that Rosa won't try anything, except for maybe a kiss. And she says if Rosa *does* try to kiss me, I should just pretend she's my grandma—a suggestion that doesn't really help.

But by last bell on Friday, I do feel a little stronger and figure that if I can survive the date, I can pretend it never happened later. All I have to do is make it to Sunday.

Luckily, Dad provides a convenient distraction all day Saturday. He always has a shitload of projects backed up, and decides today is Clean Out the Garage Day. Oh great. A whole day of listening to him go on and on about commies and black people. And if it's not bad enough having to listen to him gripe all day, it's actually worse because he forces Wally to "help" too. The Turd's about as much help as a one-legged man in an ass-kicking contest.

But I do have to give him credit for one thing though— The Turd always manages to screw things up in a way that gets Dad pissed. *At me.* And this time is no exception.

When Sunday finally rolls around, I try to keep busy right up to the time I have to leave to meet Rosa. After church, I spend time preening and trying to find just the right clothes. I don't want to look too appealing, but I don't want to look like a total dork either. I choose disco trousers and a wide-collared polyester shirt, which would look perfect except for the fact that it's turned cold, and my winter jacket is dreadful.

And what important teenage occasion would be complete without a zit the size of Montana.

I bike my way to the theater and spend thirteen minutes combing my hair so it looks slightly less like I've just escaped from a mental institution. It doesn't work. Every time I've almost got it right, the wind blows, and it's a complete mess all over again.

When Rosa arrives, unlike me, she doesn't look nervous at all. She's wearing jeans and a T-shirt clearly designed to leave no doubt she's got boobs and a navy pea coat that makes them even more obvious. She clearly wants to get a reaction.

It's working. I'm starting to feel queasy.

The ticket mistress, some ancient blue-hair with horn-rimmed glasses as thick as Coke bottles, takes our money, and we find ourselves standing in front of the concession stand. Rosa buys a box of chocolate raisins. I stick with popcorn and hope it will settle my stomach.

Armed with our snacks and sodas, we make our way into the theater. After the glare of the afternoon sun, it would probably be wise to stop long enough for our eyes to adjust to the darkness. But instead, we march forward, stop at a suitable row, and I politely wait for Rosa to go in first.

Somehow, she misses the greasy mess on the floor.

But *I* don't. Oh no, of *course* not. I step right into it and slip. Hard.

As the world goes into slow motion, I am falling forward, and I brace for impact.

The soda launches from the cup in my hand.

It doesn't just hit Rosa; it *explodes* all over her, drenching her from head to toe.

A flurry of popcorn falls like snow all around us.

But the worst part is I don't actually fall. Oh no, not a chance. That would make me look like I'm just an innocent klutz. No, I somehow manage to regain my balance and end up just standing there, looking as guilty as sin, with a squashed cup in my hand.

Rosa stares at me like I'm the Hunchback of Notre Dame.

The people at the theater are nice enough to give us our money back, as well as free tickets to come again another time. As soon as the lady hands me the tickets, Rosa snatches hers, making it clear she has no intention of coming back with me. In fact, at this point, she isn't talking to me at all. She just glares at me. Nine minutes later, she disappears down the street, still as mad as a wet cat.

The whole experience has been thoroughly embarrassing. But at least it's over, and I'm kind of relieved. For the first time since Wednesday, I don't feel nauseous.

I GET HOME only to have Wally stop me at the door.

"Hey, Shithead, some guy named Gene just called. He wants you to go over to his house. Something about the project you two are working on."

While The Turd wanders off to the kitchen, I hesitate in the doorway. Gene must have some kind of sexual tapeworm or something. I could probably tell him I didn't get the message. I mean, after all I've been through today, I'm not really in the mood to do anything physical, even with him. But I don't want him to hear about me and Rosa from somebody else.

Twenty-seven minutes later, I'm knocking on the Murphy's front door. Gene answers and shows me in. He's barefoot and wearing a pullover and cutoff shorts.

"Glad you could make it," he says as we start upstairs. "The family went out, and it's been so boring with nothing to do."

He closes his bedroom door and locks it.

"Your brother said you were out. Where'd you go?"

"I went to the movies. With...with a girl."

"With a girl?" He looks mildly surprised and breaks into an amused grin. "Who was it?"

"Rosa Martinez."

He lies back on the bed, stretches out, and rubs his hand against my leg.

"Man, I'm impressed. She's hot."

He gives me a nudge. I reach over and start massaging him.

"I would lay her in a heartbeat."

"Uh-huh."

"Yeah, she's got nice boobs," he says, and then he whispers, "Come on."

It's a routine cue between us by now. Today, he talks through a lurid fantasy about Rosa while calling me a cocksucker and playing with my hair and earlobes.

Then I see his face. His eyes are filled with lust, but he's looking at the Cheryl Tiegs poster on his wall. It's mortifying. He's not thinking about me at all. But that tidal wave of passion is rising up inside me. I close my eyes, and suddenly, it's Kerry's face I see. Then, it's happening, and it's stronger than it's ever been before. I'm literally seeing sparks and shivering. Finally, I collapse onto the bed as the fantasy Kerry fades into the real Gene still on top of me.

I'm confused as I bike away from the Murphy house. Knowing that Gene was thinking about Cheryl Tiegs the whole time we were doing it makes my relationship with him feel cheap. It makes *me* feel cheap. I know he doesn't see himself as my boyfriend, but I keep telling myself the sex with him is so great that he must be anyway. And he might think of her when we do it, but I'm the one making him feel that way. So how come I feel so worthless after I'm with him?

And what was it with that fantasy about Kerry? It's one thing to fantasize about a guy when you're by yourself, but something else when you're in another guy's arms.

I decide to put it out of my mind. The less I think about it the better.

Later that evening, I get calls from Blake and Kerry. Both are sympathetic when I tell them what a disaster the whole thing with Rosa turned out to be. Well, Blake isn't really sympathetic as much as positively heartbroken about it. The conversation ends up feeling more like me consoling him than the other way around.

For his part, Kerry is more subdued. Actually, the call is a bit awkward, given my little fantasy about him, and hearing his voice brings the whole thing back to me. So much for my idea of putting it all out of my mind.

Chapter 7: Plan B

I HAVEN'T EVEN made it through the art room door on Monday when Annie pulls me over to our table.

"You've got to tell me the truth about you and Rosa Martinez."

"What?"

"Something happened. What was it?"

"Who told you something happened?"

"Rosa told Stephanie, who talked about it to Billie Jo Jackson. She told Vickie, and Gwen overheard her telling it to Melissa, and she told me."

"What did she say? What's going around?"

Annie looks over her shoulder, sees Mike Kowalski passing, and gives him an evil look. Once she's sure he's out of earshot, and only Jeremy can hear us, she continues.

"The word is you tried to make out with Rosa, and then you tried to feel her up, and she had to slap you."

"You've got to be kidding me. I can't believe Rosa would say something like that, and I can't believe *you* would actually believe it."

"I didn't say I *believed* it, honey. I'm just telling you what I heard. Now, come on; tell me the real story."

As embarrassing as it is, I tell them everything about my date with Rosa. Annie listens attentively, and Jeremy looks up occasionally to register sympathy.

When I finish, Annie says, "That sounds more like it."

"Thanks for that vote of confidence."

"No, I just mean I knew the story I heard about you trying to feel her up couldn't be true. I knew something else must have gone down."

"Of course something else went down. I'm *gay*, remember? This is just great. All I need is for everyone to think I'm a jerk—a straight jerk. I'll never get a boyfriend with that kind of reputation."

Seconds tick by. I sulk and pretend to work while Annie amuses herself with another round of her ongoing war of aggression against Mike Kowalski. To hear her talk, you'd think he believes he's better than us. But back in September, when he tried to sit at our table, she put him down so bad it surprised me he didn't transfer to another school. At the time, I thought if he'd just return fire, she'd probably tone it down. But he never said a word, and after three days of abuse, he retreated to a different table. Ever since then, he just sits there on the other side of the room, sneaking longing glances at her when she's not looking. Or at least he tries to.

After the bell rings, we're putting our things away when Annie suddenly gets that gleam in her eye that usually spells trouble.

"I've got it," she says, with a chortling snort. "It's so simple. We need to fix you up with another girl."

"Have you lost your mind?"

"Sugar, there's only two ways to fix this. You *could* call the girl out and tell people what really happened. But if you did that, it would only be your word against hers. And even if people did believe you, it would only make you look worse. The other option is to go out with another girl. If that goes off okay, you'll sink back below the social radar screen. Then we can go back to work on fixing you up with a guy."

"But that'll just make the gay guys think I'm straight."

"You think you're the only gay guy to use a date with a girl for cover?"

"But—"

"Now, don't you worry. Your old Aunt Annie's on the job. I'll take care of everything."

She walks off grunting a giggle that for all the world sounds like a pig being strangled. Jeremy just pats me on the shoulder and leaves too.

The rest of the afternoon doesn't get any better. In PE, Brad and Ramrod use the rumors about me and Rosa as an excuse to double up on the insults. In the showers, Brad wags himself at me and says if I'd been packing what he's got, Rosa would have been all over me. It's really pathetic. He's not that "gifted."

On the way to study hall, I run into Gene. He nods towards a restroom, and I follow him inside. After a quick check that we're alone, he turns to me with a grin.

"You didn't tell me you tried to cop a feel off Rosa."

"She's lying. I didn't do anything to her."

He can hear the panic in my voice and presses his advantage. "Hey, it doesn't matter to me. I don't care. You can spend time with whoever you want. I can always find someone else to *hang out* with."

"But I want to spend time with you," I whisper. "You know, I'm...a fag—*your* fag. Do you want me to come over today?"

He smirks triumphantly. "Maybe tomorrow. I'll call you. That is, if I'm not too busy, and if you're *sure* you really want to."

"I want to. You know I do."

Gene walks out, and I slump against the wall, totally degraded. There's no mistaking where things stand between him and me now. He couldn't have made it any more clear. He's only toying with me, and I'm heartbroken. He doesn't care if I go out with a girl because the truth is, he really doesn't care about me at all. If I'm not available, he'll just find someone else. I guess I knew it all along. But even if it makes me feel empty and worthless to have to admit it, I've got to make him keep me somehow.

WHEN I WALK into study hall, Blake and Kerry are already getting our library passes from Mr. Warren. Kerry's helping me with a history project, and Blake plans to use the quiet to study his lines.

On the way, I make the mistake of mentioning Annie's Find Randy a New Girl scheme. Of course, Blake loves the idea the second he hears it. He's already heard six different versions of the story about Rosa slapping me.

"You don't know how lucky you are to have Annie Brock's help," he chirps. "She may be crazy, but she knows practically everybody."

"But I don't want Annie's help. I want to forget about the whole thing."

"You can't. Think about it. If you don't bounce back quick, no girl will ever go out with you. You don't want *that*, do you?"

Actually, that would suit me just fine. If Kerry weren't with us, I'd go ahead right now and tell Blake I'm gay just to shut him up. If I can only survive until the weekend, I'm going to tell him the truth, and maybe he'll stop harping on me about girls.

"Promise me you'll at least think about it, okay?"

I nod, and he's temporarily satisfied.

While Kerry and I find an unoccupied table, Blake takes a seat in one of the cushioned reading chairs. As predicted, he not only got a part in the show, he got the one he wanted. He's playing Lieutenant Cable. It's one of the major characters, and he's determined to get all his lines right and sing all his songs without going flat. He's always worried his singing won't be good enough.

He thinks *he's* got troubles. Between Annie and Blake pressuring me, and the fear that Gene might drop me for another guy, I'm totally stressed-out.

We've just spread our books out when Kerry looks me over and sighs.

"How bad can it be to have Annie set you up?"

"I'd just rather let it rest," I reply, my knee bouncing under the table. "Going out should be a personal decision."

"That's true," he says, with a slow nod. "Nobody should be pushed into anything they don't want. It's nobody's business if you don't want a girl."

I freeze for a split second and then clear my throat.

"It's not that I don't *want* a girl, I just don't like people trying to set me up, that's all. And I didn't want to go out with Rosa in the first place."

"Oh. Well, I'm sorry if I pressured you." He looks down at his notebook blushing, and I feel like a jerk for snapping at him.

"I'm sorry, Ker. You didn't pressure me at all. I guess I'm just still feeling a bit touchy about the whole thing. But believe me, it's not you. You didn't do anything."

We go back to our work, but I still feel bad. Maybe I *should* let Annie set me up. One successful date on top of the stories Rosa's spread about me ought to at least shut up the locker room pinheads. And Annie did promise that after this, she'll concentrate on helping me find a guy.

On the bus, I tell Blake I've decided to let Annie set me up with someone. If nothing else, it stops him from pestering me. Content that all's now right with the world, he drifts off into a monologue about the show's rehearsal schedule, and I spend the rest of the ride trying to convince myself that this date thing is a good idea.

WHEN I GET to Art class on Tuesday, I don't even need to tell Annie I'm prepared to let her set me up. She's been assuming it was a done deal from the second she thought of it. As soon as we get settled and begin working on our projects, she starts a sort of twenty questions game to find "just the right girl" for me.

"Uh, you do remember that there's *no such thing* as a 'right girl' for me, don't you?" I say, wishing she could just magically make Gene fall in love with me.

"Sugar, it's for your own good. If you've got something in common with the girl, maybe you won't be so nervous this time. And the information will also be useful to help find you a guy later. Now, let's get started."

And so the game begins. Annie asks the questions, I answer them, and Jeremy listens in.

Some of the questions are really dull:

"What's your favorite group of all time? And don't say the Village People," she warns before I even open my mouth.

"I don't know. Talking Heads or Lou Reed."

Kerry turned me on to them.

"What's your favorite food?"

"Hamburgers."

My cheeks grow warm as I remember Gene getting me that hot dog after the first time I went to his house.

Some of the questions are just silly:

"What's the one thing in the world you most want to do?"

"Duh."

If she only knew how I tingle all over when I'm with Gene.

"What eye color turns you on most?"

"Hazel."

Wait a minute. Gene's eyes are brown. Kerry's the one with hazel eyes.

"What color hair really turns you on?"

"Brown."

Kerry has that kind of beautiful coarse, wavy brown hair you just want to run your fingers through.

Okay, I admit it. I'm more attracted to Kerry than Gene—no earth-shattering news there. But Kerry's straight, and he's got a girlfriend back home. Gene may *claim* to be straight, but he's more than willing to screw a queer, so who knows? He still might fall in love with me eventually.

"What would your ideal—nonsexual—evening with your ideal date look like?"

"Listening to music and chatting about our favorite books."

Chat about a book with Gene? I can't see that ever happening. The sex with him may be unbelievable, but the truth is, sex is the only thing I like doing with him.

But Kerry's a different story. He's not only gorgeous and sexy; he's fun. We've got a lot in common, and even just talking to him makes me feel alive. He's even got me liking things I didn't used to like simply because I can see them from his perspective. He's smart, he's fun, and he's really interesting. The fact is, I enjoy being with Kerry more than just about anyone, even Blake.

As Annie's questions continue, things start adding up.

Suddenly, everything is falling into place—a place I definitely should *not* be in.

I POKE ALONG on my way from Art to PE, lost in thought. It's bad enough that Kerry's *so* hot. It's one thing to know you're gay and think a certain guy is hot, and maybe even fantasize about him every now and then. But it's something else entirely when your image of the perfect guy, the guy you'd really like to spend the rest of your life with, happens to be the guy you just met, the guy who's too handsome for words, and the guy who also just happens to be straight. It's like a double whammy. Not only is my lust gland going crazy for Kerry, but I'm falling in love with him too.

When I go inside the locker room, at first, it looks like Rick Payton is the only one still changing, and I breathe a sigh of relief. But then I see Kerry. Worse, I lay eyes on him at the exact moment he's pulling his strap up past his knees. Between that beautiful face and that gorgeous body, it's the *real* double whammy. My face flushes, and it's like someone's flipped a switch. A lump instantly forms in my throat—and somewhere else.

I unpack my things and start changing with the speed of a cheetah: sneakers fly off, trousers and boxers land on the bench, jock on, shorts up, sneakers back on.

Kerry looks over as I'm piling my things inside the locker. "You intend to wear that shirt for gym?"

I grab my gym bag and rummage around for my pullover. At the same time, I'm frantically unbuttoning my shirt.

"Hey, slow down, Randy," Rick says as he walks out of the room. "You're not that late. We've still got a minute or two."

I try to slow down, but out of the corner of my eye, I can still see Kerry's shirtless frame. The sight of his torso and his neck rising from his shoulders has me so turned on I have to turn away.

When I get up the nerve to look back, he's pulled on his shirt, but he's watching me with a funny expression.

"Are you all right?"

"I'm fine," I mumble, wishing gym shorts didn't make having a hard-on so blindingly obvious. "I'm just a little nervous about Annie setting me up."

He looks me over. "This date thing's got you that nervous? You're acting like you're about to fall apart."

"No, it's not that. I don't feel well. That crap-loaf at lunch today was rancid."

"Well, which is it—nerves or food poisoning? An inquiring public wants to know."

"I don't know. I'm just really stressed-out."

Kerry breaks into a lopsided grin, but he's still got that odd look in his eye. He walks over and puts a hand on my shoulder. His fingers move in a bewitching caress that affects me in exactly the way I don't want it to.

He fixes me squarely in the eye.

"Need a little help releasing all that pent-up tension?"

My cheeks are on fire as he raises an eyebrow and slowly looks down.

Knowing exactly what I'll see, I slowly let my eyes drop to what he's looking at.

At that second, he thumps the pointy tip of my nose, and while I stand there rubbing it, he disappears out the door snickering. Before leaving, I make a quick stop at a toilet to make sure there's nothing to see when I get inside the gym.

When class is over, I volunteer to put the volleyballs away and collect them so slowly a turtle would look faster. By the time I'm done, the locker room is empty. I grab a towel and head for a shower.

WHAT I NEED is time to think all this through and build up some immunity, but a chemistry test I'd forgotten about only adds to my stress, and when I get to study hall, I find out Blake has gone off to the music room to practice "Younger Than Springtime."

So I go to the library, but of course, Kerry does too. He pulls up a chair across from me while I pretend to be busy writing a paper for English.

I'm turning into a basket case. Trying to find my Buddha calmness isn't working. Visions of Kerry in the locker room race through my mind. The teasing sound of his voice, his touch, and even his smell—that alluring mix of cologne and sweat—all seem to slap me in the face and demand that I admit how much I want him. And every time he's ever smiled at me, every glance my way, every word he's ever said that spoke to my soul—it all shouts that I'm falling in love with him. How could I have let this happen?

"Are you sure you're okay? Do you need to go to the nurse?"

I'm already blushing to the tips of my ears before I even look up. Then the sight of those beautiful hazel eyes makes me melt and turn to stone at the same time.

"I'll be fine. The day's almost over anyway."

He still looks worried, but I give him a weak smile and go back to my pretend work. When I glance back up, he smiles back at me, and I tingle all over.

ON THE BUS, Blake studies his lines, unaware of the agony I'm going through right next to him. If only he would distract me with his latest gotta-get-a-girl fantasy, or complain about Mr. Szinhely's latest dumb stage direction. Anything. But no, he just studies his lines until his stop, and I suffer through the remainder of the ride, totally obsessing over Kerry. Not even Theo or that leggy twelfth-grade basketball player Terry Huff can shift my attention.

There's only one thing to do. As soon as I get home, I race to my room, lock the door, and flop on the bed. I try to focus on Gene, and at first, it all seems to be working, but I'm helpless to stop images of Kerry from flooding my mind. So I try to focus on every sexy guy I can remember from TV and the movies. I go down the list: Peter Frampton, Mark

Hamill, Rick Springfield, Scott Baio, John Travolta, even Leif Garrett. But right when I reach the point of no return, it's Kerry's face and body that send me over the edge.

This isn't good.

THE NEXT DAY when fifth period arrives and I take my usual seat across from Jeremy, I notice a pretty nasty-looking bruise on his arm. But as soon as he catches me looking at it, he pulls his shirtsleeve down to cover it.

"How'd you get that?"

"It's nothing," he mutters. "Some guy pushed me in the hall, and I bumped into a locker."

"He must have pushed you pretty hard."

"It's nothing."

I start to ask him if it was one of the guys Kerry and I saw pushing him the other day, but the bell starts ringing. Right on cue, Annie comes bounding in like she's the star of her own TV show and tousles my hair on the way to her seat.

Mrs. Pilt announces that for our new project, we're going to be making ceramic sculptures that will be entered in an upcoming regional contest. Before long, the sound of air pockets being pounded from twenty-nine lumps of clay echo through the room like people being flogged. Clay gets under everybody's fingernails, and an earthy smell fills the air. Chad Maddox sneezes and giggles incoherently.

At our table, the three of us discuss a few options, and we decide to make our individual pieces also work together as a group. With that plan in mind, we begin working on some preliminary models to test out options.

We've been at it for a few minutes when Annie smiles at me.

"I've got the perfect girl for you. She's in my history class. Janie Morton."

Jeremy's head bobs up like a cork out of water, and he stares at her like she's totally lost her mind.

"Janie Morton?"

"Trust me, she's just what we need," Annie says, glowing at me and totally ignoring Jeremy. "First, she's a good-looking girl, right?"

I nod, trying to recall who she is and wondering if she was in one of my classes last year.

"Second, she's—how shall I say it?—not hard to date."

"What do you mean *not hard to date*?"

"She means the girl's easy," Jeremy declares and goes back to his work.

"She's not *that* easy," Annie says, scowling at him, and adding, "Shut up. Janie is easy *to get along with. And* she's not bitchy—" she casts another reproachful eye in Jeremy's direction "—like *some* people I know."

Jeremy slowly shakes his head, while Annie hands me Janie's number with all the formality of awarding the grand prize.

At the end of class, Annie has just floated off down the hall. Jeremy throws the paper towel he's been drying his hands with in the trash can, rubs his fingers through his hair, and turns to me.

"Tell me, Randy, are you a God-fearing man?"

"I suppose so. Why?"

"Because from what I hear, a date with Janie Morton will either be a religious experience or a season in Hell."

He collects his books and leaves the room. I gather my things and head for PE. I've got to admit this whole date with Janie thing has got me more than a little worried. But I'll never get a boyfriend if everybody thinks I'm some sort of girl-crazy pervert. No, I've got to ask Janie out, despite my fears. As soon as that's out of the way, Annie can move on to helping me find a boyfriend, and then maybe I'll be able to get Kerry out of my mind once and for all.

"WALLY, STOP PLAYING with your beans."

Mom is participating in a nightly ritual with my brother. Tonight, The Turd's picking up his lima beans one by one, sniffing them, and burying them in his mashed potatoes.

"I'm not playing with them," he says matter-of-factly. "I'm checking them for fleas."

The Turd comes up with a unique disgusting reply each night.

"Watch your mouth," Dad warns before gritting his teeth and bringing a forkful of meatloaf to his mouth.

I take a deep breath, dreading what I'm about to do.

"Uh, Dad, I'm thinking of asking this girl out. If she says yes, could I use the car one night this weekend?"

It's like the room freezes. The Turd drops his fork, Mom stops in mid chew, and Dad stares at me like I've just grown a second head. My folks may not know I'm gay, and God help me if they ever find out, but this is the first time I've shown anything even remotely resembling interest in a girl.

Mom slowly starts chewing again with a look of absolute joy on her face.

Dad leans back in his chair, studying me.

The Turd raises an eyebrow, his eyes narrow, and he slides into a sarcastic grin.

"A girl? Is she blind?"

"Shut up, Wally," Dad snaps. He takes a quick glance at Mom. "Now, this girl you're planning to ask out—it's not that black girl you hang out with, is it?"

"No, Dad," I say with a sigh. "The girl I'm talking about is white."

"Okay. Well, do you think you could manage to take the girl out, get her home, and bring the car back without killing anyone?"

"I swear I'll be very careful. I won't even let a bird poop on the car, I promise."

"Well you almost killed that wetback last time."

"Dad," I whine.

The Turd snickers.

"Bill, you know he's careful," Mom says.

Dad looks at me skeptically. But then, miraculously, he surprises me with a grin. "Well, just get the car and yourself home in one piece, okay?"

"Thanks, Dad."

Somehow, I doubt it would go this easy if I ever told them I wanted to use the car so I could go out with a boy.

AFTER DINNER, I retreat to my room. Now comes the hard part. I feel ridiculous calling a girl I don't even know for a date. But I take a deep breath, bite my lip, and dial the number anyway.

"Hello?"

"May I speak with Janie, please?"

"This is Janie. Who is this?"

"Hi, Janie. This is Randy Clark."

"Randy Clark...?"

"I'm Annie Brock's friend from art class."

"Are you the tall one with dark hair?" she asks suspiciously. "The one Annie's always talking about?"

"No, that would be Mike Kowalski."

"You're not that little guy, are you?"

"No, but I sit at the same table with him and Annie."

"Oh, you're *that* one. Oh yes, Annie says *nice* things about you. Okay, what can I do for you, Randy?"

"Well...uh...Annie is always saying what a great person you are, and I was wondering if you might like to go out with me this weekend."

"Sure, I'll go out with you, Randy. When do you want to go?"

"How about Friday night? We could have a bite to eat, maybe pizza or a burger, and take in a movie."

"That sounds great."

Janie gives me her address, and we arrange for me to pick her up at six.

Amazingly, I make it through the whole call without feeling sick. And just like that, I've got a date set up.

A date.

With a girl.

My *second* date with a girl.

This is crazy, but I've got to go through with it. I can't risk letting the other gay guys—whoever they are—think I'm some straight sex maniac. As long as I don't get sick when I'm out with Janie, though, everything should be okay.

Why can't it be this easy to get a date with a guy?

Chapter 8: A Weekend of Rendezvous

DAD'S JUST GIVEN me the keys to the car, and I've successfully made it out of the driveway—without killing anybody. After a quick stop for gas, I'm on my way to Janie's house. *Eighty cents a gallon. What a rip off.* But I've got more important things than the cost of a full tank of gas to deal with, like a stomach full of butterflies. This will mark my second—and hopefully last—date with a girl. I just want to get it over with as soon as possible.

I am taking it seriously though. I've shaved (might as well practice for the day when I'll really need to), and I'm as squeaky-clean as I can be. I bought a bottle of cologne—not as sexy as Gene's, but then I don't suppose thinking about him would help things tonight—and I'm dressed smartly for the occasion in a Bee Gees pullover and disco-style bell-bottom pants.

How I've gotten through the last two days, I'll never know. It's been hell. Dad's spent every waking minute reminding me about the responsibility that comes with driving. You'd think I'd never even taken Driver's Ed, much less actually got my license.

And, of course, last night we had to have that "father-son talk."

If I'm lucky, someday I'll be able to block it out of my memory.

Speaking of things to block from memory, since Wednesday night, The Turd has been going all out to torment me. It's been open season on stupid comments about "that poor girl." I've suffered through a constant stream of remarks about how ugly Janie must be, how dumb she must be, and how bad she must smell.

And he's not left me out of the line of fire either. "Does that poor girl realize you'll cry if she pinches you? Has she had all her shots? Does she have any idea how 'little' you are? Does she know your balls haven't dropped yet?"

I swear. He must have an encyclopedia of personal putdowns he's been saving for just this occasion.

And don't even ask me about how my mom has been acting. I'm not even going there.

But the school week's finally over, and soon enough, I'll be able to put this whole unpleasant business behind me. I plan to spend the rest of the weekend quietly celebrating.

Oh, I've made Blake swear to wait until I call him or until I tell him how things went on Monday. Technically, I made Kerry swear too, but it wasn't really necessary with him. Blake's the one who can't stand not knowing every detail about everything in the world as soon as it happens.

A VERY NEAT yard—crowned with a Virgin Mary shrine—guards a conservative-looking house. I'm prepared for the third degree from parents, not so subtle threats from older brothers, and inquisitive stares from younger siblings. Even though I'm pretty sure Annie put Janie up to this, I'm still nervous. Words like "easy" and "season in Hell" ominously float through my mind as I get out of the car.

The door opens, and Janie smiles from ear to ear. She's wearing a low-cut blouse with a gold necklace supporting some kind of medal. It's snugly wedged between as generous a set of boobs as a girl could have without falling over. Her skirt stops well short of halfway between her waist and her knees. She's got firm legs and strong ankles—she needs them; she's wearing four-inch high heels. If not for the shoes, I doubt she'd come up to my shoulder.

Oh, did I say she has big tits?

She closes the door with one hand, lunges at me, and wraps me in her arms. The way she kisses me, you'd think I'm the love of her life. It's wet, and it's sloppy, and she seems to be checking my teeth for cavities with her tongue.

"Hi, Randy," she gushes when we finally come up for air.

"Hi, J-Janie," I stammer. "Do, uh, do your folks want to meet me?"

"Why would they? You're dating me, not them."

I escort her to the car and open the door for her like the gentleman I've been brought up to be. As soon as I get behind the wheel, she scoots over next to me faster than a kid going down a waterslide. She's practically on top of me.

"So, what are you in the mood for?" I ask and quickly add, "For dinner, that is."

"Burgers will be fine."

"Burgers it is."

When we go inside Jim's Burger Barn, Janie sweeps me over to a booth and pulls me in beside her. A couple of times while we eat, she squeezes my knee. Maybe she's testing my reflexes. When we're done, I pay the check and leave a generous tip.

Halfway to the car, Janie stops me.

Right there, in the middle of the street, in front of God and everybody, she kisses me. It's another slow, wet kiss, and once again, her tongue does a spot-check on my teeth. The only difference this time is the chili and onions.

"You know," she announces, "we don't *have* to go to the movies if you don't want to. I've seen all three of them anyway."

I start to worry that I've failed the cavity test, but she goes on.

"We *could* just drive around for a while, and then maybe go somewhere else."

So we drive through The District. Twice. Everybody who's anybody sees us together. There we are, in the car. Me, Randy Clark, with a girl—Janie Morton, no less—who doesn't look like she's mortified to be seen with me at all.

But I'm not really sure it's all worth it. Janie's got her arm around me, and she's playing with my hair. Her other hand keeps squeezing my knee and sliding up my thigh—on the inside. With each pass, it slides up a little higher, and I get more and more uncomfortable.

"I know another place we could go, if you'd like," she says.

"Uh...sure. Where?"

"Turn left up there."

Twenty-one minutes later, we're in the middle of nowhere. Janie tells me to turn onto a side road. It's very dark, and the houses are few and far between. After a couple of turns, the road dead-ends a good half mile from the last house.

"We can park here for a while," she says.

I turn off the headlights, and the instant the car's motor stops running, hers starts. She's all over me. I didn't know it was possible for a girl to like making out this much. The last time I saw anything close to it was in a vampire movie.

Right now, I'd gladly prefer the mark of the undead.

TWELVE TWENTY-THREE. I'M lying in bed, clutching the covers.

I practically ran to the shower as soon as I got home. After lots of soap and hot water, I'd washed all traces of Janie away from my body, but washing away the memory of what happened tonight will be a lot harder. I roll over and wonder how much a psychiatrist costs.

I should probably be congratulating myself right now. By normal standards, the date was a rollicking success. On the plus side, I didn't throw up on Janie. In fact, I didn't throw up at all, and I did almost everything she wanted me to. *And* I brought the car back home in one piece. (Señor Pedestrian survives for another day.)

But it was also the most uncomfortable night of my life. And when it was over, all it proved was that the only way I can, um, be with a girl, is through the masterful use of my Buddha focus. It took absolute concentration about a certain someone the whole time. Otherwise, my date with Janie would have been a disaster of biblical proportions.

Great, so I did it. I had a successful date with a girl. But it just confirms what I've known all along. I am a U.S. Certified Grade-A homosexual. I'm as queer as a three-dollar bill. I've climbed Mount Titicaca and seen the summit, but without a doubt, I was born to pursue Mount Dick.

I just don't understand it. Last month, I started out with a simple mission–to identify other gay guys at Chadham High, look them over, and pick one out for a boyfriend. It should have been easy. Instead, I'm no closer to finding the right guy, and the guy I'm having sex with doesn't love me, and the guy I'm falling in love with is straight.

I can hear Annie now: "You're only falling in *lust*, sugar."

And speaking of Annie, so far, her whole contribution to helping me achieve my goals has been talking me into going out with a girl. *Twice.*

That's it. Monday afternoon, I'm going to have a word with Annie and clarify the parameters of what her job is supposed to be here.

IN THE MORNING, the full extent of my traumatic date with Janie hits home. At first, I think a good-night's sleep has given me the necessary distance, but things start to go downhill the minute Mom asks me to help her with the grocery shopping. As soon as we pull out of the driveway, she starts in with the questions. All the while, she's wearing the silliest grin I've ever seen.

"So, how was your date last night?"

"Fine."

At least it's over. Now would you just let me forget the whole nightmare ever happened?

"Were you polite?"

"Yes."

If I'd been rude, maybe I wouldn't have been violated.

"Did she look pretty?"

"Up to a point."

And then she started taking her clothes off. Excuse me while I pull over and throw up.

"Did she have a good time?"

"She certainly seemed to."

I, on the other hand, have been scarred for life.

"Are you going out with her again?"

"I don't know. We'll see."

In other words, not in this *lifetime, sister.*

Mom's questions go on and on, and the more I have to think about Janie, the more uneasy I feel. By the time we get to the grocery store, I'm a nervous wreck. Then things really go downhill. As soon as we walk inside, I feel like everyone knows what happened to me. It's like I'm naked or something, and everybody's staring at me.

And every female below the age of forty looks threatening. When one woman asks me to help her put a big bag of potatoes in her cart, I actually jump, terrified she's going to pull me into the vegetable aisle and start humping me. My heart doesn't stop racing until I'm back home.

As the day wears on, the stress gets worse. By midafternoon, I feel like I'm going to crack up, so I call Annie. She agrees to meet me at the park in a half hour. I get there with nineteen minutes to spare and wait for her on a park bench, drumming my fingers on the back of it.

It's a bit warm for this time of year, and the people around me are taking advantage of it. Jogging is all the rage these days. Several men and women pass me. The females make me decidedly nervous, especially the ones who seem to slow down as they go by.

As soon as Annie sits down, I throw my arms around her, and start crying on her shoulder.

"Randy-baby, what's wrong? What happened?"

Over the next twelve minutes, between sobs, I tell her what happened.

"Oh baby, I am so disgusted Janie took advantage of you like that. I figured she might make a pass, or kiss you or something, but I swear I never thought she'd go that far."

Annie rocks me and gently pats me on the back. "You poor baby. There, there, it's okay. I know it was horrible, but it's all over now."

After I've calmed down a little, she clears her throat. "But, honey, I do have to say it: It was pretty stupid to let her direct you to a dead-end road in the middle of nowhere. Lord have mercy, boy, how could you not know what was on her mind?"

She's right, of course, even if it does make me feel like an even bigger idiot.

AFTER ANNIE AND I say goodbye, I bike around aimlessly through various neighborhood streets to kill time, trying to fill my mind with any sight or sound that might help me forget I ever heard of Janie Morton. House after house floats past me, and I turn up this or that street, not caring or paying attention to where I'm going.

But before I know it, I end up in Gene's neighborhood. Telling myself it must be fate, I leave my bike on the lawn and knock.

Gene opens the door and smirks. He's only wearing shorts. From the sounds and smells coming from the kitchen, I figure his mother is in the back, and she must be cooking.

"Just couldn't wait for me to call, huh? Well, come on up."

Once inside his room, he locks the door and rubs my thigh. Then he winks, backs me up to the bed, and pushes me down.

"It's a little warm in here."

"Gene? Could we just talk for a while first?"

"Sure," he says with a smile, but he pushes me back, rubs against me, and pinches me.

"Come on, Gene," I whisper between gasps. "Stop. I don't want to do this right now."

My hand goes up to stop him, but I end up pulling at his shorts instead. He swings free to stand, comes back naked, and kneels next to me on the bed. He tugs on my pullover. I want him to stop, but he caresses me, and I give in.

My shirt lands on the floor. He climbs on top of me and leans over close. I can't help but moan when he pinches me and tickles my earlobe. Damn him. He knows how to get me going.

It's the same old story. We are the predator and the willing prey, animals acting on pure instinct and passion. His hands glide over me and turn my body against me. I lose myself in the sensations of the moment—the taste, the smell, the feel of his arms wrapped around me, and that exquisite vibration when he's inside me.

When it's over, he lies there smiling. I lean over to kiss him, but he turns away, and I end up just kissing his neck. After I dress, he walks me to his bedroom door.

As always, the bike ride home brings me back down to reality all too quickly, and I wonder why I went anywhere near his house.

Maybe after last night, I needed something that felt natural to me, something that wouldn't sicken me like what Janie and I did. But I also needed something more than that. I needed time. I needed to feel wanted, to feel that someone cared. But Gene doesn't care what I want, and he never will. To him, I'm just someone to have sex with. Period.

The truth is, Gene and I only connect on one level—passion—and that's not enough. I used to think passion and love were pretty much the same thing, but they're not. Physical contact may feed passion, but it can't feed a starving soul—only love can do that.

"And Gene will never love me," I admit with a sigh.

I've had sex with two different people this weekend, and both times, it meant nothing to them emotionally. Neither of them cared about what *I* wanted, what *I* needed. Neither of them cared about me.

Chapter 9: A Welcome Distraction

BLAKE JUMPS ON the bus and beelines straight for me. I probably should have called over the weekend and told him how my date with Janie went, but some experiences, the traumatic ones anyway, need time to be processed.

He falls into the seat next to me as excited as a dog about to go walkies. But one good look at my face tells him my story won't be a tale of romance and passion. He actually waits a few seconds before even speaking.

"How was your weekend?"

"Peachy. I'll tell you about it in Spanish, okay?"

He nods, and we're both silent the rest of the way.

After a quick stop at my locker, I wander to homeroom. Kerry's hair is a little messy today. He's wearing a lavender button-up shirt that highlights those amazing eyes of his.

"Did you have a nice weekend?" he asks after we exchange good mornings.

"Yeah, I suppose. You?"

Before he can answer, Ramrod's voice rises like chalk on a blackboard. "Hey, Clark, I hear you took Janie Morton out Friday night. She must need psychological counseling."

"Oh yeah, she was traumatized all right—after she saw your face Friday afternoon."

Kerry and the others laugh, and Mrs. Beach warns everyone—meaning Ramrod and me—to quiet down.

Kerry leans over. "Well, if there was any doubt that the whole school would know you went out with Janie, it'll be front-page news now."

"I guess so. I'll tell you about it later," I say, and he nods.

As the morning progresses, I can tell word is spreading about my date with Janie. A few of the girls seem to show more interest in me, but most still look at me like I'm pond scum. More than a few of the guys, though, glance at me like I'm now part of some secret club, and I wonder how many of Janie's dates have ended the same way mine did.

During Spanish, I give Blake a brief account of Friday night and tell him we ended the evening just driving around before I took her home. I don't mention us stopping along the way, or where we stopped, or what happened once we did. (If I had to talk about it, I think I'd throw up.)

For once, Blake doesn't ask questions. He just listens and seems to understand that whatever went down, it wasn't something I'm very comfortable with.

My first opportunity to tell Kerry about Friday comes at lunchtime. We walk outside and find a spot that provides relative privacy. The sun shines on Kerry's hair and highlights the flecks of green and gold in his eyes. He looks so good that for a minute, I forget why we came outside in the first place.

To bring me back to reality he finally has to ask, "So, you want to tell me about you and Janie?"

I proceed to tell him, and although I skip over the more embarrassing stuff like I did with Blake, this time, I don't hold back on how uncomfortable the whole night was.

When I finish, he's silent for a few seconds. Then he says, "You know, there's no law that says you have to date girls before you're ready. Or at *all*, for that matter."

The remark hangs in the air between us. I'd think he was making a crack, but his expression is almost wistful, so I just nod and let it pass.

AFTER ART CLASS, which features Chad Maddox high-fiving me and Annie giving Mike Kowalski the evil eye, I slump along to the locker room where I totally ignore Brad and Ramrod, change, and get out fast.

Today, Coach Horne has us running around the football field. We start out all packed together, but by the time we reach the twenty-yard line, we're already spreading out. While I'm holding my own, Kerry's got the stamina of a marathon runner. Initially, Ramrod outpaces me, but before long, he's winded, and we leave him behind.

The goal line on the far side of the field marks the halfway point. I'm already exhausted by the time I get to it. The only thing keeping me moving is seeing Kerry ahead of me. By the time I cross the finish line, I'm completely drained. But then I look back. Most of the guys are still plodding along, including, to my amusement, Brad and Jamie. A red-faced, panting Ramrod is pulling up the rear.

As we each complete our third lap, the coach tells us to hit the showers. Kerry and I head inside, along with Rick Payton and a couple of the other guys. I'm so spent from the run I don't even bother invoking my Buddha focus. With every step, what little energy I've got left in me evaporates like the sweat dripping off my body.

But it's a different story as soon as the water hits me. Maybe it's the sight of four very attractive teenage males, bending and stretching as the warm spray washes over them. Maybe it's the smell of adolescent sweat dripping off slender young chests and running down freshly worked-out thighs. Whatever the reason, energy courses back through me, and within seconds, my natural reaction grows stubbornly obvious.

If I look one way, there's Rick Payton and Jeff Gray in all their glory.

If I look the other way, Billy Mason is soaping up his chest.

And turning away from him brings me face-to-face with Kerry. He's washing the shampoo out of his hair, the soapy water streaming down his face and chest. I watch it flowing down and surrender to the arousal coursing through me.

Then, I glance back up and realize Kerry's eyes are open. He's caught me checking him out. And the worst part is, he's far enough away that he doesn't even need to look down to see what's happening to me.

Talk about embarrassed. Between my face and my hard-on, I'm surprised there's enough blood left for the rest of my body. I spin back to the wall and shut off the hot water. But in this condition, even cold water has a fight on its hands. My lust gland is in full hormonal rebellion, and it refuses to take this fight lying down.

I rush to the locker room, dressing as fast as I can. But just when my brain has finally regained some control over my body, Kerry walks in, totally naked, and my lust gland goes back on full alert.

He stops. Our eyes meet. He's wearing an odd expression.

"Crazy workout today, huh?" he says.

"Yeah."

He's looking directly into my eyes. "It really...uh...gets the blood moving, doesn't it?"

He starts to say something else, but I grab my book bag. "I've got to go. Chemistry test today."

It's a good thing we really don't have a test in Chemistry. The run's effect on my lust gland continues the whole class. Stray images of Kerry in the shower haunt me like ghosts on the edge of my field of vision. As soon as I get to study hall, I ask Mr. Warren for a library pass and spend the rest of the period hiding out in case Kerry comes looking for me.

THE NEXT WEEK and a half only deepens the disaster that is my life. Report cards come out, and my grades continue a trend that guarantees I'll graduate as "Most Likely to be Mediocre." The only bright spots are Art and English. My history grade is only slightly better than it was before Kerry started studying with me. And Spanish doesn't help because even my parents know Mrs. Burnett gives anybody who shows up a B-minus, and yet, I somehow manage to only make a C-plus. Then there's the C-minus in PE, the C in Chemistry, and the D-minus in Geometry. In short, it's not a report card that inspires a lot of confidence in my academic potential.

Then, my self-esteem suffers yet another blow when Blake passes his driving exam on his first try. He's not the kind to rub it in, but he's so proud and happy to show off the picture on his license that it can't help remind me of the three attempts it took me to get mine.

But the real root of my troubles can be summed up in five words: Kerry Sawyer and Gene Murphy.

When Gene hears about me going out with another girl, Janie Morton no less, it's like he goes on some kind of campaign to make my life miserable. He invites me over Wednesday and then won't let me touch him. He preens and smirks and orders me not to come by again until he tells me to. The rest of the week, every time the phone rings, I'm dying for it to be him. And at school, whenever he sees me, he makes sure to catch my eye only to avoid me. By the time he finally does call me Sunday afternoon, I'm so desperate, I practically jump him as soon as I get there. Then, he calls me a slut and a cocksucker the whole time. It's humiliating enough to hear him say it, but the memory feels even more degrading every time I remember it.

And Kerry. Since he caught me checking him out, it's been weird. He hasn't really said anything about it, and he sort of acts normal, but there's something different in the way he looks at me now. And then there are other things—little things. Like whenever he's sitting next to me, he makes sure his leg touches mine. And he sort of poses when he's standing in front of me. It's like he's trying to see if he can get another rise out of me, which already happens all too easily. And it doesn't help that he's started wearing things he just looks so good in, like that striped pullover that clings to his chest, or those tight new-wave jeans. Really, it's like he's taunting me, and it's driving me crazy. But then again, everything he does these days drives me crazy—and makes me want him even more.

I'VE ONLY BEEN home for a half hour Tuesday afternoon when the phone rings.

"Hello?"

"Hey, Randy-man," Blake says, cheerily. "Will you be busy tonight?"

"I doubt it."

"Good. Come join me for the rehearsal. I'll drive."

"Uh-huh, 'join you' as in just watch the rehearsal or 'join you' as in join the show?"

"Well, now that you mention it, it's still not too late for you to be an extra."

"Blake."

"Yeah, there is a whole group of sailors who don't have any lines; they just sing in the chorus. You could be one of them."

"I don't sing."

"Don't worry about that. You'll be fine. *And* you'll have fun."

"No."

"Well, okay then. Just come along and sit in."

"No."

"Come on. I promise; I won't say a word about joining the show. Just come see what's happening."

"No."

"Please," he whines, and there's a full four seconds of silence.

After the fifth second, I sigh.

"You're making that puppy-dog face of yours, aren't you? I hate it when you do that, even over the phone."

"Aw, come on. I promise I won't pressure you."

"You're *already* pressuring me."

"Just come with me tonight and see what it's all about. You never know, you might change your mind, and if not, I won't say a word. I promise."

"Okay, damn it. But I'm telling you now. I'm not joining the show."

BLAKE PULLS OFF the access lane, parks the car, and we walk to the auditorium. It's a separate building and almost as large as the gym, except it only holds enough seating for seven hundred people. The rest is taken up with the stage, dressing rooms, and scenery shops.

I take a seat over to one side about halfway from the stage, hoping to make myself inconspicuous. Blake goes up to the stage. A number of students are milling about waiting for things to get underway, and he starts chatting with a few of them. There's a lot going on for nothing to be happening. The buzz of laughter and a dozen conversations overlap snatches of songs from the production. Two people bang away at "Heart and Soul" on a piano, while Blake smiles and chats animatedly with two girls. He's having a good time, and it's a cute side of him I don't get to see very often. It's funny how he doesn't have a problem talking to girls when he's not thinking about them as potential dates.

One of the guys breaks away from the group and starts up the aisle. It's Mitch Weaver. His light brown hair crowns a handsome but smooth face, and as he gets closer, his eyes fix on me.

"Hey, Randy. Are you joining the production?"

"Hi, Mitch. No, Blake's been telling me what a great show it is, so I just came along to see what it's all about. Of course, he *has* also been trying to get me to join up."

"Well, you ought to think about it. It's a lot of fun. I bet you'd like it if you gave it a chance."

While Mitch makes his own version of a Blake-like sales pitch, I make a silent appraisal of him. He's got a strong personality that doesn't invite crude insults from the Ramrods of the world, and he's always been open and nice with everybody. He's tall and has a build that's somewhere between sturdy and lanky—kind of sexy really.

Mr. Szinhely claps his hands, and the cast and crew fall silent. Mitch gives me a final smile and struts back up the aisle.

"Good evening, cast," Mr. Szinhely says, chuckling like Paul Lynde. "Tonight we're going to work on the first act, specifically the Bloody Mary-Bali Ha'i sequence. We'll do a full walk-through and then fine-tune it section by section. So, places, everyone."

Most of the guys ascend to the stage and disappear to the right. A few other guys, and all but one of the girls, grab seats in the first couple of rows. Over the next half hour, I watch the scene unfold in various stages of development. The only female on stage plays a native who tries to sell the sailors grass skirts. It's a pretty funny scene.

"Okay, people," Mr. Szinhely says, "We're going to take five. Now when we come back, I want to take some time with Billis, Cable, and Bloody Mary, and then we'll do a final walk-through of the whole bit. So the rest of you don't wander off too far."

The people in the seats stand and stretch. Those onstage drift away in twos and threes. Mitch and a couple of guys stroll up the aisle. He has his eye on me and smiles as he passes. I'm tempted to follow him, but Blake trots over and grabs a seat near mine.

"Well, what do you think?"

"I think it's actually going to be pretty good. Much better than I expected."

"This is your chance. It's not too late to get in on the act."

"Hey, I said I *liked* the circus. I didn't say I wanted to run away and *join* it."

"Ho-ho-ho."

Mr. Szinhely calls the group back to order and begins work with the principal cast members, including Blake. Meanwhile, those not needed chat quietly and otherwise entertain themselves. I notice that Mitch and a few others are not in the auditorium, so I sneak to the lobby where I hear sounds coming from outside.

People huddle and talk in several little groups. The night air has that wonderful feeling that only autumn can give. It's not too cool and has a refreshing edge that makes you really feel alive. A clean aromatic breeze challenges the fumes drifting from the cigarettes a couple of students are smoking. Mitch sees me and walks over.

"So, have you been enjoying the rehearsal?"

"Yeah, I really have. You guys are good. And you do a great job on that 'dame' song; your voice comes through really nice."

"I was afraid I was singing flat."

"Well, I don't know what it's supposed to sound like, but it certainly sounded good to me."

He breaks into a humble smile that's cute beyond words. "Thanks."

I smile back. "So, how are you doing in History? I can't believe Mrs. Molina thinks Jackson was such a great president."

"Me neither. He was such a tool. 'Let's just kick the Indians out and march them across the continent. Too bad if a lot of them die along the way.'"

"Yeah," I say with growing confidence. "So, you going to any of the football games this year?"

"No," he says. "I like to watch football on TV every now and then, but I'm not really into it the way some of the jocks around here are."

"Yeah, I know what you mean."

While we chat, I get the overpowering sense we're connecting. Mitch and I have been friendly for years. But what's significant is that he's again locking eyes with me.

If he's flirting with me, this may be my chance. I could do a lot worse than Mitch.

I decide to test the waters and take a small step closer. He doesn't step back.

That's it. He's interested in me.

"Want to get together sometime?" I'm looking directly into his eyes.

"Yeah, might be fun to hang out together," he says, matching my gaze.

"How about this weekend? We could grab a bite and take in a movie."

"Yeah, that'd be cool."

"Say, Friday night?"

"Yeah, sure."

We're staring straight into each other's eyes, we're both wearing bashful faces, and one step closer, and we'd be embracing. By the time someone calls everybody back inside, hugging him isn't the only thing I want to do to Mitch Weaver.

I follow him inside, certain we both want the same thing.

I've done it. Friday night will finally be my first real gay date.

Back home, I lie in bed. Sure, Mitch hasn't actually told me he's gay, but I haven't told him I am either. Why would we need to? If a guy wants to date a girl, he doesn't walk up and say, "Hello, I'm heterosexual. Would you like to go out with me?" so why should two gay guys?

As I look back over the years I've known Mitch, I start seeing a pattern. He's always been nice to me, and we've always gotten along. The more I think about it, the evolution of our relationship over time becomes more obvious. We've been meant for each other from the start, and tonight was that pivotal moment when we began the next phase of the life together that will soon be ours.

Chapter 10: Mitch Weaver

I DON'T SAY a word to Blake or Kerry about my plans Friday night. When the topic comes up, I just offer up a vague, "Sorry, I'll be busy." And oh boy do I plan to be busy. Over the next three days, I carefully plan out everything. Wednesday morning, when Kerry and I come into History, and we pass Mitch on the way to our seats, he nods good morning, and I respond with a shy smile. I lose track of the lesson, dwelling on the curve of his shoulders and how the sun accentuates his hair.

When I tell Annie and Jeremy about Mitch, Annie says she thinks it's just possible I might actually have a chance this time. Oddly enough, Jeremy is even more optimistic about my prospects than Annie—another first.

But both of them caution me to take it easy, and to go one step at a time. Of course, Annie goes way over the top and even claims I get carried away with things too easily.

Ridiculous. When have I ever let my mind run away with me? I mean, caution is one thing, but not being prepared is something else. And I definitely want my first date with Mitch to be special.

After History class on Thursday, I let Kerry go ahead and pull Mitch aside. I offer to drive Friday night, and he jots down his address and phone number. When he passes me the note, our fingers touch. The sensation is electrifying.

That night, I join Blake for another rehearsal. I'm fascinated by how easily Mitch dominates the stage with his handsome yet modest sexual appeal. In every song, his nasal tones are all I hear, and his voice rings out sharply above all the others.

When Mr. Szinhely calls for a break, Mitch invites me to join him and a few others outside. I follow along like a puppy chasing the wiener wagon. While I don't really participate in the conversation much, when I do, I make sure to agree with everything Mitch says.

When the cast gets called back inside, I stroll along beside him, resisting the urge to hold his hand. While he continues to the stage, I grab a seat where I'll be able to have a good view of him.

I haven't been sitting there more than forty-five seconds when Blake spies me and runs up to pull me forward. I should be suspicious, but the fifteen minutes I've just spent flirting with Mitch have left me off guard.

It's not until we pass the front row that the little voice in my head says, "Uh-oh, it's a trap."

"Mr. Szinhely, this is Randy Clark, the one I've been telling you about."

Mr. Szinhely chuckles. "Greetings, Randy, greetings. Blake's told me how disappointed you were to miss the tryouts and how much you want to be in the show. Well, cheer up there, Bunky. Blake speaks so highly of you that I'm going to make your day. You can join the cast as one of the sailors."

He sees the look of shock on my face and smiles broadly.

"Now, I'm afraid I can't give you a speaking role, but you can sing along with the sailors. How's that?"

"I...uh..."

He laughs and pats me on the shoulder. "That's okay, that's okay. I know; you're speechless. Well, congratulations."

I've been shanghaied. Blake smiles at me and blinks coyly. I could kill him.

But on the other hand...

I *would* be standing next to Mitch, so I'd get to spend that much more time with him—not exactly a bad thing. I look over and see the happy expression on his face. That settles it. Blake has finally gotten his wish. I'm in the show.

I spend the rest of the night standing close to Mitch and Hunter Shea, a guy he seems to be really good friends with. The stage directions aren't difficult, but I let Mitch guide me through things anyway. It gives us more opportunities to connect.

At nine thirty-two, Mr. Szinhely calls a halt for the night. He's pleased with everyone's progress, and after adding a stern warning to those with speaking parts about memorizing lines, he tells us to have a good weekend.

Blake's even more pleased than Szinhely with how things went, and I have to hand it to him, he has every right to be happy. The rehearsal focused on the second act. Lieutenant Cable has a song called "You've Got to Be Carefully Taught," and tonight, Blake really came into his own as a singer. If he can pull off a performance like that in front of an audience, our little production just might end up on Broadway yet.

When we descend the steps at the side of the stage, the girl Blake was talking to in the library stops him.

"Blake," she squeals. "Where did you get that voice? I've never heard anyone sing with such emotion. My God! You gave me goose bumps."

"Thanks," he says, trying not to act as proud as he must feel. "Oh, I'm sorry. Mary Beth, this is Randy Clark. He and I go way back."

"Nice to meet you, Mary Beth."

"Hi, Randy," she says, barely glancing my way and—introductions over—goes right back to fawning all over him.

Mary Beth is that most dangerous of all animals, the *Americanus femalius*. She's obviously in search of a mate, and right now, she's set her sights on Blake. Of course, he's so totally oblivious, I'm not even going to bother pointing it out to him later. He's never once considered the possibility that a girl might be interested in him. Well, if he doesn't see it in this one, he's probably better off.

I look around and notice Mitch standing next to the stage-side door. He's looking our way, and since I've already heard enough of Mary Beth slobbering on and on about Blake's dulcet tones to last a lifetime, I mosey over.

"I'm glad you joined the show," Mitch says.

"I am too. It's a lot of work, but I really enjoyed myself tonight. And thanks for all the help."

"Oh, it was nothing, just helping you get into the blocking. And you're a natural."

"Thanks."

A voice rings out from somewhere in the auditorium. "Mitch, come on; it's time to go."

"Be there in a second, Hunter," he yells back. "Got to go. See you tomorrow. I'm looking forward to hanging out."

I watch him disappear down the aisle and sigh. *From behind, he's almost as good-looking as Kerry. Wait. Stop it. No. No, he's* better *looking. He's better looking, and after tomorrow night, it'll be easy to get Kerry out of my mind.*

I have to wait another four minutes before Blake finally gets away from Mary Beth. He's not exactly trying too hard. But it doesn't matter. With fantasies about tomorrow night and what my date with Mitch will be like floating through my mind, I'm more than happy to wait.

THE WEAVERS LIVE in a nice two-story house facing the southern end of the street. I slow the car to a stop in front and blow the horn. That's the protocol: blow the horn and wait for your date to come out. Guy dates don't require door-to-door service, at least not at the beginning anyway.

My parents didn't even ask why I wanted to use the car tonight. It's funny. Since my date with Janie, they treat me like I'm a completely different person. It's like, to my father, I'm suddenly no longer the sissy embarrassment I've pretty much always been. I've somehow become something he might actually one day be proud of—you know, a competent human being. And when I ask for the keys these days, instead of another lecture, he assumes I'm going to see a girl. Hey, what he doesn't know won't hurt me, right?

I did give them enough clues that tonight is a date though. I had every minute after school planned out. The first thing I did when I got home was hit the shower. Then I spent a good half hour choosing what to wear: a loose-fitting puffy-sleeved striped shirt, with an extra button undone at the neck, pleated slacks plain enough to be casual, and the same cologne I wore when I went out with Janie, but placed in more strategically important locations. Twelve minutes of fussing over my hair capped off my preparations for the evening.

Incidentally, when I emerged from the bathroom, The Turd told me Gene had called. I guess that sexual tapeworm of his is getting hungry again, but for once, his summons didn't leave me panicked to get to his house as fast as I could. I've pretty much been ignoring him since Tuesday night. Hey, if things go right tonight, Gene can dump me. I won't care.

Mitch bounds across the yard, and I'm struck breathless. He's wearing a pullover that's just tight enough to reveal a much hotter chest than his usual school clothes let on, and those tight, flair-legged pants would enhance his looks from any direction. When he gets in, his cologne does overwhelm mine a bit—it's kind of pungent—but it's a small price to pay.

I pull the car into the street and head for The District. "Which movie do you want to see?"

"You decide."

"Well, we've got *Alien, Starting Over,* and *Quadrophenia.* I've seen *Alien,* and I hear *Quadrophenia* is kind of boring."

"Me too. So unless you want to see *Alien* again, I guess *Starting Over* it is."

"Works for me," I say, determined to make him realize how compatible we are before the end of the evening.

We start out with a bite at Jim's Burger Barn. When the waitress comes to take our order, Mitch doesn't even look at the menu.

"I'll have the Kaiser Burger with extra sauerkraut, fries, and a root beer," he says.

"I'll have the same," I chime in, but I'm thinking, *Oh God, how can anyone eat sauerkraut?*

"Wow, this is cool," he says, beaming, "I don't run into many people around here who like the Kaiser as much as me."

"Oh, I love it."

During the meal, music is the main topic of conversation. For a singer, Mitch has really bad taste—I mean, I'm sorry, but Leo Sayer? Hello? Nevertheless, I continue my agree-with-him-about-everything campaign, and I only disagree over the one group he mentions that he's not too enthusiastic about. He does most of the talking, and I spend the whole time trying not to choke on my Kaiser Burger and root beer.

At the theater, Mitch heads directly to the concession stand for snacks. I go too, even though I'm still feeling a bit nauseous from a stomach full of sauerkraut.

"I'll have Milk Duds and a root beer," Mitch tells the guy.

"The same," I say, trying to make my smile look less forced.

Someday years from now, Mitch will look back on tonight, and appreciate just how far I went to show him we were perfect for each other.

Normally, I'd take a seat somewhere in the middle of the theater, but I leave the decision up to Mitch. We end up almost in the last row. I don't mind. *Maybe he wants to make out or something.*

The movie is funny, and my only disappointment is that Mitch doesn't make a move on me. It's probably just because he doesn't want anyone to see us necking, although we are in a dark theater and the nearest other person is four rows up from us. It doesn't matter though; the night's not quite over yet.

As we stroll back to the car chatting, I parrot back his every opinion. He thinks Candice Bergen is a really good actress and goes on and on about her. Personally, I don't see it, but I nod enthusiastically anyway.

When we pull up in front of his house, I turn the engine off, and we keep talking for a few more minutes. If we were parked out in the middle of nowhere right now, I'd be much more receptive to a good grope and oral exam than I was with Janie.

We're turned towards each other. I'm so focused on him I barely even notice the dog barking somewhere in the neighborhood. It's our night, and right now, we're the only two people in the world.

"Yup, definitely a good movie," I say for the third time. "Good movie *and* good company."

"Yeah, we should do this again sometime."

"You know, I didn't realize we had so much in common."

"Me neither. You don't find many people around here who like The Stranglers."

I nod. "Yeah, it's a shame."

Actually, I have no idea who The Stranglers are, but I'm prepared to buy their album first thing in the morning and memorize every song on it.

"I'm really glad you joined the cast, Randy. I like hanging out with you like this."

"Me too."

"Well, I've got to go," he says with a sigh and starts to reach for the door handle.

"Thanks for making it such a great evening," I say.

I touch his shoulder.

He turns back to me.

I lean in for a good-night kiss.

He pushes me away with the force of a bomb blast and glares at me.

"What the hell! Are you out of your mind?"

"But—"

He slams the door, and stalks off inside. I just sit there, the blood draining from my face. The knot in my stomach is only made worse by the sauerkraut, milk duds, and root beer already churning around there.

A middle-aged lady with a little mutt of a dog passes the car. She glances at me with a sour expression. A light comes on in a second-story window of the Weaver house. Mitch's silhouette appears.

How could I have been so stupid? Mitch is straight, and I tried to kiss him. How could I have let myself get so wrapped up that I ignored what he said about the women in the movie? Oh God, he'll tell everybody I tried to kiss him, and I'll be dead meat in no time.

I start the car and slowly drive off.

Chapter 11: Aftermath

ANNIE SITS DOWN beside me on the park bench, sighs, and shakes her head.

"This is becoming a habit. Now, tell me what happened."

"I did the stupidest thing on earth last night," I whine.

"Randy, stop it. You always overdramatize everything. Now, just tell me what happened."

"Mitch *isn't* gay. And when I dropped him off after the movie, I tried to kiss him. He'll tell everyone, and Ramrod and his boys will kill me."

She purses her lips for a second before replying. "Let's just wait and see what happens."

"You *know* what's going to happen. And even if Ramrod and Brad don't kill me, no gay guy in his right mind will ever be caught dead with me after this comes out."

"I seriously doubt Mitch is going to say anything about this to anybody."

"How can you be so sure?"

"First thing's first. You took out insurance, remember? You've got two dates with girls on record, and one of them says you tried to feel her up, and the other is a well-known slut. So if Mitch Weaver talks, who's going to believe him? And another thing— The best I know, Mitch hasn't dated a single girl in his life. If he says anything, people will think he's trying to cover his *own* tracks. So calm down and stop worrying."

She hands me a tissue, and I dry my eyes. There *is* a certain logic to what she's saying. But the revelation that one of the two girls she set me up with is a well-known nymphomaniac doesn't help my mood.

"Come on; let's go for a walk." She pulls me to my feet. "Don't you worry, sugar. We'll find you the right guy. Just next time, don't be so overeager."

She continues to comfort me for another thirty-one minutes while we walk around, but although I put on a brave face, I know I'm doomed, and desperation builds inside me.

After we say goodbye, I go straight to Gene's house. This may well be my last chance to be with him before he drops me like a hot potato. By Monday, the whole world will know I'm gay, and he'll never let me touch him again.

The driveway is empty, but I knock anyway, and eventually, Gene opens the door.

For a second, we just stand there.

"Hi, Gene," I mumble.

"Oh, so you're talking to me again?"

"I never stopped."

"Hmm. I thought maybe you'd set yourself up for another date, maybe with Janie Morton again."

"No. Nothing like that. I've just been busy the last few days." I can't look him in the eye.

"Yeah, well, I'm pretty busy today myself."

"Come on, Gene; can't you spend some time with me?"

"No, I don't think so. I've got plenty of other guys I can hang out with."

"Please." I make a point of looking down at his crotch and licking my lips.

He studies me for a second, and his lips curl into a triumphant sneer. "Come on up."

I step inside. He takes me by the back of the neck and guides me upstairs. As soon as we get to his room, I fall to my knees right there in front of him.

He pushes me off. For the next hour, I totally humiliate myself. I beg, and I even cry in front of him. I want to make him moan and cry out that he wants me to be his forever. But he just calls me things like a cock-sucking bitch. I try to ignore it, but with each insult, the truth of just how worthless I really am sinks in deeper and deeper.

When it's over, and he dismisses me as usual, I stop at the door and turn back, dying for him to say something—anything—I can hang a little self-respect on.

"Gene, do you like me? I mean, are we friends?"

"Yeah, of course I like you. You're my bitch."

I stare at him for a second, unable to respond. What little self-respect I still had collapses.

As I open the door, he pinches my butt and whispers, "Be a good girl."

Without saying another word, I leave, defeated, spiritually empty, and emotionally alone.

When I get home, I go up to my bedroom and put on an old 10cc record. I sulk as the song continues, and I review everything that's happened since five o'clock yesterday.

Suddenly, I have one of those moments of clarity they're always talking about, and it doesn't paint a pretty picture.

How could I ever think Gene could be my special someone? That just proves how stupid I really am. To him, I'm not even a friend. I'm just his bitch. He doesn't give a damn about me, and he never will.

By Monday afternoon, everyone will know I'm gay and that I tried to kiss Mitch Weaver. I'll be the laughingstock of Chadham High. And after word gets out, I won't even have Gene. He won't have another thing to do with me after this. Why should he risk his reputation? Like he said, he can find other guys to hang out with—guys who will do what he wants, guys who will let him do what he wants to them, guys who won't jeopardize his straight guy image.

And oh my God! Kerry's going to find out. He'll realize that what happened in the shower wasn't just caused by locker room air. He'll never speak to me again.

I'll be lucky if even Blake still associates with me.

How could I have screwed up my life so bad?

MONDAY MORNING IS a nightmare from the moment I get on the bus. Theo Hayes is the first person I see, and the smirk on his face says it all. As each person gets on, they either cast a disgusted glance my way or ignore me completely. Blake seems to be the only one who doesn't have a clue how bad I ruined my life Friday night. Everyone else knows exactly what happened, and they know exactly what it means about me.

And I know exactly what they think about it—they're not *exactly* being subtle.

As soon as Kerry lays eyes on me in homeroom, he breaks into an all-knowing smile—he's obviously heard about what happened. His "Good morning. How was your weekend?" can't be more sarcastic. On the way to English, his arm brushes against me. He's doing it on purpose; he's taunting me.

History is an absolute torture. I don't know who looks more embarrassed, me or Mitch. I had hoped he'd just pretend I didn't exist, but as soon as Kerry and I walk in, Mitch looks right at me. He's positively red with rage and quickly looks at his book. I flush with humiliation. During class, I catch him glancing my way and half expect him to throw his book at me.

Only art class offers me any relief, and it's not much. I sit at the table, miserably playing with the clay, pretending to work on my project. Inspired by all the palm tree props crowding the back of the room, the three of us decided to make little ceramic trees—one each that can be combined as a set—but I'm not feeling very artistic at the moment.

"I just can't believe I thought he was gay," I say again. "You should have seen the look on his face when he saw me in History. I thought he was going to jump up and punch me right there on the spot."

"Stop exaggerating," Annie says. "He didn't look so traumatized when I saw him in fourth period."

"Well, I still don't believe it," Jeremy says. "I would have bet a hundred dollars that Mitch Weaver is gay."

"I'm just sorry I encouraged you," Annie says. "I really thought you'd caught a live one this time."

Mike Kowalski passes our table, and she can't resist a dig.

"Yeah, a live one," she says in a loud voice. "Not like old *Dead Fish* Kowalski."

He glances at her over his shoulder and goes back to his table.

"Annie, you should lay off Mike," Jeremy mutters, but she's not paying him any attention.

"What have you heard today?"

It's the third time I've asked.

"Honey, I haven't heard anything—nothing. I *swear*. And like I told you Saturday, I don't think the boy's gonna talk. You might have embarrassed him, but if he says anything, he's got a lot more to lose than you do. Your rep is set."

I turn to Jeremy, but he shakes his head. "I've not heard a word, not a *single* word. Really."

"Well *something's* going around. You should see the way people have been looking at me all day."

Annie and Jeremy glance at each other and sigh. They're good people. I appreciate them trying to make me feel better. But we all know the score.

Sixth period rolls around. I stand outside the locker room, trying to fight down that nauseous feeling you get when you know you're doomed. Once I go through that door, I'll have to face Brad, Jamie, Ramrod, and Kerry, and Rick Payton, Billy Mason, Jeff Gray—all of them.

Maybe I could skip, hide out in the library. Maybe I could just spend the rest of the day in there.

But before I can sneak off, Coach Horne sees me.

"Clark, get moving."

Well, that kills that idea.

I'm already blushing when I push open the door. The buzz of laughter greets me, and I know exactly who they're all laughing at. Ramrod spies me coming in and nudges Brad.

"Poor, poor Randy." His voice rises above the rest. "What's the matter? You still crying over your break up with Janie? Yeah, I saw her out with Jacob Wilson Saturday night. I guess you just didn't *measure up.*"

"Right, why date a fag when you can have a *real* man," Brad adds, playing with himself.

I bet it's the most action he ever got in his life.

They both laugh. I should probably be grateful they're not beating the hell out of me. Everyone is laughing, except for Kerry and Rick. Rick looks disappointed and angry. Kerry just watches me.

I slam my locker closed, retreat to the far end of the hall, and crumple into a cross-legged lump next to a trash can. It's a good barrier to hide me from the guys. I hear them shuffling from the locker room to the gym and purse my lips, determined not to scream out the agony that's ripping me apart.

But I can't stop the tears.

"Hey, are you all right?"

My head jerks up to see Kerry peering over the trash can at me.

"Seriously, what's wrong?" he says, sitting down next to me. "You've been acting funny all day. Come on; tell me. What's wrong?"

I choke and wipe my face. "Nothing."

"Is it because you really *do* like Janie Morton?" he whispers.

"Janie...? Oh God, no."

I want to laugh, but my throat catches, and the tears are flowing again.

"You know damn well what it is. Everybody does."

He studies me for a second.

"It doesn't matter what anyone knows, or what they *think* they know. Whatever it is, it's all right."

He throws an arm around me and squeezes me. I push him away and jump to my feet.

"Look, you don't have to play games. Just leave me alone, okay?"

I run to the locker room and start changing. My eye is on the door in case he tries to follow me. But when it opens, it's Coach Horne standing there.

"Clark, Sawyer says you're not feeling well. Do you want to go to the nurse's office?"

"No," I say and turn away so he won't see the tears on my cheeks. "I just need to throw up, that's all. I'll be fine."

If only I could barf my way out of all my life's problems.

"Okay, here." He hands me a note and takes in my tearstained cheeks and red eyes.

"Why don't you go outside and get some fresh air? There are plenty of trash cans near the lunchroom if you need one. Hell, that lunch today's probably what made you sick in the first place. But look, if you start to feel worse, get to the nurse's office, okay?"

I go outside and try to find my Buddha focus, but not even Buddha will have anything to do with me now that the word's out I'm gay.

By the time for Chemistry, though, I have calmed down some, and I stop off in a restroom to wash my face. But just as I turn to leave, Gene walks in. He takes a quick glance around and feels me up.

"Hey, man, how about a quick blowjob?"

It's more than I can stand. My life is ruined, and even if I don't deserve anything better than being Gene's bitch, I don't want it. Especially not today.

I push his hand away and storm out. He emerges and glares at me.

"Don't you ever touch me again," I growl, not trying very hard to be discreet. "And don't you ever call me again. We're through."

Several people look from me to him, but I don't care who hears me. Gene stares at me, his face a mixture of shock and outrage.

"You're pathetic," I say, turning on my heels.

I leave him standing there fuming.

When the bell rings for study hall, I go straight to Mr. Warren and get a library pass. I hide in a corner behind a bookcase so that even if Kerry and Blake come in, they won't see me.

If I only had relatives in another state, I'd move and finish high school there. But no, everyone in my family lives in Chadham County.

"HEY, STUPID!" THE Turd squawks from downstairs. "Will you pick up the damn phone? Or are you still too busy trying to find your dick so you can jerk off?"

It's the third time Wally's yelled up about a phone call. This time, I sigh, lean over, and pick up the receiver.

"Well it's about time," Blake says. "I've been trying to get up with you for over an hour. Where were you this afternoon? Kerry and I looked all over for you. Listen, you won't believe what's going around."

"Oh yeah? Try me."

"Penny Richtbacker's dropping out. She's pregnant."

"Huh? What? Who? Penny Richtbacker?"

"Penny Richtbacker, the junior. Somebody knocked her up, and she's leaving school."

"Wow."

"I know. And she won't say who the father is. Can you believe it?"

"Maybe she doesn't want to marry him."

"Probably. Damn close call for him, though, huh?"

Blake goes on to give me a full rundown of the rest of the day's gossip, but something isn't adding up. Either nothing's going around about me, or "Rona Barrett" Rogers has been totally excluded from every gossip vine in the county, which is impossible. But that would mean Mitch really *hasn't* told anyone about Friday night. But if not, what was going on with everyone looking at me today?

And they *were* looking at me—*weren't* they?

TUESDAY, I SUFFER through another day of social ostracism and humiliation. Mitch can't even look me in the eye, and people are avoiding me. My only consolation is that Brad and Ramrod haven't upped the ante in their locker room insult festival.

Actually, they pretty much act just like they did before. And so far, Coach Horne hasn't banned me from using the locker room and showers with the *normal* boys. Maybe he's hoping they'll kill me and get it over with before he has to exile me.

And apparently, Blake still hasn't heard about what happened. Maybe people are keeping it from him out of sympathy, or because they know he's my friend, and they're afraid he's got dirt on them and might retaliate.

It doesn't add up. Other than Mitch, the only person who's acting any different at all is Kerry, and it's the way he's acting different that's weird. I thought when he found out about me, he'd dump me, but it's like nothing has changed between us at all. He's even acting like that scene I made outside the locker room Monday never happened.

But there is one thing. Sometimes when we're talking now, and it's just the two of us, he touches me—like he brushes his fingers lightly over my arm. But the way he looks at me when he does it... It's like now that he knows the truth about me, he's doing it to turn me on or something. The trouble is, it works. Anyway, either I'm just imagining it—which I'm not—or he's doing it to be cruel.

Blake's got his own brand of cruelty, but it doesn't have anything to do with me being gay. I know that for certain now. I turn down his offer of a ride to the rehearsal and then skip it entirely. The last thing I want is to spend all night standing next to the straight guy I made a pass at. Instead, I take a shower after supper and lay low in my bedroom.

At nine fifty-three, my door flies open, and Blake barges in.

"Where were you tonight? You join the show and miss the very next rehearsal?"

It doesn't even register on him that I'm lying in my bed with the covers pulled up, probably looking as bad as the disaster my life has become makes me feel.

"I've been sick."

"Oh that's a relief. I was afraid there was something wrong, like you were dropping out of the show or something."

"Well...the fact is, I don't think I'm cut out for show business after all. I am quitting."

"No! You can't quit, not now, not after what's happened. Half of the guys have quit."

A chill runs through me. "What...what happened?"

"One of them told Szinhely he was quitting yesterday, and then tonight, six others didn't show up."

He gives me a curious look and takes a slow breath.

"Randy, it's silly, but I've got to ask you a question. How did you get along with the guys the other night? Okay?"

"Yeah," I say, my throat going dry. "Why?"

"Well, you see, the thing is, the guy who quit yesterday claims a guy came on to him. See, a couple of the regulars are gay, and I think that freaked him out. But he must have told some of the other guys about it, because now they've quit too. That mostly leaves just the regulars, and we really need every guy we can get."

I stare at Blake, frozen in place.

Oh God. Mitch quit the show because of me. And he may not have told the whole world, but he told the other guys in the show, and now they've all quit too. The show's in trouble and it's my fault. Damn it, Now I can't quit.

Wait a minute. What did he say? "A couple" of the regulars are gay? That means, at least one of the guys I rehearsed with must be gay too.

"Some of those guys are gay?"

"Yeah, but don't tell me you, of all people, have got a problem being around other gay guys."

The world around us seems to fall silent. It's like being struck by lightning. His words echo in my ears. I've always assumed Blake would not have a problem with me being gay, but under the circumstances, now at the moment of truth, I'm not so sure.

"What do you mean *other* gay guys?" I try to sound indignant, but Blake's having none of it.

"Oh come on, Randy. You went out with Janie Morton, and I bet it went down just like it has with every other guy she's ever gone out with. Now it did, didn't it?"

I reply with the world's smallest nod.

"So why didn't *you* react like every other guy she's ever been with? I'm telling you, no straight guy could have ever gone out with her and come back acting as upset as you did."

"I'm not—"

"Come on, Randy," he says with a grin, "it's *obvious* you're gay."

For a second, all I can do is stare at him.

"How...how *obvious* am I?"

"Dorothy, you're so *totally* obvious, all you need is a little dog and red shoes. Look, you never talk about girls, and the only girl you ever talk *to* is Annie Brock. And I've caught you staring at guys lots of times, but I've never once seen you really look at a girl, you know, *in that way*. I've been waiting for you to come out for years."

"Wait a minute. If I've been so obvious and you knew I was gay all along, why the hell have you been harping on me about girls all these years?"

"Okay," he says and chuckles. "The truth is, you really aren't *that* obvious, and I wasn't totally sure you were gay until that date with Janie. But that cinched it."

"And...and it doesn't bother you that I'm gay?"

"Look, Randy, I want to be an actor. You can't be in that profession and not expect to associate with a lot of gay people. And you and I have known each other forever, you're my best friend, and I love you—just not in that way. So just don't make a pass at me, and we'll be fine, all right?"

"Don't worry," I say, laughing out loud. "If I ever do make a pass at you, you'll know two things—I've lost my mind, *and* I've gone blind."

"Hardy-har-har," he says and laughs. "But hey, I do have one question."

"Yeah?"

"Are you going to start lisping now?"

We both laugh, and I suddenly feel better than I have in weeks—that is, until Blake brings me right back to the approaching train wreck my life's heading for.

"So that's all settled now, and you're staying on with the show, right?"

I give him a nod, and Blake leaves, happy that all's right with the world. He might as well enjoy his happiness while he can. Sooner or later, Szinhely is going to find out that I'm the reason most of his male actors have dropped out.

Chapter 12: Invitations

IT'S THURSDAY NIGHT. Over the last couple of days, I've had to admit that either Mitch really didn't rat me out, or Chadham High has become a lot more open-minded than I ever thought possible. The Ramrods of the world really aren't treating me any different than last week, and people aren't shooting me evil glances any more than usual. Annie always says I overdramatize; I guess this time maybe she's right. Maybe I have been a little bit paranoid.

My bedroom door swings open. Blake stands there with his hands on his hips.

"Okay, freeze, mister. You're coming with me."

"What?"

"Get your shoes on. I'm driving you to the rehearsal."

"Blake, I'm perfectly capable of driving myself. You go on, and I'll see you later."

The fact is, I'm still undecided about going.

"Now, we'll have none of that. I know all about it."

My stomach lurches. Szinhely knows, and he's sent Blake to get me while the cast and crew sharpen their pitchforks.

"You know all about it?"

"Of course I do. We've all been there before. Being on stage is a new experience for you, and you've just got cold feet. It happens to everybody. But it's just like learning to ride a bike—you've got to get out there and dive right back in. You've got to hold your head. You've got to make lemonade like the Romans do. Now come on."

Since you can't argue with logic like that, I shrug my shoulders and reach for my shoes. If I'm destined to be humiliated and run out of town—or at least the auditorium—I might as well get it over with.

Nineteen minutes later, Blake escorts me into the auditorium. It feels like he's ushering me onto the firing squad range. But the cast and crew don't even notice I'm there, at least they don't turn into a faggot-lynching mob as soon as I come in. They're all chatting and laughing in the same little groups just like always.

Joe Christopher, one of the stagehands, catches sight of me and walks over.

"Hey, man. Good to see you. I was afraid you were another one of the dropouts. What a bunch of douchebags."

"Uh, yeah," I say, not certain it's a compliment to have been mistaken for a douchebag.

Mr. Szinhely arrives and things get under way. He doesn't act standoffish towards me.

Must still not know I'm the culprit who caused the mass exodus of straight guys.

I take note of the guys who are still in the show. Mitch is nowhere to be seen, but I knew he wouldn't be. However, he's not the only reason I'm counting heads. According to Blake, at least two of the guys still in the show are gay, but he didn't mention any names. Hell, for all I know, he may not even know exactly which ones are gay himself.

Joe Christopher is definitely straight. During the break, I see him snuggling with one of the female extras off in a corner. I *am* surprised to see Hunter Shea. I'd assumed he and Mitch were kind of close friends. He's got a good voice, and he's also not bad-looking either, that is if you consider skinny redheads handsome. He seems friendly enough, but he doesn't act gay—like I would even know what that looks like.

By the end of the evening, I'm no closer to figuring out which of my fellow cast members is gay than I was when I came in, but I am feeling more relaxed. I decide that while Mitch may have told the guys who dropped out with him what happened, he must not have told them any of the details or who it was that tried to kiss him. Maybe Annie's right, and he really does figure he's got more to lose than me if word gets out.

But if I feel better Thursday night, by the end of Friday, I'm back in a funk. Whether Mitch tells people about me or not, my little fiasco with him does prove one thing: No one's interested in me except Gene, and since Monday, he's avoiding me like the plague. If he sees me at all now, he just glares.

No. No one's interested in me at all.

DISCIPLINE—THAT'S A word my dad loves, though he's not really big on punishment, unless you count having to listen to him yell. No, to Dad, discipline means being in control of yourself. Like when he's doing some outdoor project, and it's burning hot, he'll refuse even a sip of water until the job's done. I think he got it from his time in the military—you know, "army tough" and all that.

For me, discipline means that even though it's Saturday, and I woke up horny, I made it all the way through my shower and back to bed without touching myself for other than legitimate purposes. That counts as a major accomplishment, and I'm more than willing to reward myself for it now. All I need to decide on is who to fantasize about. Unfortunately, there's only one boy who can do that job for me these days: Kerry.

Oh well, I might as well indulge myself.

I've only just got started—although it's a very productive start—when a knock on the door breaks my concentration. It's The Turd's usual less-than-polite pounding.

I ignore it.

Suddenly, the door flies open.

Yup, it's Wally all right.

And Kerry is standing right there next to him.

In a flash, I sit up and cross my legs. The Turd grins like he's caught me jacking off. Which he hasn't. This time. Barely.

"Sorry for that," Kerry says as The Turd walks away snickering. "You did warn me about him, but I honestly thought you were exaggerating."

"And now that you've actually met the beast in the flesh, your opinion is...?"

"You were being kind."

For a moment, I just sit there taking Kerry in. It must be warm outside. He's only wearing a pullover and loose-fitting shorts. He's the perfect picture of a hot teenage boy. If eyes were teeth, I'd be eating him alive.

He gives me a lopsided grin. "So, uh...can I come in?"

"Oh, sure. Sorry, my mind isn't really working yet today."

He comes in and closes the door behind him, pulls out my desk chair, and takes a seat facing me.

The way he's dressed is getting to me, especially since I was already primed when he came in. He's got so little on, he could be naked in less than five seconds. And while he's not wearing much, I'm only in my boxers, and feeling very...uh...vulnerable.

"So," he says lazily, "just hanging out, eh? Up for a little fun?"

"I...uh...s-sure." I'm blushing, and there's no way my boxers are hiding my hard-on.

We sit there looking at each other, not speaking. He's barely two feet away from the bed.

Without warning, he stands up and takes a step closer.

"Do you ever get the feeling there's two things going on at once? Like there's *one* thing going on at one level, but something *else* is up just below the surface?"

I'm sitting there, stone-still and rock hard. He stares into my eyes, but he doesn't see how dangerous he's making me. I want to grab him and just hold on, and the willpower to stop myself is draining away.

My weakening voice of reason whimpers, *Come on. Say something, anything.*

"Uh, you want to bike into town and hang out?" I try to sound casual, but my throat is dry.

"Okay," he whispers, but his eyes are still holding me prisoner.

I scoot to the edge of the bed and stand up. We're now only inches away from each other. I can feel his body heat, and every inch of my skin is on fire. As always, he smells wonderful.

"So, uh, do you want to get dressed first, or are you going to go like that?"

As I turn to find some clothes, his arm brushes against me. The touch is electric. Desire literally oozes out of me. I fumble to pull on a pair of shorts and choose a long, loose pullover.

While I struggle with socks and sneakers, Kerry looks my room over. Except for the absence of bimbo posters, it looks just like any other teenage boy's room. Patti Smith, Lou Reed, and The Police decorate the walls. I've got a small record collection and a shelf or two of books—mostly fantasy, rock star bios, and some poetry. He nods approvingly at my two Cars records and copy of *Babel*.

Once we're on our bikes, I start to relax. We ride around with no destination, chatting about nothing in particular. It's a cool day, but I feel an inner heat that makes the air exhilarating.

We stop for fast-food burgers and take our purchases to the park. Kerry looks beautiful sitting next to me in the dappled shade.

It's funny. Usually, when I'm around Kerry, I'm in a constant turned-on state, and I definitely am today. But it's different somehow. It's like "he" and "I" have kind of disappeared into this strange but beautiful "we" moment. I'm still turned on, but I feel, I don't know, something different. I feel easy, like I'm complete.

After we've biked around another hour or so, we decide it's time to head back. When we come to the corner where we'll part company, I turn to him.

"That was fun. Thanks for coming over."

"Yeah, I enjoyed it too. I really like being with you."

"Me too."

He puts a hand on my shoulder. His fingers squeeze me seductively. Our cheeks are flushed.

"You know, Randy, we could keep it just between us. And you know I would never tell anybody. Think it over. If you want, maybe we could get together sometime and talk about it."

I nod dumbly. His eyes seem to search mine for a second, and then he rides off with an over-the-shoulder grin and a final wave.

As I turn to go home, my mind's working on overload.

What was that? An invitation to admit I'm gay? Or was it a proposition? *Oh God, if it was a proposition...*

No, wait, wait, wait. Damn it, I've got to stop making a fool out of myself. I refuse to make the same mistake with Kerry I made with Mitch and Theo. The stakes are too high. I can't afford to lose him. I may want his body—and oh God, I do—but I need him as a friend more. If I have to spend my life loving him from a distance, at least I'll still be close to him as a friend.

But if it wasn't about me admitting I'm gay or some kind of proposition, then what the hell did he mean?

AFTER SPENDING THE rest of the weekend wondering what's going on "below the surface" between me and Kerry, I'm back on the bus for the start of a new week. Amazingly, Blake is wide-awake, a rare occurrence on a Monday morning. He glances around to make sure we're a safe distance from the others and leans over.

"So, uh, tell me," he says in his conspirator voice. "Have you...uh...bagged yourself a gay-babe yet?"

"A *gay-babe*?"

"Yeah, come on; tell me. Who was it?"

"Mister," I say in my best Mae West voice, "I'm not the kind to kiss and tell."

He grins and drops the subject, which is good. I'm certainly not going to tell him how I nearly ruined the show by making a pass at Mitch Weaver, or that *I* was the one "bagged" by Gene Murphy, repeatedly, all last month.

On the way to homeroom, we stop at our lockers. A tall, dark-haired girl calls out to Blake and practically bounces her way over to us. She stands close to him and gives his arm a playful squeeze. She's all smiles.

"Hi, Blake. I'm having a party on the fifteenth after closing night. You'll come, won't you?"

He beams. "Sure, I'd love to."

I detect some serious two-way attraction going on here. And they're so focused on each other that Blake's completely forgotten I'm still standing there. To remind him, I clear my throat.

"Oh, excuse me. Marilyn Romer, this is Randy Clark." He nods in my direction, barely taking his eyes off her. "Randy's just joined up for the show. Marilyn's in the show too, Randy."

"Hi, Randy. I'm not really *in* the show. But I do play the violin, and I'll be in the orchestra, so I guess you could say I'm *kind* of in the show."

"Nice to meet you."

"Why don't you come along with Blake to my party? You can help me keep him out of trouble."

"Hey," Blake protests in mock outrage, and I grin.

"Sure, I'll bring the elephant tranquilizer gun."

We laugh, and she gives Blake's arm another playful squeeze.

"Well, got to go. Bye, Randy," she says, glancing my way. Then she tilts her head and addresses my best friend with a lot more attention. "Bye, Blake."

"Bye, Marilyn."

I grin as Blake watches Marilyn run to catch up with a couple of girls. Talk about stars in his eyes.

"She's beautiful, isn't she? Oh, sorry, I forgot who I'm talking to."

"Shut up. I can still appreciate a girl's beauty even if I'm *not* attracted to her."

"Yeah," he says glumly. "I wish *she* was attracted to me."

"Oh, I don't know. It certainly looked like she's attracted to you from where I stood."

"Ha. I wish."

"Well, why don't you just ask her out and see?"

His eyes flash into that nervous look, and his voice trembles. "M-maybe if the show's a hit, but n-not now. She'd never go out with me now."

"Whatever."

Blake wanders off to homeroom, his head still in the clouds. I'm beginning to think he's even more dense than I thought he was. Or is it denser? Whatever.

MRS. PILT'S RADIO clicks out "My Best Friend's Girl." I'm struggling to apply the last touches to my ceramic project. My original idea, a pine tree, turned out to be impossible, but the alternative I chose is almost as hard. A willow. It's so delicate I'm afraid the wind from someone passing by will blow it apart.

Annie and Jeremy have already completed major work on their choices—an oak and an elm. While Annie adds a touch of paint to her oak, she's engaged in another soliloquy about Mike Kowalski. It's a lengthy critique of his project—a ceramic elephant.

Luckily for Mike, he isn't here today.

"The fool. If he got all the air out of that piece of crap, I'm a strawberry blond. There's no way, and I mean *no* damn way, that monstrosity will *ever* survive the kiln. I told him he needed to pound it more before he started, but does he bother to listen to me? No."

Mike Kowalski and Annie Brock—I really don't get it with those two. At the end of class on Wednesday, when Annie finished washing her hands, Mike offered her a paper towel. She just gave him a mean look, grabbed her own, and walked away. But then on Thursday, he was washing his hands, and she offered one to him. At least he took it. Go figure.

As I carefully apply slurry to the last limb of my ceramic, Jeremy glances in my direction.

"So what's going on with you and Kerry Sawyer these days, Randy?"

I'm so startled, I almost knock over my willow.

"What? Why do you ask?"

"To talk about something else besides elephants," he says, cutting a glance at Annie.

She sticks out her tongue at him and continues painting.

"Well, what do you want to know?"

"Oh, I don't know— What have you guys been up to? Who's he dating?— That kind of thing."

"Honestly, I don't think he's dating anybody."

"Oh," Annie chirps. "You mean he's *still* available?"

"I mean I don't know," I snap. "You know, not everyone feels compelled to yack about every single detail of their lives."

"What's the matter, Randy?" Jeremy asks even more quietly than usual. "Why are you so touchy about it?"

"I'm not touchy. I just don't know anything about his sex life, that's all."

"You've still got a thing for him, don't you?" Annie whispers.

"No, I... If you must know, he's just been giving me a hard time lately."

Annie raises a sarcastic eyebrow, but Jeremy nods.

"Do you want to talk about it?" he asks.

"No. Well, not here anyway."

"We'll meet in the park at four," Annie announces.

Jeremy nods in agreement.

THE PARK IS chilly. I walk in circles to keep warm. Jeremy rounds the corner, and takes a seat at one of the benches overlooking the river. I sit down beside him.

"Hi, thanks for coming."

"No problem," he says.

Annie appears and sidles over to sit on his other side.

"Okay, Randy," she begins, "now, what's the trouble? What's going on between you and old *Hot Body* Sawyer?"

"Nothing."

"Come on, tell us."

I sigh. "The thing is, I'm not sure. I told Kerry I wasn't ready to date, and he kind of implied he knew I'm not into girls. And over the last couple of weeks, he's been saying and doing things that kind of...you know...get to me."

"Like what?" Jeremy asks, and Annie leans in closer.

"Well, he kind of says or does little things like he knows it'll turn me on."

Annie nods. "Mm-hmm. Does he do it all the time? Like, in front of other people?"

"No...he only does it when it's just the two of us, or if not, he does it in a way that no one else will notice."

"So, you're saying he generally only does it when there's nobody else around?"

"Uh-huh."

She raises an eyebrow and nods. "Interesting."

She glances at Jeremy, and he nods in agreement.

"You think it's all in my head, don't you."

"No, honey, I *know* it's not all in your head." She clears her throat. "Okay, Melissa overheard Billie Jo Jackson talking with Vickie. Billie Jo said she tried to catch Kerry's eye a couple of times, but he just ignored her. Then Vickie pointed out that nobody's ever really seen Kerry hanging out with anyone but you and Blake Rogers."

"So?"

"So, Billie Jo's not the only girl who's let Kerry Sawyer know she's available. Don't you think that's significant?"

"But I told you he's got a girl back home."

"And I'm telling *you*, I don't know *what* he's got back home. But around here, he seems to be no more interested in girls than you are."

"But that's stupid. I'm gay."

A guy jogging past us looks our way. Annie rolls her eyes, I blush, and Jeremy snickers.

"Honey, are you *sure* he's not gay too?"

"Of course I am."

"I think you should tell him you're gay," Jeremy says abruptly.

"I can't. I might lose him as a friend."

Annie shakes her head. "Sugar, if he can't deal with you being gay, you're going to end up losing him eventually anyway."

"And you never know; he might not even care," Jeremy says, still watching the jogger disappear in the distance.

I look over at Annie, and she nods. "Could be he's already figured it out. Maybe that's why he's been hinting around about it—you know, encouraging you to come out and admit it."

"You really think I should just tell him?"

"Sugar," she says, "you've got nothing to lose that you wouldn't lose one way or the other anyway."

Jeremy nods.

I STARE AT the phone on my desk, and my hand shakes as I pick up the receiver. Taking a final breath, I dial Kerry's number.

"Hello?"

"Hey, man. It's me."

"What's up, Randy-man?"

"Got a minute to talk?"

"A minute? Well, let me see." I can hear the grin in his voice. "Yeah, I might even be able to spare a minute and a half."

"There's...uh...something I've been meaning to tell you...and I—"

"Hey, Stupid." Wally's voice cuts through the receiver like fingernails on a chalkboard. "Mom says dinner is ready."

"Get off the phone, Turd!"

"You better come now, Shithead. Trust me, you're gonna want to eat this crap before it gets cold."

Kerry laughs. "Sounds like whatever you want to tell me will have to wait."

"Yeah, I guess so. Well, later, dude." I hang up the phone and wonder if I can get to Wally and kill him before he gets to the table.

When I try to call Kerry back after dinner, his line is busy. Then as luck would have it, between The Turd and Mom, our phone is in use the rest of the evening.

This is worse than a nightmare. Kerry knows I want to tell him *something*, and if he suspects what it is, tomorrow could be horrendous. And Mom never buys my "I feel sick" routine, so my chances of avoiding him are zero. I'm doomed.

TO MY RELIEF, Kerry acts like he's forgotten all about my phone call when I see him the next day. But I haven't. I've had enough second thoughts to fill a book, and they all say the same thing: Keep your mouth shut and pretend the conversation never happened.

At lunchtime, we're trying to guess what today's nutritional offering is supposed to be, while ignoring the shouts of a junior vainly trying to remind everyone about the dance Friday night. As the junior gives up and storms off, Annie breezes over to us, grinning from ear to ear. She's wearing a big floppy denim hat with spangles, magenta bell-bottoms, and the kind of printed disco shirt I thought they only wore on *Soul Train.*

There is nobody else within five spots of where we're sitting, but she pulls up a seat so close to Kerry, it looks like they're Siamese twins. She gives me a quizzical look and makes a small nod in Kerry's direction. When I respond with a slight shake of my head, she purses her lips and rolls her eyes at me.

Meanwhile, Kerry's delighted to have his first real up-close experience of Miss Personality 1979. I've told him a lot about Annie, but she and Jeremy usually sit with a different group of kids for lunch. From the expression on his face, I can tell he's just dying to know how the real Annie will compare to the picture I've painted of her.

He doesn't have to wait long.

"Guess what happened to Mike Kowalski's elephant?" she says, bursting into a snort-giggle. Mike's sitting a couple of tables over from us, and she's talking more than loud enough for him to hear her.

At the sound of Annie's laughter, Kerry's eyes widen. I've told him about it before, but this is his first encounter with the real thing.

"It blew up in the kiln," she says and laughs. "I mean KABOOM!"

Jeremy is walking over to join us and is about to sit down, but when he hears Annie talking about Mike, he shakes his head and keeps moving.

As he walks off, Annie glances over at Mike again. He catches her looking at him, but for the first time, he doesn't look away. Instead, he waves to some girl I don't know who's just passing by his table. She sits down next to him, and then he wraps his arm around her shoulder and gives her a quick peck on the cheek.

Annie freezes for a split second. Then she whips her head around in another direction.

"When did the explosion happen?" Kerry asks.

Another split second passes while Annie stares at him like she doesn't know what he's talking about.

Suddenly, she cackles. "Second period. BLAM!" Her laughter doesn't sound genuine now.

Kerry turns to me. “So that’s what that noise was. I thought it was thunder.”

“Nope. That was just ole Mickey’s art grade self-destructing,” she says, but there’s a touch of bitterness in her voice, and she seems distracted.

Without warning, she straightens her shoulders, turns to Kerry, and clears her throat.

“So Kerry, has Randall here asked you out to the dance Friday night yet?”

My cheeks feel like they’re on fire, and I start shaking. How could she say such a thing?

To my shock, Kerry says, “Well, it wouldn’t really matter because I don’t dance. I’m no good at it.”

“Honey,” she says, batting her eyes at him. “That don’t matter none when you’re with the right partner. And believe me, the slow songs are *especially* easy. You know, the *belly-rubbing* kind. You just get up real close to him and rub against each other.”

Kerry raises his eyebrows and smiles. Annie turns to me. I hold my breath. She’s wearing a strange expression—like her mind is somewhere else.

Unfortunately, her mouth is right here.

“Well, what about it, Clark Kent? Are you going to be Superman and ask old *Hot Body* here out? ’Cause, if not”—she suddenly gets loud enough to be heard five tables away—“I just happen to know a tall ebony beauty who’s available Friday night.”

“Let’s just say that Randy’s gonna have his hands full Friday night,” Kerry says with a wink, making my nerve level peak even higher.

Annie glances at him with a raised eyebrow and turns back to me with a knowing smile.

“Really? With what, I wonder?”

“Getting ready for Hanukkah!” I shriek, grabbing my tray and dashing for the trash can as fast as I can without running. Kerry follows me outside, laughing.

“Hanukkah?” he says, giggling, and shakes his head. “I can’t *believe* you said ‘Hanukkah.’ Hanukkah’s not until next month. And since when did you become Jewish? I don’t remember seeing you around the synagogue on Yom Kippur.”

“Yeah, yeah,” I mumble.

“Hey, I’ve got an idea,” he says. “Why don’t you stay over at my house Friday night? We can grab a pizza, kick back, and listen to some music. It would be the perfect opportunity to talk without interruptions.”

I stare at him in disbelief. The very idea is crazy.

It was all I could do to keep from jumping him Saturday. How could I handle being alone with him for hours? At night? In a bedroom? No. This is an absolutely terrible idea. I can’t do it. It’s just too dangerous.

“Okay,” I hear myself say, and wonder where it came from.

Chapter 13: Confrontations

I PRETEND TO glance at my watch and then tell Kerry I've got to go work on my art project. It's an excuse, but I'm so freaked out by what Annie just did, and even more so by Kerry's invitation to stay over Friday night, that I need to find a little quiet time to try and calm down.

The room appears to be empty. Even Mrs. Pilt isn't here. Perfect. I go to our usual table, plop down in a chair, and sigh.

"So did you tell Kerry?"

I nearly jump out of my skin as Jeremy walks up from the back of the room and sits down.

"Well, sort of."

"What do you mean *sort of*? Did you or didn't you?"

"I started to last night, but we got interrupted."

"And...?"

"And I didn't get a chance to call him back. But it doesn't matter. I'm certain he knows what I was going to tell him now."

"What do you mean?"

"I guess you were out of earshot and didn't hear what Annie said just now."

"All I heard was her trying to embarrass Mike Kowalski as usual. That was more than enough for me."

"Yeah, well he wasn't the only one she embarrassed. She did everything but come right out and tell Kerry I'm gay."

Jeremy's eyes go wide. "You're kidding. What did she say?"

"Let's just say she made some pretty broad hints."

"Typical. So what happened? Is he still talking to you?"

"He invited me to stay over at his house Friday."

Jeremy raises an eyebrow. "Really? Well, if he does know, then it would appear he doesn't care. Looks like you can stop worrying."

The bell rings. Mrs. Pilt and the other students come in. Annie finally arrives, takes her seat, and drops what has to be the biggest chartreuse paisley handbag in the history of fashion on the floor next to her. She seems agitated, rapping her fingers on the table, and glancing here and there like she's thinking about something. When Mike comes in, she glares at him but says nothing. He walks right on by her and sits at his usual table.

We spend the period painting our ceramics. It's delicate, time-consuming work. And for once, even Annie doesn't talk, which is fine with me. After that little stunt in the lunchroom, I'm giving her the cold shoulder, and she's lucky I don't cuss her out.

But after a few minutes, her silence becomes unnerving. I keep waiting for her to say something, anything, but she's not paying me, or Jeremy, any attention at all. In fact, the only thing she pays any attention to, besides her ceramic, is Mike. Every now and then, I catch her looking over at him.

The thing is, Mike's ignoring her—I mean *really* ignoring her. And the longer he does, the more it seems to irritate her, and the more stressed-out I get. I keep expecting her to lash out any minute with one of her trademark Kowalski put-downs. It's like waiting for an explosion. But the whole class passes without her saying a single word.

When the bell rings, she stays behind, putting her supplies away with exaggerated slowness. Jeremy and I leave together.

Just as we approach the intersection where I'll turn off for the gym, I spy Gene Murphy walking our way. He's got his arm wrapped around a tall, very shapely girl. Even from a distance, I can see the bulge in his pants, which fills me with a strange mixture of jealousy and self-loathing.

He looks up and sees me walking next to Jeremy, and his eyes narrow. As he passes us, he brings a fist to his mouth and grunts out a fake cough.

"Cocksucker."

He might as well have slapped me. All those times he's called me a fag race through my mind. I relive how pathetic and desperate I was to please him, and how worthless he made me feel the last time we were together.

Fortunately, either Jeremy didn't hear what Gene said, or he pretends not to. But after a few steps, he peeks over his shoulder and shakes his head.

"Did you see who he's with?"

When I don't respond, he continues. "That's Amanda Worthingham. He just broke up with her sister not a month ago. I bet you anything Becky doesn't even know he's going after Amanda. What a bastard. And neither of them have a clue how mean he can be—yet."

At the next intersection, Jeremy continues on his way while I turn off for the gym. I'm moving slow. My stomach feels sour, and my head stings. Seeing Gene with a girl, knowing he's playing two sisters off against each other, and having him call me a cocksucker in front of Jeremy like that—it all just makes it hit home. I may have been the one to say Gene and I were through, but in the end, it didn't matter.

*I need—needed—*him. *He never needed me. He was just using me the whole time—using me like a piece of garbage.*

I'm so upset, I don't even rev up my Buddha focus before walking into the locker room. Of course, the first thing I see is Kerry. At least he's already finished changing. But he flashes me a smile and tousles my hair before walking out, leaving me thoroughly preoccupied for the rest of the period.

Between Annie's stunt in the lunchroom, the way Kerry's acting, and that little encounter with Gene, this whole day is blowing my mind. I feel like I'm losing it.

Chemistry is a lost cause. My mind flips back and forth between hating myself for ever getting involved with Gene, wanting him back, and desperately wanting Kerry, all at the same time. Thinking about Gene makes me feel so worthless it's absolutely painful, but the images I keep seeing of Kerry are dangerous. I've got to suppress my feelings for him before I mess things up worse. But the way he's been acting...I'm so confused.

Kerry arrives in study hall, gives Mr. Warren a note, and comes over to me.

"Listen," he says without sitting down. "I've got to work on a project for Physics, so I won't be here. Call me tonight when you get home."

He squeezes my shoulder and walks away, while the effect of his touch races to tickle my lust gland. For a second, the confusion, the doubt, the fear all vanish, and I surrender to the sensation. I can't help it; I'm hopeless. I've become a full-fledged addict, and Kerry Sawyer is my drug. Right now, I'd be happy just to be a freckle on his butt, if it meant I could be with him every second for the rest of my life.

BLAKE DRIVES US to rehearsal because he's still not convinced he can trust me to show up if he doesn't. I'd be offended at his lack of trust—if it wasn't justified.

The only good thing about rehearsal is—there *isn't* anything good about rehearsal. If not for this stupid show, I wouldn't have made a fool out of myself with Mitch. Now I've got to be in it because I ran him and the other straight guys off.

At least my role as an extra is easy. For the most part, I just have to stand there and react to the main characters. The guys who can actually sing handle the more difficult songs, and the rest are so easy all we have to do is shout out the lines.

The guys I'm with are all very friendly. When we're not on stage, we hang out with some of the tech crew. I keep my eyes open, still trying to figure out who the "couple of gay guys" Blake mentioned are. So far, I'm not having any luck, but they are an interesting group of people.

We're chatting quietly, when I hear someone approaching from behind me, and Hunter looks up.

"There you are," he says. "About time you showed up. I guess you can't get anywhere on time if I don't drive you."

"Very funny. I told you I had to help my dad with something before I could leave."

My blood runs cold. It's Mitch. *What the hell is he doing here?*

"Where were you Thursday?" Joe Christopher asks.

"It was my sister's birthday," he says and adds, "I cleared it with Szinhely."

He says hello to a couple of the other guys, and then his eyes turn to me.

"Hi, Randy," he says with a forced smile.

"Hi, Mitch. How's it going?" I can't hide the slight crack in my voice.

"Fine."

Without another word, he turns to one of the stagehands and picks up on some long-running topic they've been debating. My face is glowing so red you could find your way home in the dark by it. But everybody goes back to their conversations and pretends not to notice. I stand there wanting to disappear and cursing myself for having let Blake drive. But I'm stuck.

After an hour of rehearsal, Mr. Szinhely calls for a break. People stretch and either congregate in little groups or head for the lobby. Blake is busy going over "You've Got to Be Carefully Taught," much to the delight of his one-member fan club. I'm about to find somewhere to hide when Mitch motions for me to follow him. A queasy feeling erupts in my stomach.

We go outside. He leads me away from the others and stops at the old oak tree across from the lunchroom.

"You know, you had one hell of a nerve the other night."

"Look," I say, watching my shoes, "I'm sorry about what happened. I shouldn't have done it."

"You're damn right you shouldn't have done it," he hisses. "Trying to pull something like that right there on a public street? What the hell were you thinking?"

"Look. I'm queer, and I liked you, and I thought you liked me. I'm sorry. It won't happen again."

He stares at me for a second and takes a step closer. I'm ready for him to punch me in the face, but a voice rings out that we all need to get back inside. He sidesteps me and walks away. I poke along, giving him as much distance as possible, and wishing the rehearsal would magically be over before I get inside.

Up ahead, a group of four guys starts back in as well. One of them tosses a cigarette to the ground. I start to step on it but pick it up instead. Wiping off the filter, I take a deep drag only to choke for the next four minutes. So much for using cigarettes to calm nerves. What a stupid habit.

The rest of the rehearsal is surreal. Mitch and I have to stand next to each other every moment we're on stage. The thing is, he's now acting like nothing ever happened between us. He even compliments my reactions to one of the main character's dialogue. But his pretend goodwill doesn't make me feel any better, and I count the minutes until Mr. Szinhely calls it a night.

When it's finally time to go, I can't get out fast enough. It doesn't help that I've got to wait for Blake. After twelve infuriating minutes of Mary Beth drooling all over him about how much she loves his singing, I pull him away and drag him to the parking lot.

As soon as we're on the road, I clear my throat and say, "I don't think I'm right for the show."

"Nonsense. You're doing great. Besides, it won't look right if we don't have enough extras. And you're a perfect fit for one of the costumes. They've already made it."

"Look, I gave it a chance and, well, I'm just not comfortable."

"Wait a minute. You can't mean you're uncomfortable being so close to other gay guys? What are you trying to tell me, you're prejudiced against fags?"

"Shut up. I just don't want to do it."

"Randy, what's the real trouble here? What's changed your mind so suddenly?"

"Nothing."

"Good. Then you're still good to stay in. Now let's hear no more about it."

I'm trapped, fated to go through with the show.

We drive the rest of the way in silence while the radio slobbers out one crappy disco song after another.

WEDNESDAY CONTINUES MY new twilight-zone journey into surrealism. Kerry's still acting strange and giving me friendly little touches when no one is looking. When he asks why I didn't call him last night and I make a lame excuse, he just grins like it's a compliment.

In History, Mitch looks up as Kerry and I enter. As we pass him, he surprises me with a friendly-looking smile. When Mrs. Molina calls on a girl who sits near me in the back, Mitch turns around to listen to her answer, but his eye is on me. At least I have Spanish and Geometry to relax and work myself into a calmer frame of mind. But after another lunch period of Kerry's smiles and friendly little touches, I'm more than ready for Art.

As I fall into my chair, Mrs. Pilt glances at our table. I've often suspected that she hears more of our conversations than she lets on. After all the tension between Annie and me yesterday, she's probably wondering how our table talk will go today.

Jeremy wanders in and plops into his chair. His jacket collar is ripped, one of his cheeks is red—it almost looks like someone slapped him—and he's breathing a little raggedly. I'm about to ask him what happened when the bell rings, and right on cue, Annie bounds into the room. I imagine Doc Severinsen blasting out the *Tonight Show* theme song. Today, she's wearing a bright orange button-up and hip-hugger jeans with a fringed purple wraparound sash. It's up for grabs whether her grand entrances are supposed to be about the outrageous clothes she's wearing on any given day or just the outrageousness that is Annie herself. Someday, she's got to end up famous.

She coasts to her seat and surveys the room, showing no hint of whatever was going on with her yesterday. But her eyes narrow when they fall on Mike Kowalski, and her mood turns sullen. She stares at him until he notices her, then she quickly looks away. A few minutes later, he's staring at her, and as soon as she catches him, his attention snaps back to his new project—a second ceramic elephant.

They're both frowning.

For seventeen minutes, Annie works in silence while Jeremy and I trade wary glances. It's like the calm before the storm.

And the storm finally breaks not five seconds after Mrs. Pilt steps out to check the kiln in the storage room. Her footsteps have barely faded away when Annie unleashes her wrath.

"Have you seen that girl he's been slobbering all over for the past two days at lunch?" she says to no one, but loud enough that everyone, especially Mike, can hear her. I shake my head, and Jeremy grits his teeth.

"It wouldn't be so bad that the girl's ugly, if he didn't look like such a pathetic loser drooling all over her."

Jeremy and I stare from Annie to Mike and back again. Mike doesn't say a word. But his usual hurt puppy-dog look has been replaced by steely silence.

"I'm telling you, it's pathetic, just plain pathetic."

"Annie, you really ought to lay off him," I whisper.

Totally ignoring me, she opens her mouth to continue her tirade. But without warning, Jeremy pounds the table so hard Annie jumps, and I shield my willow.

"Shirley Ann Brock!" he roars. "For once in your life, can you please just let it go and keep your mouth shut? You've been riding Mike's ass ever since September, and now that he's given up on you and found somebody else, you're just jealous. Well, too bad. It's your own damn fault. Why should he waste his time on someone who's afraid to face her own feelings?"

"W-what are you t-talking about?" she stammers.

"You know damn well what I'm talking about. You're afraid to admit you're in love with a white boy. You treat Mike like crap because you're black and he's white, and you're scared of what other people might say if they knew you're in love with him. And now you're upset because he's found another girl. Well, too bad. You've got no one to blame but yourself."

The room has gone totally quiet. Annie stares at Jeremy in utter shock. This is the first time I've ever seen him confront her about anything serious. And it's the *only* time I've ever seen Annie Brock silenced by anybody.

At that moment, Mrs. Pilt walks back in and looks around at all the heads bobbing between Annie and Mike and Jeremy. The tension in the room is unbearable.

Finally, Mike breaks the silence. "That girl in the lunchroom is just my cousin, Annie. I asked her to sit with me to make you jealous. You have to know there could never be anybody for me but you."

For a heartbeat, Annie just stares at him. Then, quicker than I can take it all in, she jumps across the room, grabs Mike's head in both hands, pulls him to his feet, and plants the sloppiest, most amorous kiss on him I've ever seen. It's so sensual, even *my* lips start tingling.

He takes her into his arms in the most delicate of embraces. All we need are violins and it'd be exactly like one of those old Hollywood movies—the ones I only watch when I'm alone because they make me cry. As it is, there's a catch in my throat even without the violins.

Slowly, Jeremy begins clapping his hands, and the whole class breaks into the wildest round of applause ever heard in Chadham High. Mrs. Pilt opens her mouth like she's going to say something, but stops, and starts clapping too.

When Annie finally lets go of him, Mike's face is frozen in absolute ecstasy. She saunters back to her seat, the tears on her cheeks framing a soft smile. A couple of the other girls are sniffing and wiping their faces. Even Mrs. Pilt's eyes are watery.

And my God! Now *I'm* crying. Someone will probably wind up calling me a faggot for this later, but I don't care. I've just witnessed one of the most romantic moments of the twentieth century.

"Okay, that's enough of that," Mrs. Pilt finally says, but she's smiling just like everybody else.

"Next stop, the *Love Boat*," I say, trying to pull myself back together and wiping tears off my face.

"Waiter, a glass of water for Mr. Clark, please," Jeremy deadpans, and we all start laughing.

By seventh period, the word has spread that Annie Brock and Mike Kowalski are in love, that they had a major smooching session in Art, and that fifteen years after the Civil Rights Act, the racial barrier has finally fallen at Chadham High. It may offend some people, but not me. I'll always treasure the memory of watching Annie and Mike holding hands as they walked down the hallway after class.

Of course, several different versions of the story are going around. Luckily for Mrs. Pilt, none of them mentions that she was in the room when the smooching went down, let alone that she applauded the kiss of the century along with everyone else. I'm glad. There are too many bigots in Chadham County, and that's just the kind of thing some of them would raise a stink over.

The funny thing though is that all the stories going around have somehow mixed up the parts Jeremy and I played. They all have me as the one who confronted Annie, and Jeremy as the one who broke down crying.

I DRIVE TO rehearsal by myself Thursday evening. Blake had to go back early so he could practice a couple of solo scenes, and I told him there was no way I was going to spend the whole night listening to him sing. He only relented after I swore up and down that I really would show up, even without the Blake Rogers police escort.

I'd rather be by myself for the drive home anyway. I'll need that time to build up my Buddha focus. After I get home, I'm going to call Kerry and tell him I'm gay. Better to have him reject me over the phone tonight than in person at his house tomorrow.

I arrive a little early and grab a seat off to the side. My plan is to avoid Mitch. He's chatting with a few people, but as soon as he sees me, he walks over, and my anxiety level starts to rise.

"Hey, Randy, how's it going?"

"Okay. You?"

"Fine," he says. "Look, we've still got a little while before we get started. Want to take a walk?"

I study his face for a second before saying, “Okay, sure.”

This is confusing. After our last conversation, nice is not what I expected out of Mitch Weaver.

He leads the way outside, and I follow apprehensively. It’s chilly, but at least it’s not raining. I follow him past the lunchroom to the loading bay, wondering if he’s looking for a more private place to punch me. He leans against the little wall and looks me over for a second.

“So when did you first realize you were gay?”

“What does it matter to you?”

After everything that’s been going on over the last couple of days, I’m in no condition for a cross-examination about my queerness.

“I’m just curious,” he says.

“Look, I told you I’m sorry for what I did, and it won’t happen again. Can’t we just forget about it?”

“But I don’t want to forget about it. When did you first know? Come on; tell me.”

That’s it. I can’t take it anymore. I turn and hightail it to the parking lot, with Mitch yelling after me to stop. Before he can get to me, I jump in the car and race out for the highway. All I can think about is telling Kerry I’m gay, and the sooner I get it over with the better.

I get home, dodge my parents, and run straight to my room. But, as if I’m not stressed-out enough already, I can’t get up with him. I keep trying, but by bedtime, every call has ended in a busy signal. If I don’t have a nervous breakdown by Saturday, it’ll be a miracle.

Chapter 14: The Cage Door Opens

"OKAY, PERHAPS YOU'D like to tell me what happened to you last night," Blake demands as soon as he gets on the bus Friday morning. "Mitch Weaver said you took off like a bat out of Hell. What the hell is going on?"

"I don't want to be in the show."

"Oh, here we go again," he scoffs. "Will you just give me one good reason why you keep deciding you don't want to be in the show?"

"I just don't."

"Don't give me that, Randy Clark. I've known you too long. Now what's the problem?"

"Okay, look—" I lower my voice to a whisper "—I'm the reason all the straight guys dropped out. A couple of weeks ago, Mitch and I went to the movies, and I...uh...I tried to kiss him."

Blake just stares at me like he doesn't get it.

"Look, it's kind of awkward being around the straight guy you made a stupid pass at."

Blake shakes his head. "Randy, didn't I tell you that the straight guys dropped out claiming one of our *regulars* hit on one of them?"

"Yeah?"

"Well, hello, Einstein. *Mitch* is a regular. *And* he's *still* in the show."

It takes a few seconds for me to digest this information.

"Mitch is gay?"

Blake's lips curl into a sarcastic pursed grin, and he nods.

"But if Mitch is gay, why did he get freaked out when I tried to kiss him?"

"I don't know. Maybe you're not his type. Maybe he's not the kind to kiss on the first date. Maybe he likes somebody else. Hey, I've got a *great* idea— Why don't you ask him tomorrow at the rehearsal and find out?"

"Tomorrow?"

"Yeah, from here on out, we have weekend rehearsals. Now, can we stop all this 'drop out of the show' nonsense once and for all?"

I nod, wondering just how many other things I've misunderstood recently.

When I get to homeroom, Kerry isn't there. It makes me feel guilty, but I kind of hope he's out sick. If so, I'm off the hook. He won't be able to have visitors if he's sick.

Freed up from one issue, I can move on to deal with another. As I pass Mitch on the way to my seat in History, he glances up, and I whisper in his ear.

"I'm sorry about last night. Can we talk tomorrow at the rehearsal?"

He looks back at me for a second and nods slowly. I wonder just how crazy he must think I am.

The first thing I see when I walk into the lunchroom is Mike, Annie, and Jeremy. Mike has his arm around Annie, and Jeremy is sitting across from them. They make quite a contrasting little group. Jeremy is in his trademark black windbreaker, and today, he's wearing a black pullover with his black jeans and sneakers. Mike is sporting a plaid shirt, slacks, and Doc Martens, while Annie is decked out in a lavender blouse, peach skirt, and clogs. I laugh out loud because Mike's talking very animatedly to Jeremy, and for once in her life, Annie's actually just listening. Hilarious. From the expression on Jeremy's face, I'd guess he's not sure it's an improvement to now have two blabbermouths chattering at him instead of just the one.

Mentally rolling the dice, I decide to take my life in my own hands and walk over to the serving line. One of the lunchroom ladies tells me today's featured menu item is hamburgers, but I swear I never saw one with a red crust before.

I've just set my tray down and pulled up a chair next to Jeremy, when Mr. Allen appears out of nowhere.

"Young man," he barks to Mike, "take your hands off of that young lady. It's against school policy to paw over girls. Don't let me catch you doing that again."

While Mike slowly removes his arm from around Annie, Jeremy catches my eye. He cocks his head towards Billie Jo Jackson and Terry Huff, who are passing by, each with a firm hold on each other's waists.

"What about *them*?" I say, but Mr. Allen is already walking away in the opposite direction.

"They match," Annie comments sourly.

"Damn double standard," Mike says and snorts.

Nobody feels much like talking after that, and we just chew our lunchroom mystery food in silence. Without the distraction of conversation, my eyes wander, and I notice more than a few people looking our way. More specifically, they seem to be staring at Mike and Annie, and there's something hostile, if not openly angry and downright mean in their eyes. The room suddenly feels a lot colder.

We deposit our trays and pass back through the room on our way to the courtyard. Voices follow us like growling beasts.

"Nigger...stupid Polack...faggot...crybaby."

Just before Mike opens the courtyard door, we're all startled by a fork clattering against the glass. Snickering and laughter breaks out around us. Right as the door closes behind us, something else crashes against it. We keep moving.

When we get to Art, Mrs. Pilt can tell something's up. Mike's at our table, but no one's talking—not even Annie. Compared to the glad romance of yesterday's class, today, we might as well all be at a funeral. We're lost in thought about what we've all just experienced, each in our own way. Most of the name-calling might have been directed at Annie and Mike, but from the look on Jeremy's face, it got to him too. And it definitely got to me.

When the bell rings after class, I take as long as possible to get to the locker room. I'm not in the mood to deal with Ramrod, Brad, and the rest of the six-million-dollar jackasses today. And besides, Coach Horne may yell at you for being late, but he never reports it.

As I turn the last corner to the locker room, the sound of a basketball game pounding away in the gym echoes in the hall. Breathing a sigh of relief, I push open the door and go inside. At first, the room looks empty. Mission accomplished.

But when I turn to sit down, I'm surprised to see Kerry changing on the bench across from me.

"Kerry, where have you been all day? I thought you were out sick or something."

"I forgot to tell you. I had a dentist checkup, so Mom let me skip this morning. Don't worry, though; we're still good for tonight."

"Listen, Kerry, about tonight—"

"You know, you'll be my first friend to come over since we moved here. My mom's letting us use the guest room. You'll love it. It's even got a private bathroom. We'll have the whole thing to ourselves. And my dad's springing for pizza, just for the two of us. We can talk more on the bus."

"Kerry, I'm not going to be on the bus."

Kerry's smile fades. *Damn it. He looks so disappointed.*

"See, Kerry...the thing is...I...uh...I didn't pack my things."

I'm sorry, but I just can't take it. I'm already too stressed-out from the last twenty-four hours, especially after witnessing all that bigotry in the lunchroom. I heave a sigh and force myself to say it.

"I'm not going to take the bus to your house... I'm going home...and...and when I've got my things, I'll bike into town. It'll make it easier on our folks. No one will have to drive me home."

Why can't I ever say no to him?

THE SAWYERS LIVE in a large two-story house in the upscale part of town. Kerry greets me with a broad smile from a swing on the wide front porch. He leads me inside and positively beams while introducing me to his mother. Mrs. Sawyer has the same dark hair as Kerry, but her eyes are almost like black pools, and her chin is softer. She's very nice.

The guest room could almost be a small apartment on its own. Besides the usual bedroom furnishings, it's got a sitting area with a TV and comfortable chairs. It's very cozy and kind of romantic looking, like it would be the perfect room to...

No. I'm not going to even think about it.

After putting my things down, we go upstairs to Kerry's room and bring down his stereo and a stack of records. Kerry's really into new wave. He's got posters of The Clash, Squeeze, and several new wave bands I've never even heard of. Otherwise, his room is a lot like mine, including the Police poster I've got on my wall.

Setting up the stereo takes several trips, and I meet Kerry's sisters along the way. Janice is in the same grade as Wally. She's parked herself in front of the living room TV, and grumbles each time we walk in front of her. When Kerry introduces me as Wally's brother, she wrinkles her nose. I can't say I blame her.

Monica is a twelfth grader. I've seen her before in the hallway at school. She is everything to feminine teenage beauty Kerry is to the masculine variety. Seeing her also reveals a glimpse of how Kerry will look as he matures over the next couple of years. It's an appealing vision.

We've just got the stereo set up, when Mr. Sawyer pops in. He's the other half of Kerry's good looks, with the same hazel eyes, a surprisingly good build for a man his age, and the same lopsided smile Kerry has. After double-checking that Kerry has enough money for the pizza, he tells us to have a good time and leaves. Having met both of them, I decide Kerry's parents are cool. The Sawyers are a nice family.

Kerry and I hang out in the guest room for a couple of hours, chatting and listening to records. Mrs. Sawyer lets us borrow the car, and we drive to Tino's Pizza Nook and pick up a large pepperoni. After eating, we play cards and chat while listening to more music. The TV is on with the sound turned down. *The Rockford Files* takes on a whole different feeling when you're listening to Patti Smith singing "Land."

At seven minutes after ten, there's a knock on the door. Mrs. Sawyer pokes her head in to tell us Blake is on the phone. Kerry picks up the receiver, and I listen in.

"Guys, you're not going to believe it. The police had to be called to the dance. Somebody beat the crap out of Jeremy Smith. He had to be taken away in an ambulance."

The blood drains from my face. "What happened? Who did it?"

"Nobody knows. Annie Brock and Mike Kowalski found him outside on the ground all beat to hell. He looked bad, man. I saw him. Whoever did it did a real number on him. And they smeared his lips with red paint. The police talked to a bunch of people, but the best I know, they didn't arrest anybody."

"Oh God, I bet Annie's beside herself."

Kerry asks Blake a few more questions, but I'm too stunned to speak. My mind races, and the more I think about it, the more upset I get.

Oh my God. Jeremy got beat up. The guy who did it probably thought he was the one who cried in art class yesterday instead of me. That's the way all the stories going around had it. Oh God, he got beat up, and he's in the hospital, and it's all my fault. If someone had come after me, I could have at least gotten in a hit or two, but Jeremy's so little, I bet he couldn't punch his way out of a wet paper bag. He didn't deserve it. It should have been me. It's all my fault.

Kerry hangs up the phone. "Why would anybody beat up Jeremy?"

"Because they thought he was me," I say, my stomach twisting up in knots.

"How could anyone possibly mistake Jeremy for you? You've got a good four inches on him."

"It's that damn story going around about Annie and Mike Kowalski. The story's all wrong. Jeremy didn't cry when they kissed, I did."

"I don't get it."

"Don't you see? Whoever did this thought they were beating up the queer, but they got him instead of me."

I freeze and a chill runs through me. *My God! What have I said?*

Kerry stares at me. "So you *are* gay."

What's left of my nerves go haywire. My hands are shaking, and I can't catch my breath.

"I've got to go," I shriek, snatching my bag.

"Randy, wait."

I bolt to the door. Kerry grabs my arm. I strain to break free of his grip, but he's stronger than I am. Panic is overwhelming me, and I stare at him with the wild-eyed desperation of a caged animal.

"Let me go, damn it!"

Then the world seems to go into slow motion. Kerry pulls me close, and swings me into an embrace. I try to push him off, still struggling, but those hazel eyes are staring into mine.

"Randy, it's okay. I'm gay too."

The words hang in the air like smoke. I stop struggling.

Then he kisses me. At the touch of his lips to mine, a gentle stream of emotion winds its way through me, and panic gives way to the most exquisite peacefulness. I close my eyes and open them again just to confirm that I'm not hallucinating. A voice in my head finally says, *Breathe.*

"I've wanted to do that since the first day I met you," he whispers.

"Me too... Wait, you said you dated a lot of girls back in Petersburg."

He breaks into a lopsided grin. "I said I *knew* a lot of girls back in Petersburg."

"You said you had a girlfriend."

"No, I said there was a special *someone.* I never said he was a girl. I guess we've got a lot to talk about."

Kerry leads me to the bed, and we sit, facing each other. I'm still trying to take it all in.

"I thought you were straight," I say.

"When I first got here, mentioning a special someone, and being vague about it, was an easy way to stop people from asking questions. And even though I was pretty sure you were gay the moment I met you, I wasn't certain, and I didn't want to damage our friendship if I was wrong, so I didn't say anything."

"Wait. You were pretty sure I was gay when you first met me? How did you know? What, do I have like a sign on my head that says 'homo' or something?"

"No. I could just sort of tell. I call it 'gaydar.' It's like the old 'it takes one to know one' thing. Anyway, like I said, I wasn't sure. See, when you went out with Rosa and Janie, it seemed like the only reason you were doing it was because Annie and Blake put you up to it. But you said you just didn't like people setting you up. Then there was that time you got the hard-on in the shower...but sometimes a good workout *will* do that to a guy. So in the end, to be safe, I decided to hint around and see if you'd say something."

"I thought you were making fun of me."

"Oh God, no, it's just that I still wasn't sure, and I couldn't chance our friendship. I felt a *little* more confident after you had that meltdown outside the locker room, but even then, I still wasn't one hundred percent certain. And when you called Monday night, for all I knew, you were going to tell me to back off. But when Annie started joking around at lunch the next day, the way you reacted left no doubt. That's why I invited you over, so we could get it all out in the open just the two of us."

"When I called, I *was* going to tell you I'm gay"—I surprise myself by taking his hand—"*and* I was going to tell you that I'm really attracted to you."

"Randy, I'm really attracted to you too."

I lean into him, and we kiss again. For the first time, I'm in the arms of the guy I want, and I'm kissing him, and he's kissing me back. And for now, the world and all its troubles can wait.

Chapter 15: Families

WHEN I WAKE up, Kerry's lying on his back, cradling the arm I've wrapped around him. My head is nestled against his shoulder. The smell of his hair is like a cool spring breeze. I could gladly spend the rest of my life right here, just watching the rise and fall of his chest. I leave a light kiss on his shoulder, slide away from him, and crawl out of bed. His eyes flutter. I wonder what he's dreaming about.

It's seven-thirty. I'd usually be grumbling about waking up this early on a Saturday, but today, I'll take as much time with Kerry as I can get.

I retreat to the bathroom for a much-needed shower and have just dressed when there's a light rap on the door. Mrs. Sawyer peeks in.

"So you're the early bird. I thought I heard the shower. Are you ready for breakfast?"

"Yes, ma'am."

She grabs Kerry by his big toe and pinches it hard. "Wake up, sleepyhead. Time for breakfast."

As she disappears out the door, he blinks in shock and stares at the ceiling. He looks so cute.

"Good morning."

He yawns and stretches. "Morning."

After he showers, we spend a few minutes cuddling and kissing before we reluctantly head to the kitchen. I'm surprised to see bacon on the menu. Mrs. Sawyer explains that it's kosher bacon and actually made from beef. It's pretty good, but Kerry whispers that he really prefers the regular kind.

We've barely finished eating when the phone rings. Kerry answers it and calls me over.

"It's Annie Brock," he whispers, passing me the receiver and leaning in to listen.

"Annie, how's Jeremy? Is he all right?"

"Oh Randy, they beat him up so bad." The stress in her voice is dreadful. "Could you meet me and Mike in the park? I need to tell you something."

"Sure, Annie. I can be there in half an hour."

Kerry squeezes my shoulder as we walk back to the table. "I'm coming with you."

CLOUDS SWEEP BY above us, threatening a chilly rain. Kerry and I follow the riverside boardwalk until we see Annie and Mike. She looks shaken and haggard. Mike is obviously exhausted too, but he's standing straight, with his arm protectively wrapped around her. We all go to a bench.

"How's Jeremy?"

"He's in bad shape, Randy," Annie says, choking up. Her eyes are bleary from crying and lack of sleep.

After a second, Mike speaks for her. "We were there pretty late last night. Man, whoever did it knew how to make it hurt. He's got some cracked or broken ribs, and they really did a number on his face."

"But he is going to be all right, isn't he?"

"It's going to take time," Annie says without looking up.

"Did he say who did it?" Kerry asks.

Mike just shakes his head, but Annie's eyes are suddenly hard.

"It was Ramrod." She spits out the words while trying to control her emotions. "It was Ramrod and his boys. They've bullied Jeremy for two years now."

My mouth drops open. "Do you know that for sure? Is that what Jeremy said?"

"No," Mike says, "he's not said anything about who beat him. He was out cold when we found him. And later, he was drifting in and out of consciousness, so what he did say didn't make much sense."

Annie cuts in. "He said *you* know. He said, 'Randy knows' a couple of times. What did he mean?"

There's only one answer I can think of, and I tell them. "He meant it's all my fault."

Annie stares at me. "What are you talking about?"

"After you guys did your Romeo and Juliet scene in art class, the stories going around had it that Jeremy was the one who cried. That's all it would take for some people to go after him."

Kerry squeezes my shoulder. "Randy, it's not your fault. And look, I don't really know Jeremy that well, but I doubt he's the kind of guy to be laying a guilt trip on you, especially right now. It's more likely he thinks you know something about who did it."

"But I *don't* know anything."

"Maybe you know something but you just don't realize it," Mike says.

The conversation continues, mostly between Kerry and Mike. Annie and I aren't really listening. I sit slouched forward with only the touch of Kerry's body next to mine giving me any comfort. Annie stares into the distance, her arms crossed tight, her jaw set, no doubt lost in conflicting emotions over the changes her life has gone through in the last two days. The happiness she and Mike should be celebrating has been scarred by ugly prejudice and bigotry for no other reason than being an interracial couple. And now she's found her best friend brutalized and left for dead. I can only imagine how hard it all must be for her.

I sit back and stare at the river, wondering what it is I know about whoever did this to Jeremy.

BLAKE PICKS ME up for our one o'clock rehearsal. I'm even less into it than normal, but after the news last night, it's a much-needed distraction.

When Mr. Szinhely calls it quits for the day, I go outside to wait for Blake. I'm really getting tired of his all-female fan club, which has doubled its usual turnout today because Marilyn came to the rehearsal and she's competing with Mary Beth to see who can flatter him the most.

It must have rained while we were inside. The cars are all damp, and the air has a fresh autumn smell. I walk over to the lunchroom area and look around for the spot where they found Jeremy. But the rain must have washed away any blood that would have given the location away.

I've been standing there thinking about Jeremy for a few minutes when Mitch walks up to me.

"Sorry to hear about your friend."

"Yeah, thanks."

"I hope they crucify whoever did this to him," he says grimly.

"Me too."

We wander out near the service road and stop, facing each other.

"Mitch, are you gay?"

"Yes."

"Then why did you get so pissed that night?"

"Because that bitch neighbor of ours was out walking her dog. If she'd seen us kissing she'd have blabbed her head off, and I don't know about you, but I don't need that kind of crap in my life these days."

"I'm sorry. I barely noticed her."

"And you and I were *only* hanging out, remember? No one said anything about it being a date. Plus, how was I to know you were really gay and not just trying to set me up? And...I already have a boyfriend."

"Hunter?"

"Yeah," Mitch says with a sheepish smile.

"I'm really sorry. I didn't know at the time."

"Hey, don't worry about it. But, Randy, you really do have to be more careful. This isn't New York or California, you know."

"Yeah, I guess you're right. I'm kind of new at all of this."

"No problem. So tell me. Are you interested in anyone in particular?"

"Well, there is this one guy," I say with a smile, oddly less embarrassed than I'd have thought I would be to say it out loud.

Mitch smiles too and nods. "Look, if you want to, call me sometime—if you haven't torn up my number, that is. Maybe we can get together and just talk."

"Thanks, I'd like that. Oh, and Mitch? Hunter's a lucky guy." He smiles, and I continue, "But the next time you and I get together, I have one thing I really need to tell you. Mitch, I *hate* sauerkraut. *And* root beer."

Hunter comes out and calls Mitch. He runs off to join him, still laughing.

At last, Blake appears, having finally broken free from Mary Beth and Marilyn. We hop in the car and are soon cruising down the highway.

"So," he says, "did you and Mitch get everything straightened out?"

"Yeah. Yeah, we did."

"Good. Then we don't have to hear any more of that 'I've got to quit the show' crap."

We drive along in silence for a minute, and I smile.

"It was certainly a nice surprise seeing Marilyn," I say, watching him out of the corner of my eye. "I wonder what brought her here today."

"She told me she came to pick up some music she left in her locker and decided to stay for the rehearsal."

"You amaze me sometimes," I say.

He looks over at me with a puzzled expression, but I just shake my head.

I could tell him, but I've decided to let someone else tell Blake the only bit of gossip he seems to have missed recently. I already know it on good authority.

Gwen told Annie that Marilyn overheard Mary Beth telling Stephanie Brigham how wonderful Blake—and his voice—is. Apparently, when Marilyn heard that, she turned red with rage and green with jealousy. Then Vickie heard Marilyn tell Allyson Horbach that she thought she just might start attending all the rehearsals to make sure she "had a good feel" for things.

From the look on Marilyn's face today, I'm not sure what she wants to feel more—the touch of Blake's lips, or her fingers around Mary Beth's throat.

I CALL KERRY as soon as I get home, and he invites me to stay over at his house again tonight. I ask my mother, but she counters with an offer for him to come for dinner and stay the night with us. Of course, while I'm still on the phone, she adds that he can also join us for church. I have no choice but to pass along the invitation, but I whisper that we'll figure out a way to get him out of the church part. To my surprise, he says he'd love to go to church with us.

"You don't know our church," I hiss.

Of course, that's not what really worries me. What worries me is the thought of him having to be in close proximity to my family for an extended period of time. But now that I know he's gay, *and* that he likes me, *and* how good a kisser he is, I'll take any opportunity I can get to spend more time with him—even if it means exposing him to my family.

Not twenty minutes after we get off the phone, Kerry's bike is lying next to mine in the yard. We hide out in my room until we're called to the table.

Dinner promises to be the most frightening part of the evening; it requires that Kerry sit face-to-face with my family. I warn him that my dad's very opinionated, and he's not the most diplomatic person on earth. And I tell him Mom can be very stuffy over things like class and social standing. And Wally? Well, he's just what he's always been. A turd.

At least there are no worries on the food front. Mom's gone all out. The table is piled high with roast beef, Yorkshire pudding, creamed spinach, and steamed carrots.

"Thank you for having me over, Mrs. Clark," Kerry says. "This is all so delicious. My mom's going to be jealous when I tell her about it."

"Why thank you, Kerry," Mom says, her eyes beaming. "But I'm sure your mother's an excellent cook in her own right."

"Oh she's good, but there's something about this Yorkshire pudding that just outdoes any I've ever tasted."

Mom smiles and promptly dishes another helping onto Kerry's already overloaded plate.

"Hear anything about how your friend's doing?" Dad says through a mouthful of roast beef.

I hesitate before answering him, afraid of where this will probably end up going. "The best we know, he's going to be all right. From what Annie tells us, they really knocked him around bad and broke a few ribs, but nothing that time won't heal."

"Well thank God for that," Mom says, and I'm ready to breathe a sigh of relief and change the subject.

But no. Dad goes on.

"Now which one is he?"

I clear my throat. "You remember last year when I tied for second prize at the art competition? Well, Jeremy was the guy I tied with."

"Oh yeah, I remember him now. He's that little Jewish fag that hangs out with the nigger girl."

Kerry and I both flinch.

"Bill Clark!" Mom exclaims, I'm sure more embarrassed that he said it in front of Kerry than from disagreeing with him.

"Freda, let's face it," Dad says, spooning more creamed spinach onto his plate. "You can look that boy in the eye and tell he's a fag. Now, I'm sorry he got hurt, but I'll bet you dollars to donuts he had it coming. He probably came on to some guy and got the shit beat out of him for it."

"Dad," I protest, "you don't know anything about Jeremy. And he's not Jewish, he's Presbyterian."

"Um..." Kerry says quietly. "*I'm* Jewish."

"Oh, well then," Dad says while filling his mouth with a forkful of steamed carrots, "coming to church with us tomorrow will be doubly good for you."

"Don't worry, Kerry," my mother says. "Our church is very progressive. We've even got a few former Methodists. And I promise, the next time you come over, I'll cook something Jewish for you. Do you like roast pork?"

This is a nightmare. I'm so angry I could scream. It's bad enough I have to hear this kind of thing all the time, but I'm absolutely mortified that Kerry's getting it the very first time he eats with us.

And the nightmare only gets worse. Out of the corner of my eye, I see Wally leaning over—in my general direction, of course.

Oh no! He wouldn't dare. Not now. Not in front of Kerry.

It's the last thing I can coherently think before The Turd adds his own special contribution to the conversation.

Pffffffffft...

"My compliments to the chef," he says with a nod to my mother as a cloud of stench spreads throughout the room.

And with that, all conversation comes to a screeching halt.

A HALF HOUR later, Kerry and I are back safely behind my locked bedroom door.

"God," I say, pounding my fist into the bed between us. "I just can't believe he'd say things like that in front of you. And you *don't* have to go to church with us."

"Don't worry. It won't be the first time I've ever set foot in a church."

"And The Turd. I just... It's so, so embarrassing."

"Really, it's all right. So, your brother's a turd. It's okay. It's no reflection on you. And as for your father, look, he's a man of his generation; it's just the way he was raised. Old prejudices die hard. And hey, he may know I'm Jewish now, but at least he doesn't know I'm a little Jewish *faggot*."

"Yeah, but what's he going to say when he finds out his son's a 'little faggot,' too?" I pound the bed again. "God, I hate living like this."

"Then let the skeleton out."

"The skeleton...?"

"Yeah, the skeleton in your closet. Let it out and see what happens. Just have a little talk with your old man. Tell him you're gay and see what he says."

"See what he says? Are you kidding? I can tell you *exactly* what he'd say. He wouldn't say anything; he'd just beat the crap out of me, kick me out, and never speak to me again. Tell him I'm gay... You tell me, have *you* had that little talk with *your* father?"

"Yes, actually, I have. My whole family all know I'm gay. We're big on honesty. *And* after I met you, I told them I was pretty sure *you* were gay too."

"You told them I...? Wait a minute. Your parents know you're gay, *and* they know I'm gay, *and* they let me spend the night with you? In the same bed?"

"Well, I'm pretty sure they weren't worried you'd get me pregnant."

For a moment, I just marvel that there are really people in the world who can find out their son is gay and not totally freak out over it. But then I compare Kerry's family to my own and come to a sad conclusion.

"You're lucky. Your folks accept you. My folks would never accept me if they knew I was gay. Hell, my dad doesn't accept me now, and he doesn't even know the truth. They don't really know me at all. And the sad thing is, they'll never know who I am because they'll never accept what I am. I'll always be alone."

Kerry scoots closer and wraps an arm around me. "Hey, you're not alone. I'm here."

"But you can't be here forever."

"Maybe not," he says softly, "but I am here now. And who knows what's in the future?"

I shake my head. He brings his other arm around. For the longest time, we just sit that way, the emptiness inside me giving way to a warm, protected feeling. Kerry's here, for me, giving me his support, his strength. And it feels like love.

Sometime later, we undress and crawl into bed. The radio is tuned to an all-night FM station. In the darkness, Kerry takes me in his arms. His skin is firm, warm, and yielding to my touch. I'm at peace. He kisses me, and we cuddle as I fall asleep in his arms to Christine McVie singing "Songbird."

WHEN I OPEN my eyes, Kerry is lying next to me, watching me.

"Good morning," he whispers. "Ready to face a new day?"

"I'd rather just stay here like this with you."

"Well, if you think your father will go for it, I'm all in."

When I start to sit up, he pulls me back. We look into each other's eyes, and our lips touch. I'm melting into stone, and so is he.

Unfortunately, the pounding on my door makes us both jump.

"Hey, Shithead," The Turd screeches. "Dad says you better get moving if you're going to church."

"Kerry, you really *don't* have to do this. I—"

"I told you. It's not a problem. Now go ahead and shower. I've already cleaned up."

And so the morning goes. In the shower, I'm lost in the memory of Kerry lying in my bed, the two of us holding each other throughout the night. In the car, the heat of his body next to mine consumes me. In church, I wish I could hold his hand like the guy and girl a couple of rows ahead of us.

My parents take us to lunch downtown where we listen to my mother go on and on about the sermon, the minister, and several people who were, or weren't, in church. My father ignores her, The Turd plays with his food, and Kerry and I pretend to listen while stealing glances at each other and playing footsie under the table.

When we get home, I ask Mom if Kerry and I can use the car to visit Jeremy in the hospital. After motherly warnings to behave—to me, she's certain Kerry will be the perfect gentleman—he and I drive back across town. We aren't sitting close to each other in the car, but we are holding hands.

After parking the car, we ask for Jeremy's room number in the lobby and take the elevator to his floor. Annie is sitting in a waiting area with Jeremy's mother. Annie's reading the latest issue of *Seventeen*, but as soon as she spots us, she bounds over.

"How is he?" I ask.

"He's awake, and he's doing a lot better."

Then she stops, and I can see the wheels turning in her head. It's the second time in two days she's seen me, and Kerry's been with me both times. She breaks out into a typically over-the-top Annie-grin.

Kerry smiles back innocently, but I blush way too easily these days.

"Hush," I warn her before she can say anything.

She makes a kissy-face before taking us over to introduce us to Jeremy's mother.

I've met Mrs. Smith before. She's a couple of inches shorter than Jeremy, with the same stringy auburn hair. Normally, she's quite cheery, but right now, the hours of worrying over her son are telling on her. She explains that visitors are only allowed in two at a time, but at the moment, nobody is allowed in because the doctor and a nurse are checking him out.

While we wait, she talks about Jeremy—how much she always worries about him, about how his father died when he was just a toddler, about how she had to raise him by herself, and how special he's always been. I can't imagine how hard her life must be, and I can't help but admire her strength in bringing up Jeremy on her own.

Of course, Jeremy would probably try to muzzle her if he knew some of the things she's saying. When he feels better, I've got to ask him for his side of the toddler-spaghetti story.

After a few minutes, the doctor and nurse come out, and the doctor sits down to update Mrs. Smith. She asks him if it's okay for me and Kerry to go in, and he says yes.

We turn to go, but just as we get to the door, Annie stops us.

"You need to be prepared," she whispers. "He looks bad. Real bad."

We both take a deep breath.

Chapter 16: The Hospital and the School

THE ROOM IS dimly lit. It reeks of disinfectant. Jeremy's lying on his back. Mummy-like bandages encircle his skinny torso. The one wrapped around his head looks like a turban. An IV drip leads to one bruise-pocked arm. Two black eyes bullet his face. Stitches hold together a gash above one brow. His jaw is swollen. The area around his mouth, coated with some kind of ointment, looks raw, puffy, and wet. His eyes are so swollen I can't tell if he's awake or asleep.

"Jeremy?" I whisper.

"Hey, Randy." His voice is weak, scratchy, and slurred. "And is that Kerry?"

"Hi, Jeremy," Kerry says.

I step forward and brush my fingers over his hand. "Man, what happened to you?"

"I don't suppose you'd believe me if I said I tripped in the dark, would you?"

I can't help but smile. "No, not really."

Jeremy smiles too and immediately winces.

"Why would anyone do this to you?" Kerry asks.

"Because he knows I'm gay. Isn't that reason enough?"

It takes me a second to take in this new revelation. How could I have known Jeremy all these years and never even once considered the possibility that he was gay?

"Do you remember anything about it?" I ask.

Jeremy pauses and answers slowly. "I'm beginning to. He started hitting me and calling me a cocksucker... That's about all I can remember."

"But you do know who did it," Kerry says.

"Oh, I know exactly who did it."

I grip the bed's handrail. "And you've reported him, right? You've told the police."

"No," Jeremy replies. "And I don't intend to."

"But he should be locked up," I exclaim, trying to keep my voice down.

Jeremy tries to shake his head and groans at the pain. "Listen, you know how things are around here. It would just be the fag's word against his... And besides...there's someone else involved, so I'm not saying anything."

I'm about to argue with him, but Kerry takes my hand in his. "It's his decision, Randy. Come on. I'm sure Annie and his mother want to come in."

I lightly rub Jeremy's bruised arm. "I hope you know what you're doing."

"I do. Trust me."

We start to the door, but I turn back.

"Jeremy—Annie and Mike told me you said I know something. That you kept saying, 'Randy knows.' What do I know? How do I know anything about who did this to you?"

He looks down and pauses. "Oh...I was pretty out of it for a while there. I don't remember saying that."

I turn back to leave, but Jeremy speaks again.

"Randy? Did you...uh...ever get that thing we were talking about the other day straightened out?"

"You mean telling Kerry I'm gay?"

Kerry wraps an arm around me. "He did. And I told him I am too."

Jeremy forces a smile that must be agonizing. "I knew it. Do me a favor, Kerry. Keep close to this one; he's needed someone to look after him for a long time."

I grin evilly. "Hey, do you want me to get Annie and Mike both in here at the same time? They're dying to talk to you."

"Oh God, please, no," he says with a final painful smile. "I think I'd lose my mind if I had to lie in here like this and listen to both of them at the same time."

KERRY AND I are driving back home, sitting a respectful distance from each other, but again holding hands.

"I can't believe I never knew he was gay. I must have the worst gaydar in history."

"Good thing. I might never have had a chance with you otherwise.

He's cute."

"Hey, I don't make it a practice to fall in love with all my friends, you know."

My cheeks burn, and I glance over. Kerry squeezes my hand and smiles.

A few minutes pass before either of us speaks again.

"God, he looked awful," I say. "Damn it. I wish I understood what he meant about me knowing who did it and who the other person involved is."

"And why somebody else being involved would stop him telling the police who did it."

"Oh no!"

"What?"

"What if he's protecting the guy he was with? What if somebody saw him with another guy and that's why they beat him up?"

"Unless your father was right and it really *was* the same guy who did it."

"I don't believe that for a minute."

"Well, anyway, at least you can stop kicking yourself. He didn't get beat up because of you."

MONDAY MORNING OF Thanksgiving week turns chilly, and, predictably, the heater on the bus isn't working. It's cold in more ways than one. What conversation there is focuses on Jeremy's attack. I wish more of the talk was sympathetic, but this is Chadham County.

Theo Hayes is typical of most. He may say he's sorry Jeremy got beat up, but his eyes tell the real story. He doesn't approve of the violence, but he's certainly not going to lose any sleep over it. As far as he's concerned, Jeremy had it coming. He'd care just as little if somebody had beaten me to within an inch of my life.

I can't understand how somebody could be friends with a guy for years and then turn on him just because he's gay. You'd think gays conducted satanic rituals and made human sacrifices or something.

As the day progresses, I get more and more depressed at how callous everyone is. It's one long series of shrugged shoulders and condescending smirks. Everyone is whispering about the act of barbarism that happened Friday night, including the teachers. But none of them even bothers to mention it out loud, let alone condemn it. They'd all rather just pretend it never happened.

I bet over the years, there's been enough dirt swept under the rug in this place to make a mountain.

Kerry and I sit across from Annie and Mike in the lunchroom. None of us feels like talking, and given the hostile glances Annie and Mike are still getting, and the constant buzz of "queer" comments muttered all around us, all we want is to be left alone so we can finish our food and get out of there.

I'd have thought the expression on Annie's face alone would be enough to warn people off, but it's apparently not enough to stop Billy Mason.

"I hear they did a real number on Jeremy Smith," he says, pulling up a chair next to me and Kerry.

I glance over at Annie. She's glaring at Billy out of the corner of her eye.

"Is it true they painted his lips red?"

How stupid can he be? Even Wally knows about the red paint. It was in the newspaper.

"Maybe you should ask the police," Mike says.

Annie's glaring straight at Billy now.

"I heard the reason he got beaten up was, you know, he tried to blow the guy. Man, that's just gross."

At this point, I expect to see steam blowing out of Annie's ears any second. But Billy's still not smart enough to quit while he's behind.

"You know, I bet—"

"William Mason!" Annie explodes. "Why don't you just shut the hell up? What are you trying to say? You think he deserved what happened to him?"

"No!" Billy splutters in shock. "I'm just saying he might have, you know, offended the guy."

"Oh, so being offended justifies attempted murder—is that it?"

"No, but the guy might have felt threatened."

"Oh, so big bad Jeremy, all five and a half feet of him, scared the asshole so bad that he had to nearly kill him in an act of self-defense? Is that what you're saying?"

"No, I just mean if it's true he's a fag, that may be why the guy did it."

"Oh, so *that* makes it all right!" Annie's yelling now. "You know what, Billy? Those brown eyes of yours are no lie. You're full of shit!"

Before any of us can see it coming, she's on her feet. If Billy were smarter, he'd be on his feet too and running like hell.

"Billy, would you please do the world one little damn favor? From now on, don't speak with your stupid mouth open."

She storms away from the table with Mike in hot pursuit. Just before she gets to the courtyard door, somebody must be dumb enough to say something she can hear. She wheels around and takes a sudden step towards some guy. He jumps back away from her. As she and Mike disappear out the door, several people laugh at the guy.

Kerry and I stack Mike and Annie's trays on top of our own.

"What did I do?" Billy asks. "I mean, it's not like the guy lynched him or anything, is it?"

He still doesn't get it, and I'm amazed that someone so good-looking could be so dumb.

"Billy," Kerry says, "I think the point is it's wrong to beat somebody up, period. And even if Jeremy *had* done something that offended the guy, *which I sincerely doubt*, beating the hell out of him was overkill, don't you think? I mean, it takes a sick mind to do what he did to Jeremy. And yes, if you think about it, it *is* kind of the same thing as lynching a guy for being black. So it wasn't okay."

"I didn't say it was okay; I was just saying maybe that's why the guy did it, that's all."

"I know," I say. "But think about it. From the way people are talking and those stupid rumors going around, you'd think it was Jeremy's fault he got beat up. I've known him for a long time, and believe me, Jeremy didn't deserve what happened to him. And I've actually *seen* what that bastard did. No one deserves that."

We leave Billy to ponder the emptiness of his mind and catch up with Annie and Mike at a table outside in the courtyard. Everything is damp, but I doubt Annie even notices. She seems to be somewhere between wanting to cry and wanting to beat Billy up for being such an idiot. Her arms are crossed tight, and she snorts out her breath like a bull ready to charge.

"That son of a bitch! Somebody ought to 'do a real number' on him for being such a dumb ass and see how he likes it!"

"He didn't mean it that way," Kerry says. "He just didn't know what to say."

"Oh, you think that's *all* it was? Well, honey, let me tell you something– You don't know these people around here like I do. I've been going to school with these *little angels* since kindergarten, and they're not all quite as sweet and innocent as they pretend. I've been called a nigger, a coon, a pickaninny, and worse. And some of the parents of these little angels are the same damn ones who hung my uncle from a goddamn tree. Hung him from a goddamn tree!"

She breaks down. Mike hugs her, and she cries on his shoulder.

The bell for fifth period rings. Kerry and I give Mike a nod and leave him to console her. When we get to the corner where Kerry will turn off for his business class, he gives my arm a quick squeeze. It's as much consolation as either of us can risk displaying in public.

Making my way to the art room, I can't get what Annie said out of my mind. It never occurred to me that any of the people around here would do something like lynching a man. And I shudder at the thought that somebody I know could actually be related to whoever killed Annie's uncle.

Why would anybody lynch a man just because of the color of his skin? What does it matter to anyone if somebody's skin is different than theirs?

And what exactly is the problem that people have with gays? Why should Ramrod and Brad care if I'm gay? What does it take away from them? What do they think—it's like measles, and if they get too close, they'll break out in gay? Seriously, what are they afraid of?

Of all the times I've worried about what would happen if people found out I was gay, I never even considered the possibility I could really get hurt because of it. I simply had no idea how threatening some people's hatred can be. I thought I lived in a safe world. School was a safe place—boring and unpleasant—but safe. A guy might punch you in the arm, but not hard enough to do real damage. It never occurred to me that there are people out there who really would go out of their way to hurt you in a major way. Real violence just didn't happen in my world, and if it did, it would never happen to me or to anyone I knew.

But the world suddenly feels dangerous, alien, brutal. What happened to Jeremy was hate, *real* hate, not the childish kind where you say, "I hate that guy" just because he irritates you. This kind of hatred is aimed at who you are, not what you do. It's the kind of hatred that beats the hell out of a guy and feels smug about it. And all because you're different. It just doesn't make sense.

Hating people because they're different is so stupid. And my folks are no better. They insulted Kerry to his face simply because he's Jewish.

They even made him go to church with us. God, I'm so ashamed of how they treated him, and Kerry just sat there and took it like it was nothing. And his family welcomed me into their home even though they knew I was gay. I've got to do something to show him how much I appreciate him.

I get an idea and make a mental note to remember it later.

CHAD MADDOX, HIS eyes pink with drooping lids, stumbles into Mrs. Pilt's room just ahead of Annie and Mike. As he passes me, I catch a whiff of what he's been smoking for lunch. He drops his bag at the less-artistically-inclined table, and wanders back to retrieve his ceramic project—a wad of clay that he optimistically refers to as abstract art. Chad's not stupid. He's been known to come up with halfway good ideas for art projects, and last year he was even in my English class. If only he didn't let the pot stand in his way.

We've been in class twenty-three minutes when Chad floats back over to our table and slides into a chair. For a second or so, he pretends to be looking for a better paintbrush—like he'd even know one if he found it. Annie scowls and rolls her eyes. Mike watches him suspiciously, fisting a brush like he's prepared to jump up and punch Chad the instant he says something stupid.

But then he speaks.

"Tell me: is Jeremy going to be all right?"

"Eventually," Mike says, while a stone-faced Annie stares down Chad's stoned face.

"Well, tell him I said if he ever needs anything, or if anybody bothers him from now on, just let me know, okay? Tell him I said after he gets better maybe we can hang out sometime."

"Oh," Annie snarls. "So you're going to risk being seen with him after he comes back?"

Chad shrugs a shoulder. "Sure. Why not?"

"You better be careful. Someone might think you're *queer*, you know."

"What do I care what anyone thinks? Jeremy's always been nice to me, and he's one of the few people around here who never called me names or said I was stupid. A lot of people could take a lesson from him.

He's cool."

He picks out a brush, stands up, and nods to Annie and Mike.

"Oh yeah, and don't let the assholes in the lunchroom get you down. I think it's cool that the two of you are together, even if it *will* make things a lot less entertaining in here from now on since you won't be fighting all the time."

"Thanks, Chad," Mike says.

"You know, not everybody's an idiot around here, even if you'd never know it listening to the people always running their mouths and putting others down."

He starts to go but pauses and turns back. "Remember to tell Jeremy what I said about getting together to hang out, all right?"

"Sure," Mike says, and Chad drifts back to his table.

"Wow," I say. "I guess I misunderestimated him."

"*Under*estimated," Mike says.

"Whatever."

"You know," Annie says, "for an asshole, he's really not such an idiot after all."

She pauses and cocks her head to one side. Her lip twitches, and she pulls at a strand of hair. She gets up and crosses the distance to the less-artistically-inclined table. The people at the table all look up at her warily. She says something that Mike and I can't hear and offers her hand. Chad, with his usual whacked-out grin, slowly shakes it.

"Stay cool, Madman," she says as she walks back our way.

"What was that all about?" I ask.

"I just wanted him to know he's off the Chadham High Asshole Registry."

For such a brief exchange, it is a tiny spot of sunlight in an otherwise miserably depressing day. It also proves to be the catalyst for a profound change in Annie. Over the next two days, I notice that while she's just as talkative and outspoken as ever, all references to the Asshole Registry have disappeared.

Somehow, her outrageous personality seems to grow that much bigger because of it.

BUT IF I had any hope that Chad's show of support for Jeremy indicated a change in the tide of public opinion, I was delusional. The chatter in the locker room is even more crude and hate-filled than what passes for normal. Rick Payton and Jamie are the only two who show even the remotest bit of sorrow that Jeremy nearly got killed. Brad and Ramrod lead a chorus of wisecracks about Jeremy's lips being painted red that threatens to go on forever, until Kerry wonders out loud why they all seem to be so interested in lipstick. It doesn't change any attitudes, but at least it shuts them up.

During Chemistry, I don't have a clue what we're doing and just let my lab partner for the day do all the work. I spend the whole class bored and depressed until I get an idea. Since Thanksgiving is a four-day weekend, it would be the perfect opportunity to invite Kerry to stay over one night. Suffering through another meal with my dad and The Turd would be a small price to pay since the two of us could spend most of the day in my bedroom practicing our new hobby—making out.

And an even better thing would be if I wound up staying at Kerry's house. Either way, we could kiss and cuddle, and fall asleep in each other's arms. Of course, sometime in the night, we'd wake up deep in the throes of having sex together for the first time. After exhausting ourselves in shared passion, we'd fall asleep again, and in the morning, I'd wake up to find myself in his arms.

When the bell rings, I run to Mr. Warren's room. The three minutes it takes for Blake and Kerry to show up seems like an eternity. When they come in, and Blake sees me checking my watch, he snickers and shakes his head. Kerry smiles when our eyes meet, and I blush.

Blake stays just long enough to let us know he's going to be rehearsing in the music room. Kerry and I get passes for the library and settle down at a table by ourselves. There are still people roaming around, so I try to sound casual.

"Hey, Ker, want to stay over one night this weekend? I could probably even wangle you a Thanksgiving invitation if your folks would let you."

"Oh." He suddenly looks as sad as I'm already starting to feel. "With everything going on I forgot to tell you. We're going out of town Thanksgiving weekend. My grandparents invited us to spend it with them and my cousins in Petersburg. We're leaving Wednesday right after school and won't be back until sometime Sunday."

"Oh." I try not to look disappointed. "Well, maybe another time."

Chapter 17: The Long Weekend

THANKSGIVING IS THE most ritualized holiday in the world. Every family has their own variation on the ritual, but once they begin observing it, it doesn't take long for things to fall into place. It's pretty amazing, especially since Thanksgiving only comes around once a year. But the ritual happens anyway, and once it does, it's set in stone forever.

In our house, the big meal has always been supper. The menu never changes: roast turkey, stuffing, mashed potatoes, green bean casserole, candied yams, cranberry sauce, corn on the cob, and a choice of either pumpkin or apple pie with melted cheese. The funny thing, though, is not the unvarying menu—it's that people say the same thing every year. A typical Thanksgiving in our house goes like this:

As Mom sets the turkey in front of Dad, I say, "Wow, look at that bird. It's huge."

After sampling a bite with gravy, Dad says, "The best damn turkey in the world."

I chime in with, "It's delicious, Mom. Thank you."

"Yes," she says, "we've all got so much to be thankful for."

Wally pipes up with, "Yep, we're lucky we only have to eat this crap once a year."

This year, when Thanksgiving morning rolls around, instead of waking up in Kerry's arms like I'd hoped, I wake up alone, hugging a pillow, and hard as a rock. I've got a whole miserable day stretching before me—a whole day of Wally complaining about having to eat turkey, Dad cursing about the iffy TV reception and because his team is losing, and Mom fussing about everything in the kitchen.

Wonderful...

After a quick trip to the kitchen (quick because Mom shoos me out almost before I even set foot in it), I wander into the living room sipping a cup of coffee and turn on the TV.

Oh, joy. The Thanksgiving Day parade.

It's not just that I'm disappointed that Kerry's out of town, I'm downright confused about it. I mean, yeah, this could have been the perfect opportunity for a four-day necking marathon, but it's not just that.

When I look back over it, Kerry was acting strange all week. We'd had a couple of chances to make out—and we did, and believe me it was great—but there was just something about him I couldn't put my finger on. It was like he was distracted or, I don't know, hesitant or something.

It's probably just my imagination. Blake and Annie have both accused me on more than one occasion of overdramatizing things and of letting my imagination run away with me. Okay, they're probably right. I certainly spent more time on Fantasy Island than in reality during that whole Mitch Weaver episode. But this is different; I really am picking up on something. I just don't know what, and that's what bothers me.

I've been staring at the TV for thirty-seven minutes when the phone rings.

"Hey, Randy-man. Let's go to the parade this afternoon."

"Parade? Blake, why would I want to go downtown for a boring parade when I've already got a boring parade on TV right now?"

"Well, the truth is, Marilyn's going to be there with Allyson Horbach, and I was kind of hoping to, uh, run in to them."

"I think you can guess why I find the very thought of that about as appealing as having needles shoved under my fingernails. Besides, like I already told you, it's obvious Marilyn likes you. If you want to meet up with her, just do it."

"Come on; I need moral support."

"Look, I don't want Allyson Horbach to get the wrong idea. I mean—" I drop my voice to a whisper "—not only is she a punk rocker, she *is* a girl, you know."

"I promise you, you won't have anything to worry about."

"Famous last words."

"Come on—please."

"No."

Two seconds of silence follow before I roll my eyes and sigh. "You're making that pouty face, aren't you? I hate it when you do that. It's even annoying over the phone."

"Please."

"Oh damn it, fine, if it'll shut you up. But I'd better not end up with another girl liking me."

"I promise. I'll tell Allyson you're an ABBA fan."

AT ONE-THIRTY, Blake and I are walking down Main Street in The District. It's a cool day with a light breeze. We've still got thirty minutes before the parade starts, but people have already begun to crowd the sidewalks.

"Does Marilyn even know you're planning this little accidental encounter?"

"Well, maybe," Blake says, scanning the block. "She mentioned that she and Allyson were thinking of coming, and I said I'd keep an eye out for them."

"Oh, so you're telling me this could all just be a colossal waste of time."

His shoulders slump. "I suppose so."

"Well, don't get too worried." I smile and nudge him in the arm. "Like I told you before, I'm absolutely positive the girl likes you, and I bet if she even thinks you *might* be here, she'll show up with bells on."

Blake grins broadly. A couple vacates a bench near us. We wander over to it and sit down.

"So what about you?" Blake says. "What's going on in your love life these days? Have you and Kerry tied the knot, or whatever it is your kind do?"

"Kerry and me?" I scoff with a fake chuckle.

"Yeah, you and Kerry. Come on; it's obvious he's gay, and it's totally obvious you two are into each other. I mean, sheesh. You two have been making googly-eyes at each other for weeks."

At this point, I'm beginning to wonder if I'm the only one in the world who missed out on the free gaydar installation offer.

"Well, I suppose it *is* possible that Kerry *might* be gay," I mumble, "and I guess we could...uh...kind of like each other."

Blake laughs. "*Kind* of like each other? Man, I thought you were going to start crying when you told me he was going to be in Petersburg this weekend."

"You're crazy. It's no big deal to me one way or the other. We may like each other, but we're just friends."

"So you're saying you wouldn't care if right now he's spending some quality nuggy time with his *special someone* back in Petersburg?"

"It wouldn't bother me at all," I say nonchalantly, but my mood collapses.

Embarrassment washes over me, and I suddenly feel like I'm naked and everyone on the street is sneering.

Kerry and I have made out, and it's seemed obvious—at least to me—that we're into each other, but when I sort of told him I loved him in the car the other day, he didn't say he loved me back. Why not?

My whole world begins to crumble into a giant ball of humiliation.

Damn it. I probably don't mean anything more to Kerry than I did to Gene. Gene treated me like crap, and I deserved it. I was stupid to think he would fall in love with me.

And I certainly made a fool of myself with Mitch.

And now, here I've been, dreaming that Kerry's fallen in love with me, but when I told him *I* was falling in love with *him*, he didn't say a single word. He didn't even tell me he was going to Petersburg until I cornered him.

God, how stupid could I be? I've done it again. I bet he doesn't even really like me. He certainly hasn't been very eager to have sex. And he said Jeremy was cute. For all I know, he could have just been using me to get to Jeremy all this time.

Hell, for all I know, he could be making out with his slutty Petersburg boyfriend this very minute.

Damn it! That's why he's been acting funny. He's only been using me.

Marilyn's voice rings out. "Hi, Blake. Hi, Randy."

Luckily, she's without Allyson Horbach.

"Hi, Marilyn," Blake says, his eyes sparkling.

She joins us on the bench, and the two lovebirds happily chat about how *surprising* this little chance meeting is. I roll my eyes and let them chatter on.

Blake's enjoying the conversation, and there's none of that stuttering goofiness he'd be suffering with if he thought of this as a date. And Marilyn is absolutely glowing in the joy of his company. No doubt about it, she's really into him. Blake is the only one in Chadham who doesn't get it.

They continue talking, and I quietly get up and walk away. Well, why should I hang around? I've done my part. It's like teaching a kid to ride a bike. I've just let go, and it's time for Blake to ride it out on his own.

The sidewalks are filling up, but I find a spot about two blocks away. Somewhere in the distance, I hear the rumble of drums. The parade has started.

As the floats and different groups march by, I scan the crowd. Here and there, I see a few people from school. Jeff Gray is with his family, and so is Stephanie Brigham. There's Billie Jo Jackson with Terry Huff. And I laugh when I catch sight of Allyson Horbach. She's in her usual punk attire, which looks even wilder right now since she's standing next to her very conservatively dressed mother.

Then I spy Gene Murphy. It's the first time I've seen him all week. He's standing near the front with his arm around Amanda Worthingham, and he's wearing a ridiculous looking pair of gloves. Seeing him brings back all the demeaning times I spent with him. Shame begins to mix with depression as I replay how he treated me and all the names he called me—not that I didn't deserve it. But as it all plays over and over in my head, it becomes Kerry's voice calling me his bitch, Kerry laughing at me.

A fire engine with someone dressed as Santa Claus passes. The firemen throw out suckers for the kids, and the parade is finally over. As the crowds break up, I wander down the street brooding over how Kerry just left me and took off to be with his old boyfriend.

Slowly, humiliation gives way to anger.

How could he do this to me? He knows how much I'm into him. He knows, but he doesn't care. He's just been using me, just like Gene did. God, I'm so pathetic.

"Randy! Hey, Randy."

Jamie Becker walks up, smiling like he's encountering some long-lost friend.

"Good parade, huh?"

"Yeah." I'm in no mood to even pretend to be polite. He doesn't seem to notice.

"You having a nice Thanksgiving?"

"Jamie, why are you talking to me? For the past year and a half all you've ever done is insult me and put me down."

"Hey, man, that's just locker room talk; it doesn't mean anything. Besides, you give it back as good as you take it. You're good."

"Thanks." But I'm even more suspicious.

"So, what are you up to this weekend?"

"Not much."

"Me neither. Brad's up in Reston visiting his grandparents, so I'm just hanging out."

"Uh-huh."

"Hey, want to hang out tomorrow?"

Now I'm really suspicious. But Jamie does look as cute as ever, and he seems to be trying really hard to be nice. And what trouble could he cause in a public place?

"Sure, we can hang out tomorrow," I say.

"Okay, meet at the park?"

"Great. What time?"

"Say ten?"

"All right. I'll see you there."

Jamie walks off, and I go to find my bike. At least hanging out with Jamie will give me something to take my mind off Kerry and how worthless I am.

IT'S A COOL morning. I arrive at the park still depressed over Kerry and even more suspicious about meeting Jamie like this.

Jamie may be hot, but he hangs out with Brad and Ramrod, and while I don't *think* they've got it in them to beat a guy up, I'm not certain. I could be walking into a trap. For all I know, I could just as easily end up sharing that hospital room with Jeremy by lunchtime.

But I've had a thing for Jamie since, like, forever. So despite my better judgment, here I am. And despite it being too cold for it, I'm wearing the kind of pullover and shorts I used to wear when I was going to Gene's house—quick off, quick on.

I'm so pathetic. Why did I wear these clothes? And now it's too late to run home and change.

I come across Jamie leaning against the boardwalk railing, watching the river. He spies me and smiles. He's wearing running shorts and a sweatshirt. His cheeks are flushed, and his skin has the light glow of a good run.

Oh God! Why did he have to wear those shorts? And why does he have to look so damn hot in them?

"Hi, Jamie."

"Hey, Randy. Glad you could make it."

"Hope I didn't keep you waiting long."

"No, man, I just got here. Been jogging." He's grinning while he reaches down and rearranges himself. "Sorry, you know how it is when you run."

I grin back awkwardly and blush a little, but he doesn't seem to notice.

We stroll along, talking, and I'm surprised that he doesn't mention girls or sports even once. Instead, he talks about music. He's really into music, and he likes a surprising variety. He mentions Pink Floyd, The Clash, ELP, The O'Jays, and Bob Marley, as well as several new-wave acts I've never heard of.

"What do you think about that new Van Morrison record? Have you heard it?"

"I've only heard the single. It's okay."

"Oh, man, the album's great. You've really got to hear it."

"I'll keep an ear out."

"Hey, why don't we stop off at my house, and you can hear it right now? I live just around the corner."

Alarm bells go off in my mind. This smells like a setup.

I shake my head. "I don't know, Jamie. Maybe another time."

"Aw, come on. I really think you'll like it."

I calculate how long we've been walking around—an hour and eight minutes. It seems like too long for him to have left guys waiting to ambush me in his room. So even though I'm still suspicious, we collect my bike and start off.

I discover he's not kidding about his house being right around the corner. It's not even two blocks away, in a nice neighborhood with a bit of roll to the land. The Becker house is split-level and elegant but not loud.

Jamie's bedroom is at the far end of the top floor. He closes the door and puts on the LP. The music is nice, but I'm too busy looking around for surprise attackers. Plus, it's hard for me to concentrate on the music while I battle my reactionary instincts. I mean, Jamie's sitting right next to me and he's wearing those shorts and the sweat from his run is mixing with his cologne. He could sell it as Eau de Sexy.

The album finishes, he puts on *Get the Knack,* and things start to get weird. As the first song starts playing, he sits down so close to me that when he taps his foot his leg rubs against mine. I try to be inconspicuous as my eyes continue to search the room for guys waiting to jump out and beat me up. But the closet door is open, and it's too full of Jamie's clothes and junk to hide someone.

Could he really just want to spend some time with me and listen to music?

And then...

"Hey, let's jerk off."

I stare at him in utter shock and amazement. He takes my hesitation for agreement, stands up and pulls down his shorts, and I come face-to-face with something I've only seen from a distance in the locker room—and never quite like I'm seeing it now.

"Come on," he urges, and for a second, it's Gene's voice I hear.

I stand up and take a step to the door.

"I've got to go."

"Wait, wait! Don't go. I'm sorry."

I turn back to find him stuffing himself back into his running shorts. He looks embarrassed, and, as always, the sight is so cute it tugs at me.

"Jamie, why are you doing this?"

"I just thought it would be fun to do it together, that's all. It feels good, you know."

It's like one of those scenes where everything freezes, and in the space of a heartbeat, I have an entire argument with myself.

God, this could be a dream come true. I've wanted him for so long, and we could end up doing a lot more here than jerking off together.

No, damn it. If I do anything with him, he'll own me. Gene might not have been the kind to tell on me, but I simply can't trust Jamie. And even if he is serious, he hangs out with Brad and Ramrod. One slip, and they'll find out, and I'll be dead meat.

And it would be like betraying Kerry.

But Kerry is already cheating on me. He's never cared about me. He's out there in Petersburg, probably getting it on with his old flame right now. He's just been using me for when he can't be with him—that is, until he finds somebody better. Somebody like Jeremy probably.

It's no different letting Jamie use me than Kerry. Or Gene.

Jamie looks worried, and he's blushing.

"You just want an excuse to go blabbing to Brad."

"Are you kidding?" There's panic in his voice. "Brad would kill me if he knew about this."

I sit back down and look him straight in the eye. "Okay, what do you *really* want to do?"

The beat of the music is primal and driving. We're sitting even closer to each other now. Neither of us really knows what to expect at this point. We both wait for the other to make the first move, to define the limits of what's about to happen. Then, slowly, timid fingers begin to reach out.

BACK IN MY room, I put on side two of *Wish You Were Here*. The music is slow and melancholy, and I identify with every word. My life is one big fishbowl, but I'm the only fish in it.

I misjudged Jamie. He's not the wannabe-bully like Brad that I thought he was. He's just a kid aching to find someone special of his own, just like everybody else. Today, we were both desperate to fill the emptiness we felt inside, but instead, we just settled for what was in reach. It was like filling up on water when you're starving. And what we did was clumsy and self-conscious and needy. We both got off, but it was also something we both know we'll never do again.

So far, Kerry and I haven't even done what Jamie and I did today. But I have touched Kerry. I've run my fingers through his hair, and I've tasted his kisses. Kissing Jamie would have just made what we did today even more awkward.

I wonder if that guy in Petersburg knows how lucky he is to have Kerry. Probably not. But he's the one Kerry wants, the one he needs, and he's the one Kerry's probably holding right now. I'm jealous, and I'm angry, and I feel sorry for myself. But mostly, I'm just hurt. Bitterness rises like lava inside me, and I start crying.

Chapter 18: Days that Change Everything

ANOTHER MONDAY MORNING. I ignore Blake the whole ride to school—not that he notices. He just goes on and on about how much he likes Marilyn and how he wishes she liked him. The fool still doesn't get it. God, how stupid can a guy be? She might actually be his special someone, and he doesn't even have a clue. What an idiot.

Meanwhile, there's me. I don't have a special someone at all. I only get guys who use me like the piece of trash I am. Damn it! I hate it.

After my little visit with Jamie, I hung out by myself all weekend. I went to the movies, listened to records, read, and biked around. Hey, I'm making progress—no running off to grovel at Gene's feet this time.

Last night, Kerry called. I told Wally to tell him I'd try to call him back, which I didn't. Why should I? He was either going to lie to me or, worse, tell me how he reconnected with his slutty boyfriend back home. If I wanted somebody to rub it in how worthless I am, I could just give Gene a call.

When we get to school, I stop at my locker and try to rev up my Buddha focus before I have to see Kerry, but it doesn't work. I'm too angry and hurt—and the truth is, I'm afraid. I still want him despite myself, and I dread facing him because I know how bad he can hurt me.

I finally give up and head to homeroom with less than a minute to spare. When I walk in, there he is. He looks up and sees me, and he's all smiles. It's heartbreaking and maddening. All I want is for one of us to be anywhere else but here. But after considering whether to choose a seat away from him, I decide to plop down in my usual desk. Why should I let him run me off? This was *my* homeroom first.

"Hey," he says.

"Hey." I'm so cold he should be freezing.

"Did you have a good Thanksgiving?"

"It was okay."

"I had a really interesting time back in Petersburg."

"I bet."

He pauses. "Are you okay?"

"I'm fine."

The bell rings, and I'm spared having to talk to him for a while. When it rings again for first period, he leans over and whispers, "Can we talk for a second? I've got something I want to tell you."

"Okay," I say. But I use the crowds to my advantage and slip off to the restroom where I hide out until just before the bell. After English, I make a detour and stop by my locker to avoid him. In History, I give Mitch a friendly good morning, which I hope makes it clear to Kerry that it's him I'm giving him the cold shoulder to.

When lunch rolls around, I hide out in the library. Then I skip Art because I don't want to listen to Annie Brock run her mouth. My plans to skip PE, though, are ruined when Mrs. Becker asks to see my library pass and tells me to get where I belong. She's the kind who follows up, so I have to go.

I march to the locker room and don't even bother gearing up a Buddha trance. But when I get in there, I wish I had. Everybody's in mid-change, which means almost everyone's half-naked. It's bad enough I can't find a single person to be my special someone, but I've also got some kind of weakness for any guy with skin. And today it's worse than usual. Kerry's taking his time changing, which just adds that much more overstimulation to my lust gland.

The only good thing is Jamie. He and I share a split second's glance at each other, but as soon as he sees me, he blushes and looks away. That settles that. If I had any lingering worries that he'd rat me out, I can now rest assured. He'll never tell anyone what we did. For him, it was just an experiment—one he'll probably never repeat.

As the room thins out, Kerry sits down next to me.

"Where were you during lunch?"

"I was busy." This is even more irritating. Despite being angry at him, I'm sitting here with lips itching to kiss him.

"Busy? Doing what?"

"I went to the library."

When I don't make eye contact, he asks, "What's wrong? What's up with you today?"

"There's nothing wrong with me."

"Well, you're acting like something's wrong."

"I'm not acting like anything," I say and leave the room.

We ignore each other the rest of the period.

On the way to Chemistry, I encounter another headache when I stop off at the rest room and almost walk head-on into Gene Murphy.

"I guess you must be pretty hard up these days, not getting any," he says with a smirk. "This weekend, I laid a girl so hot, I almost caught fire."

"Good for you."

"*You* know how *hard* it can get when you haven't done it in a while, don't you?" He gives himself a quick rub. Bruises on his hand draw my attention and help me avoid reacting in the way he's hoping I will.

"What do you do," I bark, "hang out in here all day waiting for me? Or would just any guy do?"

His expression changes from smug to outrage and back in a flash. Then he smirks and walks away. I make a mental note to avoid this restroom from now on.

Study hall turns out to be my easiest class to avoid people I don't want to deal with. As soon as I get there, I ask for a library pass. After handing in the pass to a junior who's half a sleep, I sneak off and hide out behind the lunchroom kitchen. It's not really much of an escape though. My mind fills with the memory of sitting here with Kerry last month.

The bus home is quiet because Blake is staying after school to work on his songs for *South Pacific*. The steps up to my bedroom are like climbing to heaven, and the clicking of the lock sounds like music. I put on the radio and stretch out on the bed. Deborah Harry is singing about a love who turned out to be a pain in the ass. Tell me about it.

The Turd's knock brings me out of the nap I was just drifting into. I shuffle to the door and open it.

But instead of Wally, it's Kerry standing there with a shy grin.

"Your brother told me to come on up."

"What do you want?"

"I want to talk to you."

"I don't feel like talking," I say, still holding the doorknob.

"Well, will you let me talk for a couple of minutes?"

"Make it short."

I turn back and sit on the bed. He closes the door and sits down next to me, despite my glance of disapproval.

"I wanted to tell you about my trip to Petersburg. While I was there I called up Owen—that's the guy I used to be close to."

Oh great, my worst nightmare. He's going to tell me how he got back together with his slutty old boyfriend.

"He and I went for a walk."

"Ha. I bet you did. I bet you had a real good time together."

"What is the matter with you today?"

"Look, I'm not stupid. Ever since you got here you've been talking about that 'special someone' back home. So you went back and screwed good old Owen. Well, good for you."

"Is that what you think? That's why you've been acting so weird all day?"

"Well? That's what happened, isn't it?"

"No. Randy, believe me, he and I broke up long before I moved here. I told you before; talking about a special someone back home was just a convenient way to avoid questions about dating."

"So you're telling me you didn't fool around with him?"

"No, I didn't fool around with him. We went for a walk. And I told him that I met this really hot guy here, and how special he is, and that I really like him. I told him that when I got back, I was going to ask you to be my boyfriend."

I suddenly feel ridiculous. For three seconds, I just sit there blinking.

"You want me to be your boyfriend?"

"Yeah, that is, if you want to."

"Yes, I do."

"So...do I get to kiss my boyfriend?"

I nod before leaning over.

I WANGLE AN invitation out of my mother for Kerry to stay for dinner. It's not hard to do. She fell in love with him as soon as he complimented her cooking. Tonight, he continues doling out compliments, even though it's only the last of the Thanksgiving leftovers. Wally just shakes his head.

After a meal in which The Turd keeps complaining about the turkey, and Dad's too busy telling him to shut up to say anything racist or embarrassing, Kerry and I retreat back to my room for some after-dinner necking.

We step inside, and I lock the door. The radio is still on, and soft jazz-rock fusion—just loud enough to cover any sounds we'll be making—floats from my stereo speakers. I pull Kerry to me for a little "belly-rub" dancing to start the ball rolling.

He sways with me for a second, but blushes and pulls me over to the bed.

"I'm sorry. I really wasn't joking when I said I'm not much of a dancer."

"Oh? I'm disappointed. Well, if I can't dance with you, how about kissing you instead?"

"Yeah, I think I could handle that," he says with a lopsided grin so hot and enticing it could seduce a statue.

So we kiss and cuddle, and I'm in heaven. Believe me, if kissing were a sport, Kerry's lips would be Olympic champions. He's tender yet powerful, and while he might not be a dancer, his tongue darts and frolics with an elegance that would put any ballet dancer to shame.

After some time, we pause for a short breather. I rest my head on his shoulder and sigh in contentment. It's so good to have him back and to be in his arms.

"So have you been with a guy before?" he asks, running his fingers through my hair.

It's like this giant rock lands in the pit of my stomach. How can I tell him about the pass I made at Mitch? Or that I was having sex with Gene Murphy all last month? And what would he say if he found out I was with Jamie only three days ago? There Kerry was in Petersburg telling Owen he loved me and how great I am, while I was— Oh God, I can't ever let him find out.

"No. What about you?"

"Just Owen. He was the only one back home, and the minute I got here and laid eyes on you, I didn't look anywhere else."

He takes me in his arms and kisses me. I return it with all the passion I can. He's my prince, but I'm no Cinderella. I'm a slut who doesn't deserve him. But somehow, despite myself, I've gotten lucky enough to be in the arms of the man of my dreams. I make a silent vow to never do anything as stupid as running around on him again and seal it in slow, devoted worship of his lips.

FRIDAY AT LAST! Yes, I'm counting down the minutes until the weekend. It's been the academic week from hell, at least for me anyway. Mrs. Jezik has us working on term papers. Mrs. Molina is determined that we memorize everything that has ever happened, no matter how insignificant, from the beginning of the world to the Civil War. Mrs. Dawson has started a grueling review of everything geometrical. And Mr. Ferguson wants to turn us all into teenage Einsteins before Christmas.

And then there's *South Pacific.* Rehearsals are getting even more boring than I thought possible, and they're taking longer and longer each time. The good thing, though, is we've only got two more weeks until this project is finally over. I wish I could say the same for school.

But despite it all, Kerry has made the week magic. For once in my life, I'm in love with someone who actually loves me too, and it's like a new world. Just being with him makes anything the world can throw at me survivable. It's as if my life has become a beautiful series of "us" moments. Little things, even just walking down the hall together, now have a special significance I wouldn't have thought possible before. We can't hold hands, but as we make our way through the crowded halls, I tingle each time we "accidentally" bump against each other. And we may be talking about dull everyday things, but it's also like a secret code only we understand. No matter what we're doing, the fact that we're sharing it together makes it special.

Tonight, we're going to see a horror movie called *Nosferatu the Vampyre,* and then I'm going to stay over at his house. I've been counting the minutes ever since he mentioned the idea on Tuesday. See, I've made up a little plan to surprise him, and just thinking about it makes every second today seem like an hour. But that final bell is getting closer and closer, and my stomach flutters at the thought of being alone with him all night.

In study hall, Kerry is helping Mrs. Ari with something for his business class, so Blake and I spend the last hour of the day in the library. We're wandering among the shelves, pretending to be looking for books.

I've just told Blake that Kerry and I are now officially a couple, and I've accepted his congratulations.

"Well, I've got to hand it to you. You've definitely bagged yourself one hot gay-babe."

"Hey," I say with a snicker, "I know he's hot, but since when did *you* turn queer?"

"I'm not, but I can appreciate a guy's gay-babe appeal even if I'm *not* attracted to him."

"Touché." I try not to laugh too loud. "So, how are things going between you and Marilyn these days?"

He frowns. "They're not going anywhere."

"What do you mean? She won't go out with you?"

"Well, yes and no."

"Hey, look, it can't be 'yes *and* no.' It's got to be one or the other. So which is it?"

"Well, that's the thing." He flips through the pages of a book he's holding upside down. "See, I haven't really asked her out. I'm not sure she likes me that way."

"Not sure she—? Hold on. Let's just step back for a minute here. Every time she sees you, her eyes light up, and she stands as close to you as she can get without being inside you. And last week, you two were so into each other I'm surprised you even noticed the parade. How can you know everything that goes on in this place before it even happens and *not* know how obviously *into you* she is? Just ask her out."

"I...can't bring myself to ask her. I guess I'm just a little nervous."

"Just a *little* nervous? Okay, look, let's go through this logically. If you meet her, say in the hall or in class, you don't have a problem talking to her, do you?"

"No."

"Okay. Now if you happened to show up for a movie and she did too, could you sit next to her and hang out to talk about it when it was over?"

"Yeah, we've done that a couple of times actually."

"Then what's so hard about just asking her to go with you in the first place?"

He puts the upside-down book back on the shelf and slouches. "I don't know."

"Maybe if you eased into it. How about this? Annie Brock, Mike Kowalski, and Kerry and I are taking Jeremy out to eat this weekend to celebrate him coming back to school next week. You could come with us and invite Marilyn along? That way, it's a date but it's not a date."

"Oh, I don't know about that. Annie's a little wild, you know."

"All the more reason to give it a shot. Annie's the perfect distraction to keep you from getting nervous."

"Which night are you all talking about?"

"Saturday."

"Marilyn's busy Saturday night. They're holding a special rehearsal for the orchestra."

"Okay, well how about if we change it and take Jeremy out Sunday?"

"It's my mother's birthday. We're taking her out to dinner."

"Too bad. It would have been the perfect opportunity. But don't worry; maybe we can work something out later."

"Thanks."

It's difficult to tell if he's grateful he'll get another chance to ask Marilyn out or just glad the pressure is off this time.

"Look, why don't you come along with us Saturday? You need a night off."

"Yeah, sure, if it's okay."

"Of course it is."

"Well, okay then. I'll tell you what, I'll drive."

"Thanks, but I was going to pick Kerry up."

"That's no problem. I'll pick you both up."

He flashes me a Cheshire cat grin that makes me wonder what he's got up his sleeve, but I let it pass.

FOR KERRY AND me, the weekend begins when the bus drops us off at the elementary school. By now, the little children are all at home, so it's only little groups of high school students heading off in different directions. Kerry and I start walking to his house. It's a chilly afternoon, and I ponder the fact that those of us who live outside the town limits pretty much get door-to-door bus service, while some of the townie kids face long walks twice a day.

Even though it's a cold day and Kerry's house is about seven blocks from the elementary school, I don't mind the long walk since I'm with him. And the pot of gold at the end of the rainbow is the warmth we'll soon be sharing in his bedroom. Ahead of us, a couple is arm in arm, and

I'm jealous because we can't do that. People would freak out if Kerry and I even held hands.

"What do you know about the movie tonight?"

"It's based on some old silent film that's supposed to be a classic," he says.

"Do you think it'll be scary?"

"I read a review that says it's *very* scary. Don't worry though. I'll protect you."

I give him a wink. "Warning— I scare easily. You might have to hold me close and comfort me all night long."

He gives me a playful shove, and I return the favor. It feels good to flirt a little, even if we can only do it when we're sure nobody can overhear us. We both grin the rest of the way home.

Mrs. Sawyer greets us, and Janice—who's much friendlier now that she knows I hate The Turd almost as much as she does—says hello. Then we retreat to Kerry's bedroom. The next hour and forty-seven minutes are spent in the most hard-on-straining make-out session in the history of the commonwealth.

The Sawyers are excellent hosts, and I sincerely compliment Mrs. Sawyer on the food. It's funny. When it was time for dinner, Kerry and I straightened out our clothes, and I had a very hard time getting my hair to look unmolested. But Kerry didn't even bother combing his. And here's the thing, no one said a word about the state of his hair, although Monica and Mrs. Sawyer betrayed tiny smiles when we first entered the dining room. The thought that they all know we're obviously much more than good friends and yet don't have a problem with us sleeping in the same bed tonight amazes me. It also makes me wish my parents could be just as accepting.

The movie turns out to be more spooky than scary, but the eeriness works on me all the same. By the time it's over, I'm glad to have Kerry around to protect me. On the way home, we hold hands in the car.

We'll be sleeping in the guest room again. Kerry quietly locks the door and sneaks up behind me. He whispers a line from the movie in a perfect Dracula voice that makes me shiver. But he turns me around, embraces me, and we begin exploring each other. His lips are salty from the popcorn, but his tongue is sweet as it freely explores my mouth.

Soon, we're lying on the bed, and Kerry starts unbuttoning my shirt. My fingers glide across his chest. He caresses me while I slowly bring my hand around to tickle him. Our lips engage in a gentle dance, stopping only long enough for Kerry to nibble on my ear. His breath skims the surface of my neck, and I gasp.

An urgency starts building in us. His every touch drives me on. I want to please him, to ignite his passion. My hand slips down. I need to feel him. His fingers slide below the waistline of my trousers.

Without saying a word, we agree it's time. Our clothes fall to the floor, and we stretch out on the bed. My consciousness is filled with the taste of his lips, his aroma, and the touch of his fingers as they play with me.

In a quick, commanding motion, he rolls us over so he's on top of me. His kisses are hot and almost animal-like. He nibbles and licks, and teases his way along my chest. His lips surround me, and I moan.

One hand holds me while the other continues to tease and explore. He's sensitive to the tiniest effect his caresses bring out in me. The dance of his tongue tempts me and entices all my senses to surrender.

A sweet tension begins to rise, possessing me, and sudden waves of pleasure overwhelm me. He brings his lips back to mine, and I run my fingers through his hair.

After a few minutes contentedly luxuriating in the touch of his skin against mine, I roll him off me, and climb up, straddling him.

His eyes pop wide open and search mine.

"What—?"

"Make love to me," I whisper.

He looks confused and hesitates. "Are...are you sure?"

"Yes. Please, make me yours."

I smile to reassure him. We watch each other, and slowly, all his hesitation gives way. That feeling awakens inside me, but it's more powerful than it's ever been before, and it's electric and yet somehow soothing. He pulls me to him and kisses me.

We roll over, and his eyes stare down into mine. I'm tingling with emotions so powerful I can barely even put words to them. But it's not just passion, it's love. With each movement, we're becoming one. The feeling is building up inside us both. And then it's like his very soul flows into me and plunges me over a waterfall of desire. We moan and writhe, clutching each other as it surges through us.

A tender silence unfolds as he collapses on top of me, and we kiss. His lips are moist. We cling to each other, unwilling to break the connection that unites us, and fall asleep, still embracing, forever united.

Chapter 19: Some ~~Enchanted~~ *Ill-fated* Evening

BLAKE STEERS US closer and closer to the Sawyer house. My body is alive with anticipation, and I want wings so I can jump out and fly there all the faster. When Kerry drove me home yesterday afternoon, he came inside for a few minutes. We kissed each other goodbye like two lovers facing eternal exile. After he left, I felt empty and incomplete. But somehow, I've survived, and now, here I am, sitting next to Blake, excitement building up inside me.

We turn the corner onto Kerry's block, and Blake slows down. We're almost there.

"It's the fourth house on the left."

"Are you going to the door to get him, or do I honk the horn?"

I giggle, blushing. "I'm going to the door." For Kerry and me, it's that kind of date now.

I press the buzzer, and seconds later, Kerry's standing before me, wearing a striped pullover that brings out the gold in his eyes. *Oh God, he's so beautiful.*

He steps out onto the porch and closes the door.

"Anyone in the car besides Blake?"

"Nope."

He takes a quick look around, slides his arms around my waist, and kisses me. I can now honestly say I've been to cloud nine.

When we get to the car, I go to the passenger-side front door, but it's locked.

I rap on the window. "Hey, Porcupine, unlock the door."

"Get in the back," Blake says with a grin.

I go to the rear door, half-expecting that one to be locked too. But I press the handle, and it opens freely. Kerry sits next to me with a coy smile. By the time I turn my attention to the front seat, Blake is already pulling back out onto the street.

"Well, ladies," he says, snickering, "you better make the most of the time you've got. I don't think they'll allow you to neck much in the restaurant."

"You know what, Blake Rogers, you're beautiful. I could just kiss you."

"Now we'll have none of that. A— I already know I'm beautiful. B— there'll be no smooching the straight guy in this car unless it's a *female* doing it. And C— if you two are going to kiss each other, shouldn't you get busy?"

"Always obey the driver," Kerry says, and before I can say anything else, he pulls me over and kisses me, ending it with a loud smacking noise. We hear Blake snickering in the driver's seat but soon forget he's even there.

FOR TONIGHT'S FESTIVITIES, we've unanimously chosen the most renowned location possible—the culinary summit of The District, famous countywide for fine food and elegant dining—Jim's Burger Barn. The quality of the cuisine at Jim's is so legendary truck drivers have even been known to stop in and partake of the fare.

Blake parks the car over to the side. This gives Kerry and me the opportunity to finish off a last round of necking before we get out. As the three of us walk to the door, Blake can't resist one final joke.

"Randy, Randy, Randy," he whispers. "Quick! Check your lipstick for smears."

Kerry laughs, Blake sniggers, and I give him a good-natured punch in the arm.

We've only been standing out front for a few minutes when we see Mike's car turning into the parking lot and take a spot near the building. Jeremy looks a hundred percent better than he did when we saw him in the hospital, but it's still painfully obvious he's a recent victim of violence. His black pullover contrasts sharply with his milky-pale skin and makes his bruises all the more noticeable.

"And here's the star of the evening," Annie proclaims as she nudges Jeremy forward.

"Hey, guys," he says.

"Hi, Jeremy," I say. "How're you feeling?"

"Better than I look I expect."

We go inside and grab a booth. Kerry scoots in on one side, followed by me and Blake. Annie pushes Mike in and follows him. Jeremy fills out the seating order. Not needing to see the menu or ask about house specials, we start by ordering drinks—no root beers requested—and a large plate of Jim's famous house fries. The waitress can't help but react to Jeremy's bruised face, and she seems a little put out to see Mike and Annie holding hands. I smile at the thought of what her expression would be if she could see my hand resting on Kerry's knee under the table.

"So, Blake," Mike says, "is *South Pacific* going to be worth the price of admission?"

"Oh man, is it ever," he says, delighted.

I roll my eyes and groan. "Oh no. Mike, you don't know what you've done. You've turned on the Blake Rogers Publicity Machine."

For the next six and three-quarter minutes (I time him), Blake goes on and on about how the Chadham High production of *South Pacific* is destined to be the biggest off-Broadway success since *The Fantasticks.* I've got to hand it to him. His sales pitch is so enthusiastic and entertaining that anyone eavesdropping on our conversation would probably rush out to buy tickets. If Blake doesn't make it as an actor, he's certainly got a future in advertising.

Presently, our waitress brings the drinks and house fries. I drown a small plate in ketchup while she starts taking our orders. When it comes to my turn, I look up, and I'm mildly surprised to notice that we now have a different waitress.

She leaves with our orders, and we turn back to our conversation, slowed by the munching of fries and the sipping of drinks. Kerry asks about our ceramics projects, and with that, it's Annie's turn to be off and running.

"Well, honey, let me tell you. After Mikey's poor elephant broke in the kiln, he worked hard to do another one. And it's so pretty, some rich guy will just *have* to buy it along with our little forest collection, so he can arrange them all together next to his other masterpieces. We're sure to all tie for first place."

Three minutes later, Annie and Blake are officially competing for most talkative person at the table, and they're really enjoying themselves. It's funny that the two biggest gossip hounds in school are only now really getting to know each other. And it's a good thing I have Kerry, because Annie's heart may belong to Mike, but I think she's just stolen my best friend.

While Annie and Blake continue to chatter, with Mike's able help, I glance around the dining room and immediately wish I hadn't. No one at our table is being particularly loud, but several people are openly staring at us. None of them looks pleased.

"Blake, see if you can catch the waitress's attention for refills," Kerry says.

Blake turns to hail the nearest waitress, but at that moment, Jim himself comes to our table. He's a big guy, bald, and usually good-natured. But right now, he's stone-faced as he stands in front of us with his hands on his hips.

"All right, get out."

"What?" Blake and Mike say at the same time.

"I'm not going to have you destroying my reputation."

Confused, I ask, "What have we done? We're just sitting here talking and waiting for our food."

"This is a family restaurant, and I'm not having any of you low-morality punks in here. Now get out."

"What are you talking about?" Kerry says.

"You listen to me, and you listen good," Jim growls. "I don't have to explain shit to you, kid. You can just go parade around somewhere else. Now get the hell out of here. Now!"

Blake stands up, and I scoot over. While the others get up, Jim towers over us and glares down at me and Jeremy. Blake throws five dollars on the table. Kerry does too.

"Here, maybe you can use it to buy some manners," he says as we proceed to the door.

Outside, Blake looks around, bewildered. "What the hell was that all about?"

"Yeah, we weren't doing anything," Mike adds.

"It's not about what we were or weren't doing," I mutter. "It's about who we are and what people think."

"Exactly," Annie says grimly. "It was because you nice little *white* boys showed *low* morals by coming in with a *nigger* girl."

"Come on," Blake says, "let's go to the fast-food joint. Maybe we can eat in peace there."

"Yeah," Kerry says. "And we better get out of here before that bastard calls the cops."

TUESDAY NIGHT IS the first of the full cast and crew rehearsals that will be the norm until the show premiers next week on Friday night. This week, we only meet tonight and Thursday, but beginning with Monday next week, it's every night, with a full dress rehearsal next Thursday.

The big national news is that last night, eleven people were trampled to death in Cincinnati at a Who concert. It's scary to think that you could get killed just by going to a rock concert. But that's not what's got everybody talking at Chadham High. Since Saturday, the word's gone around about us being thrown out of Jim's Burger Barn. While variations on the details abound, the consensus seems to be that it was all about race, just like Annie said. Sadly, it seems more people side with Jim than us on the issue.

Blake, Mitch, and I are sitting in the fourth row waiting for Mr. Szinhely to call everyone to order.

"It really sucks that Jim kicked you guys out," Mitch says.

Blake nods. "Tell me about it. I used to like him. I never knew he was a racist. What a dork."

"The thing is," I say, shaking my head, "I'm not sure it was just a white guy holding hands with a black chick that set Jim off."

"What do you mean?"

"Well—" I lower my voice "—when Jim was kicking us out, he said something about us 'parading around,' and he was looking right at Jeremy when he said it. I think he kicked us out because of the rumors about Jeremy. You know the newspaper wasn't too subtle in hinting around about the possible reason he got beat up."

Blake scratches his chin. "You really think Jim would kick out a whole table full of people for something like that?"

"Yes, I do."

"Me too," Mitch adds.

"Oh come on," he scoffs.

"Of course he would, Blake," Mitch says. "Prejudice is prejudice. The only difference in the way some people treat me versus a black person is they can't tell I'm gay just by looking at me."

"Yeah," I add. "And until those bruises heal, Jeremy's an easy target. The bruises make him as easy to pick out in a crowd as Annie and Mike."

"Well," Blake says, "any way you cut it, it's just screwed up. Where in the hell do people get that from?"

"I don't know," I say as we hear Mr. Szinhely clapping for everyone's attention.

FORTY-SEVEN MINUTES LATER, we take a break at the intermission point. Mr. Szinhely and Mr. Harmon, the band director, are exhausted. They've been running from one corner of the auditorium to the other all night, making sure everyone will be able to hear the actors. They must have already lost five pounds each.

As I jump from the stage, I'm surprised to spy Kerry sitting near the back—well, surprised, delighted, and more than a little aroused at the very sight of him. Even from this distance in the semidarkness, he looks gorgeous. Fighting the impulse to run up and kiss him, I casually saunter my way down the aisle instead.

"Hey, what are you doing here?"

"Nothing," he says. "I didn't have any homework and was bored, so I thought I'd come take in a sneak preview of the show. It looks good. And you're clearly the star."

"Hush," I say, blushing in spite of myself. "Come on."

He follows me outside. We turn the corner and walk back to a basement stairwell and backstage side door. After descending a few steps, we're more or less out of sight, and Kerry pulls me in for a kiss.

For the next few minutes, my entire focus is on the taste of his lips. But all too soon, we hear someone approaching and slowly start back up the steps to meet whoever it is.

It turns out to be Mitch.

"Chilly night, huh?" he says with a sly grin.

"Uh-huh. Say, Mitch, do you know Kerry Sawyer? Kerry, this is Mitchel Weaver."

"Hey, Mitchel."

"Nice to meet you. Call me Mitch. Randy, is Kerry here the guy you were telling me about the other day?"

I'm not sure how to respond because I don't want Kerry to think I've been blabbing around about our relationship. But before I can think of what to say, Kerry slips into a lopsided grin.

"I hope I am."

"Well," Mitch says, looking him over lecherously and nodding, "it's easy to see why Randy likes you so much."

"Hey, he's mine!"

Mitch just chuckles. "Did you catch any of the rehearsal, Kerry?"

"Yes. It looks good. You guys are really doing a great job."

We continue talking and start back for the front of the building. It's just the three of us, three gay friends, all in good spirits, enjoying each other's company. We're joking around, and having a good time. While we talk, I lean against Kerry a little, imagining a world where we could openly walk around holding hands like other couples do. It's such a wonderful dream that I wrap my arm around him and give him a squeeze.

Mitch laughs. "I better warn you, Kerry. Randy here has got a habit of taking risks in public. I even had to stop him from getting frisky in front of our neighborhood busybody once."

"Sorry," I mutter with a shy smile.

But when I look back at Kerry, my stomach drops, and I'm suddenly all too conscious of the cold. He's staring at me with a look in his eyes I can't read, but even in the darkness, I can see the color draining from his face.

The three of us are momentarily frozen in time. Mitch looks from one of us to the other, sensing the mounting tension.

"Uh, I'll talk to you guys later," he says, retreating around the corner.

For an agonizing minute, Kerry and I just stand there.

When he finally speaks, there's a distressing quiver in his voice.

"I thought you said you've never been with another guy."

"I...uh..."

"Well? What's the truth?"

"I tried to kiss Mitch after we went to a movie once."

"When did that happen?"

"A long time ago."

"When?"

"Like, last month."

"Last month?"

"When I drove him home, I went to kiss him, and he shoved me off. See, he saw the old woman coming, but I hadn't noticed her. Anyway, I thought it meant he was straight and he'd tell everybody about me. You remember that time I freaked out in the locker room—the time you had Coach Horne check on me? That was why. We didn't straighten things out until later."

"When you joined the cast."

"Right."

"So you joined the show so you could be with Mitch."

"No, I just mean Mitch and I became friends after I joined the show."

"But you went out with him *before* you joined the show."

"Kerry, listen. I thought you were straight. And I thought if I found somebody else, maybe I'd be able to stop wanting you. So I tried to make myself interested in Mitch, but it didn't work."

"It obviously worked well enough that you wanted to kiss him."

"Even if I *had* kissed him it wouldn't have mattered. You've been the only one I've truly wanted since the first time I laid eyes on you."

"Uh-huh." He doesn't look convinced.

The silence that follows may only last seconds, but for me, an eternity of mounting guilt ticks by. I search Kerry's eyes. All I see is sadness and an escalating coldness that's breaking my heart.

"I wasn't the first one you ever made love with, was I?" he says suddenly. "Friday night, you came prepared, and you knew just what to do. You'd been with someone before, hadn't you?"

I hang my head. "Yes."

"Who was it? Mitch?"

"No! Kerry, I told you. Mitch and I are *just* friends. We only went to the movies that one time, and that was it."

"Then who?"

Realizing that I've got to come clean, I sigh and tell him. "Gene Murphy. He's a senior. He started coming on to me before I met you. At the time, I thought he was kind of cute, and I...well, I kind of ended up having an ongoing thing with him for a while. But the whole time, he was just using me to get him off, so I broke up with him, and I haven't been with him since."

"Was there anyone else?"

I swallow hard and look down.

"Just one...Jamie Becker. But it was only the one time."

"Jamie Becker? When?"

I feel a stabbing pain in my chest.

"Thanksgiving weekend."

"Thanksgiving weekend? You mean while I was telling Owen how much I loved you, you were screwing around with Jamie Becker?"

He stares at me, a struggle visible in his eyes.

Oh God! He's crying.

"How could you do that to me?" His voice is strained and halting. "I...I was honest with you, I...trusted you, and...and you lied to me. I...I'm sorry, Randy, I can't be with you like this."

The words ripple through me, and I feel like I'm being electrocuted. A crushing tightness wraps around my chest and the blood is pounding in my head. But before I can say anything, a voice rings out, calling everybody back to the rehearsal.

"Kerry… "

He shakes his head, the tears flowing down his cheeks.

I want to grab him and hold on until all the pain goes away. I step forward but he backs up.

"You better get back; they're calling you," he whispers. "I've got to go."

He turns to walk away but then breaks into a run. I start off after him, but I can't catch up, and when I call out his name, he keeps running. He jumps in his car.

And then he's gone.

Chapter 20: Consequences and Conspiracy

MY STOMACH'S IN knots all morning.

In homeroom, it's now Kerry's turn to give me the cold shoulder. He's not as melodramatic about it as I was with him, but it has the same effect. His response to my good morning doesn't come with the iciness of anger, but there's still a distinct note of aloofness only I can hear. And it stings all the more because we both know *I* actually deserve it.

Sitting next to him in Literature is almost unbearable. Mrs. Jezik likes to move around while she teaches. That means for half the class, I can't avoid seeing him ignore me out of the corner of my eye. He just sits there looking at her with a focus that takes in everything in the room, except me.

And history class is an absolute nightmare. As we walk in, Mitch sees the hurt in Kerry's eyes and the guilt in mine. The expression on his face makes it clear he feels guilty himself. Between the three of us, the tension in the room is excruciating. As much as I want to be near Kerry, to find some way to say something to make everything all right, it's actually a relief when the bell finally rings, and I've got two periods away from him to recuperate.

In Spanish, the chatter of conversations buzzes through the room. We're supposed to be translating some lame text from the book, but I'm the only one even pretending to work—and it's not helping.

For a few minutes, Blake sits next to me tapping his pencil on his textbook. Finally, he sighs and turns to me.

"Okay, you want to tell me what the hell happened?"

I don't answer.

"Look, Kerry showed up last night, and you were so happy I thought you were going to wet yourself, and when you came back from the break, you looked like hell. You didn't speak the whole way home, and today, you're acting like the world's coming to an end. Now what happened? Talk to me."

"Kerry and I broke up last night," I mumble.

Blake purses his lips and shakes his head like this was what he suspected all along. "Why'd you break up?"

"Because I lied to him. He asked me if I'd ever been with anyone before him, and I said no. See, I didn't tell him about the thing with Mitch, and while we were outside last night, Mitch was there, and he kind of mentioned it. Now, Kerry knows I lied, and he thinks I've been cheating on him too."

"Wow," Blake says and sighs. "So what are you going to do?"

"I don't know."

Things don't get any better. Mrs. Dawson surprises us with a test in Geometry, but I don't even try to pass it; I just wait out the time for the bell and hand it in. I'm pinning my hopes on talking to Kerry at lunch. But my hopes are dashed when I scan the lunchroom and spot him sitting at a table full of people. He doesn't get up to leave until one of the other guys does too, and he sticks with him right up until the bell rings for fifth period.

I mope through Art, and mercifully, Annie, Mike, and Jeremy leave me alone. They can see I'm shattered and exchange worried glances, but they don't ask questions. In PE, Kerry's as distant as the finish line in a hundred-mile dash. Chemistry seems to go on forever.

Finally, the bell rings for study hall, and I race to Mr. Warren's room, but Blake catches me before I turn the corner and pulls me aside.

"Look, I'll suggest we go to the library. Maybe you can talk to him there."

We take our seats and wait, but when the tardy bell rings, Kerry's nowhere in sight. After Mr. Warren takes roll, Blake and I go up to ask for library passes.

"Where's the other musketeer?"

"I don't know," Blake says while I just shrug my shoulders.

The silence in the library is suffocating. Time seems to poke along. About halfway through the period, Blake sneaks back to check on whether Kerry ever showed up for study hall. He didn't.

"So what are you going to do now?" he whispers.

I just shake my head.

"Take a word of advice? You need to talk to him today; don't wait until tomorrow. These kinds of things can get set in stone if they go on too long."

I sigh, giving in to the growing despair I've been fighting ever since last night. "What's the point? I screwed up, and it's over."

"Over?" he says, raising an eyebrow and going into his John Belushi voice. "It's not over until *you* say it's over."

"What could I ever say to change things?"

"How about the truth? Go to him and confess everything. Tell him you're sorry, and you'll never do it again. And I mean tell him *everything* this time, right down to the time you messed in your pants in third grade."

"I never!" I retort, but he's grinning, and I can't help but smile back.

"Look, tell him the truth, the whole truth, and nothing but the fact that you're a dork. You never know, it couldn't hurt—and it just might work."

As soon as I get home, I ask Mom if I can use the car. I tell her I need to meet with Kerry for a project and say I might miss dinner. With each passing block, I get more and more anxious. By the time I pull up in front of Kerry's house, my stomach has so many butterflies I could have saved the gas and flown here.

I could use those butterflies now. When I get out of the car, my legs struggle to hold me up.

Monica answers the door. When she sees it's me, she steps onto the porch, quietly closing the door behind her. For a second, she stands there, studying me.

"Randy, I don't think it's a good idea for you to be here. Kerry's pretty upset."

"But I need to talk to him. I've got to tell him I'm sorry."

She leads me over to the swing. "Look, I don't know what's going on, but when he came home last night, he was a mess, and he's not much better today. What happened?"

"It's all my fault," I whisper. "He asked me if I'd ever been with another boy, and I lied to him. And he found out. That's why I've got to talk to him. I've got to explain and tell him how sorry I am. I don't want him to hate me."

She nods slowly and sighs. "I think I understand now. Look, Randy, he doesn't hate you, but he is hurt, and he's going to need time."

She leans forward, elbows on her knees.

"Did he ever tell you anything about Petersburg?"

"You mean about Owen? Yeah, he told me about him."

"But did he tell you what actually happened between the two of them?"

I shake my head.

"Kerry was in love with Owen; I mean totally head over heels. But Owen hooked up with another guy behind his back and lied to him for weeks. And when Kerry found out, Owen was a real asshole and blamed it all on him. He told Kerry he'd never loved him—that nobody could—and then he just walked away. That really hurt Kerry bad."

"But Kerry said they got together over Thanksgiving and talked."

"Believe me, it wasn't a reunion; it was a clearing of the air. And it wasn't easy for him. But he thought he had you, and he felt he had to face Owen. And then he comes back and finds out you lied to him. Why?"

"Because I was afraid if he knew the truth I'd lose him," I whisper, choking up. "I love him, Monica."

She searches my tear-filled eyes for a moment, gives me a hug, and walks to the door.

"I'll talk to him. But you've got to give him time. And Randy? It *is* going to take time. Now, you should go."

"Thanks, Monica."

She nods, and I walk back to the car.

If I went straight back home, my mother would ask questions that I don't want to answer. So to kill time, I stop by the park and wander around for half an hour. Although the wind is chilly, I hardly notice it. But I do shudder when I remember meeting Jamie here.

Over and over, I keep asking myself how I could have been so stupid. It's getting to be a constant refrain in my life.

When I finally go home, I bypass my parents and The Turd, telling my mother I ate while I was out. Later, sitting in my room, I stare at the wall and wish I could just call Kerry. But Monica's right; he needs time. All I can do is wait and hope that eventually he'll forgive me. But how can I ever make him trust me again?

So I do the only thing I can think to do; I pick up the phone.

"I was expecting you to call sometime," Annie says.

"You were expecting it?"

"Honey, I know you like a book. And I'm getting to know Kerry pretty well too. Suddenly you're not sitting together at lunch today, and both of you looked like somebody died, and you were so depressed in Art we were afraid you'd fall apart if we said anything to you."

"I screwed things up with Kerry, and he broke up with me."

"Oh Lord, child, what did you do this time?"

"I told him I'd never been with another guy, and last night, he found out about the thing with Mitch."

"Well, what did you expect? Why did you lie to him?"

"Because I was afraid he'd think he couldn't trust me."

"So instead you proved *you* didn't trust *him*."

"What are you talking about?"

"Randy, don't you get it? It's not just that you lied to him. When you lied, you basically told him you didn't trust *him*. You didn't give him a chance to know the truth and want you in spite of it. That's what hurt him. And, Randy, I saw the look in his eyes today—that boy was hurt. He was hurt because you didn't trust him. You didn't believe in him."

The silence on the phone is deafening.

"Then what do I do?"

"If you can get him to listen, you need to tell him everything. In detail. Come completely clean."

"But what if he hates me for it?"

"If you want him, if you love him, you've got to chance it. Take it from someone who's been there. It's the only possible way to get him back."

THE STRAIN GETS even worse Thursday. If anything, Kerry and I look into each other's eyes more now than when we were together, but it's torture. The sadness, the disappointment in his eyes when he looks at me only confirms how bad I hurt him. By lunchtime, I can't take it anymore and hide out behind the I-C-E shop—nobody ever goes there. Then he ignores me in PE and disappears to work on a project for his business class during study hall.

I barely say a word on the bus ride home, or when Blake picks me up for rehearsal. He's good enough to not try and get me to talk on the ride.

When we walk into the auditorium, we're the very picture of contrasts. Blake struts in with the confident stride of Lieutenant Cable himself. I follow like a teenaged version of Charlie Brown. Mitch spots us and runs over.

"Randy, I'm so sorry about the other night. I wish I'd never opened my mouth."

"It's not your fault."

"Is there anything I can do to help?"

"Actually, there might be," Blake says. "Mike Kowalski told me about a plan he, Jeremy Smith, and Annie Brock have cooked up."

Mitch nods. "Sure, I'll do whatever I can."

Blake goes on to explain the plan, and for the first time since Tuesday, I feel a little bit better. At this point, any glimmer of hope, however tiny, is welcome. I never appreciated just how lucky I am to have such great friends before.

In homeroom the next morning, I slip Kerry a piece of paper. At first, I'm afraid he's going to tear it up, but he stares at it for a few seconds, sighs, and opens it.

The note reads: *I was wrong, and I want to tell you how sorry I am. Please let me talk to you.*

His eyes scan the page and glance my way, but he shakes his head. When the bell rings, he leaves without saying a word.

In English, we take our seats, and as soon as Mrs. Jezik turns her back, I drop another scrap of paper on his desk.

I promise to tell the truth this time—all of it. I love you.

He balls it up and stuffs it in his pocket.

When we get to History, Mitch gives me a slight nod that he's prepared to do his part. As Kerry passes him, Mitch holds out a piece of paper. Kerry rolls his eyes, blows out a breath, and opens it.

I know what the note says: *Give him a chance. The fool really is sorry.*

I take a couple of deep breaths before I walk into the lunchroom. Annie and Mike have already cornered Kerry and led him over to an out-of-the-way table. Seconds later, Jeremy joins them and puts his books down in the chair across from Kerry. Taking one more breath, I plow forward.

As I get near the table, I hear Annie talking.

"Of course, Mikey and I were attracted to each other even when we thought we hated each other. You know how *easy* it is for misunderstandings to happen. And, you know, sometimes people do some really *dumb* things that you just *have* to *forgive them for*. But like they say, 'love conquers all'." She says it all in one breath and ends by giving Mike an affectionate squeeze.

Seeing me coming, Annie nods at Jeremy, who moves his books out of the way. I sit down and stare at the table, but I can see Kerry put his fork down, wipe his mouth, and begin to gather his tray up. Mike gives me a nod of encouragement.

"Kerry, I'm so sorry I hurt you. Please meet me in the park this afternoon and let me explain."

"Talking it over couldn't hurt, and the park's a great choice," Mike says.

Jeremy nods. "Yup. Nice public, neutral territory."

"You really do owe it to yourselves to at least clear the air before you do anything silly like breaking up for good," Annie says.

"Please," I whisper.

Kerry stares at me for a second and opens his mouth to speak. But an unexpected—and untimely—explosion of spikey hair suddenly looms over us.

"Hey guys, s'up?"

Of all days, Allyson Horbach chooses today to join us for lunch and plops down in the one open seat. Kerry stands up, mutters a "See ya" to no one, and walks away. Jeremy rolls his eyes, Mike shrugs his shoulders, and Annie turns to deflect Allyson's attention.

"Don't give up yet," Mike whispers. "Blake's on duty to make a last-minute pitch in study hall."

"And you never know," Jeremy adds quietly, "Kerry might even agree to meet you when you see him in PE."

But he doesn't; he avoids me like the plague. During Chemistry, I count the seconds and daydream about finding a love potion to make Kerry fall in love with me again.

IN STUDY HALL, Kerry goes straight to Mr. Warren and asks for a library pass. Blake jumps up to join him. I stay behind.

I'm sitting there, contemplating the laws of the universe, and how time actually *can* stand still, when Mr. Warren's voice brings me out of my trance.

"Randy, got a minute to give me a hand with something?"

I shuffle over and follow him to the storage room in the corner. It's lined with counters and shelves filled with jars, test tubes, bottles, and various props he uses in his lectures. In the middle, a table is piled high with stacks of paper. The air has a bitter tinge to it.

"Have a seat," he says, pulling out a chair.

He leans back against one of the counters and stares across the room. "You know, one of the hardest things in life is when things get tough, and you don't know what to do about it."

I shift my position and try to read his expression, curious where all this is going.

"For instance, sooner or later, every teenager falls in love, and maybe somewhere along the line, they could use some advice, but they don't know who to talk to. That can be a hard thing. And it's even tougher for some kids than others. For example, two people might fall in love when others think they shouldn't. That kind of thing can make it very hard for them."

Now I get it. He's going to give me some advice to pass along to Mike and Annie; I'm sure they could use it. But I wish he'd just talk to them directly and leave me out of it. I've got enough problems of my own.

He continues, "In most cases, a guy might go to his father for advice. But what if his father is one of the people who might disapprove?"

I start rapping my fingers on the table quietly.

"What if his father is the very last person to talk to about a relationship problem? What then? I mean, I've known parents who would kick a boy out just because he fell in love with a girl who's a different color—or with another boy."

I stop rapping the table. My heart skips a beat, and my cheeks burn.

"The thing is, whether it's a girl of another race or another boy, he needs to know that despite any opposition, he's got just as much right to fall in love as anyone else. And he needs to know there are some adults out there who are willing to listen, and help—if he ever wants to talk, that is. Do you understand what I'm saying, Randy?"

"Uh, yes, sir, I think so." The lump in my throat is threatening to choke me. "So...uh...what would *you* say to a guy in that kind of situation?"

Mr. Warren folds his arms and looks right at me. "I'd tell him don't give up, and if you hit a rough patch in your relationship make sure you talk it all out. Believe me, that's the most important thing. Talk it out. I've known cases—" a sad expression comes over him "—when talking it out could have prevented very unhappy consequences."

"And what if he, I mean, *the other person* won't listen?"

"Not listening is not the same thing as not hearing. Just ask the...other person for a hearing. And, Randy?"

"Yes, sir?"

"If things don't work out after that, then comes the real hard part."

"What's that?"

"Learning how to let go."

WHEN THE FINAL bell rings, I go straight to the bus and wait for Blake.

"Okay, this is a bit complicated," he whispers while we file in to find seats.

For a Friday afternoon, it's maddening how damn slow everybody is. And for some reason, today everyone chooses to sit as close to us as humanly possible. Blake sighs and suggests I get off at his stop so we can talk, and then he'll drive me home.

By the time we get into his car, I feel like I'm ready to explode.

"Okay, this is what happened," he says. "When we got to the library, I gave it a few minutes before bringing up the subject. Of course, he immediately told me in no uncertain terms he didn't want to talk about it. To tell you the truth, I was actually kind of afraid he was going to get up and leave.

"So I said, 'Look, I know Randy's a stupid dope, but he really didn't mean to hurt you. You ought to hear the fool out. Then, if you still want to dump the pathetic little idiot, go ahead.'

"And he said, 'Listen, I don't want to talk to him.'"

"Blake, just tell me what he said."

"And I said, 'Then don't talk; just give him five minutes, and if what you hear doesn't change things, fine.'

"And he said, 'Damn it! I don't want to deal with this...,' And you know, I almost thought he was going to say 'again.'"

I'm ready to scream.

"And I said—"

"Blake, will you get to the point! Did he agree to meet with me today or not?"

"No. But he did say he'd think about meeting you in the park tomorrow at eleven. I told him I'd pass on the message."

Blake brings the car to a stop in my driveway. “One more thing. Kerry only said he *might* meet you. He wanted me to emphasize that. He’s only *thinking* about it. And he said if he doesn’t show up, it means he wants you to leave him alone. Permanently.”

When I get to my room and close the door, it’s one of the rare occasions I wish I was a pothead—at least the evening would drift by quickly.

Chapter 21: Intermission

JOGGERS ARE FUNNY people. It's freezing and yet there they go. The only difference between today and summer is they're wearing sweats instead of shorts. Stay healthy through catching a cold—yeah, that makes sense.

I'm slowly walking back and forth at the boardwalk. The river looks angry—it doesn't like the cold either. I've been here since ten-thirty.

Somewhere nearby a church bell rings eleven o'clock—two and a half minutes slow. There's no sane reason I should expect Kerry to show up before the last ring chimes, but I still look around hoping to see him.

No such luck.

I try to tell myself he's always running late and count the seconds thinking up reasons why he's not here yet.

His mother probably demanded he take the trash out at the last minute. His bike could have a flat. He's stuck in traffic. His clock is running slow. He's looking for me in some other section of the park.

As seconds are drifting into minutes, there's still no sign of him. The knot in my stomach is tightening up, and my breath feels shallow.

I leave the boardwalk and cross the lawn to a bench. A quick look at my watch confirms it's twelve minutes after eleven. I revise my justifications for his absence.

He had to take the trash out, and *then he found his bike had a flat tire,* and *his mother wouldn't let him use the car, so he had to walk, and once he gets here he still has to find me. He's just late, that's all.*

I keep glancing at my watch.

Eleven-nineteen.

Three women jog by.

Eleven twenty-six.

I stand up and fidget to keep warm.

Eleven thirty-three.

An old man is pulled along by an eager dog.

Quarter to twelve.

The knot in my stomach snaps. My eyes burn, and the lump in my throat is starting to strangle me. I collapse back onto the bench.

He's not coming.

I don't want to leave. I'll just keep waiting, keep waiting forever. I imagine Kerry passing by days from now. He finds me still sitting here, keeping vigil for him.

I fantasize about how different things could have been if I'd just told him the truth in the first place. I daydream about not trying to kiss Mitch and turning down Jamie's invitation. I think about the emptiness in my life without Kerry—an emptiness that will haunt me forever. A tear starts to slide down my cheek.

I let it.

"Do you know what time it is?" A voice asks, and I look at my watch.

"It's eleven fifty-six."

"So I'm guessing you were supposed to meet Kerry this morning, but he didn't show up."

I look up to see the wind blowing auburn locks across Jeremy's face. He sits down next to me and throws an arm across my shoulder.

"Kerry just needs time."

"No," I say, failing to hold back a tear. "He told Blake if he didn't show up, it means he wants me to leave him alone."

"Well, he may have *said* that, but I've seen the two of you together, and I saw the look on his face when you sat down at the table yesterday. That boy loves you. He may be hurt, but he still loves you."

We stare at nothing for a few minutes.

"The thing I just don't understand is why Kerry flipped out so bad about a one-time thing with Mitch where nothing even happened. I mean, okay, you shouldn't have lied to him about it. But, God, why is he making such a big deal out of it?"

"It's worse than that. Mitch wasn't the only guy I didn't tell him about."

Jeremy's eyes are wide with astonishment.

"There were more guys? You? But you can't even pick out which guys are gay."

"There were two guys I did things with."

"Including Mitch?"

"No. The kiss thing was it with him—" I take a deep breath "—but I had kind of a thing with one guy for a month or so. And...there was a one-time thing with another guy."

"And you told all that to Kerry?"

"Yeah, after he found out I'd lied about Mitch. That's what killed things between us."

"Well, did any of this go on after you two got together?"

"The thing with the one guy sort of started before I met Kerry, and it ended before Kerry and I really got together. But the one-time thing happened over Thanksgiving. I think that's what really hurt him most."

Jeremy whistles. More cold-weather joggers pass us, huffing like steam engines.

"Do you mind me asking who the guys were?"

If it was anyone else, even Blake, I wouldn't answer. But Jeremy is the most trustworthy person I've ever met. He's the one person who will never repeat what I tell him.

"The one-time thing was with Jamie Becker."

"Well, I can see why Kerry would be upset. Jamie *is* hot. But Randy, by Thanksgiving you and Kerry were already together. Why did you do it?"

"I don't know. I got it in my head that he had gone back to Petersburg to be with his old boyfriend, and I got scared that he was just using me. I guess I didn't believe he could really love me."

"Hmmm," Jeremy says. "So that was the one-time thing. That means the ongoing thing was with Gene Murphy."

My head swings around so fast I almost give myself whiplash. "How did you know?"

"That day you asked about him in class, I figured he must have set his sights on you." Jeremy shakes his head. "Gene Murphy. That explains why you didn't think Kerry could love you."

"What do you mean?"

Jeremy stares off in the distance before he continues.

"It's how he operates. He gets you to do what he wants and then makes you feel like he's doing you a favor. He really knows how to screw with your mind. Believe me, I know. He did the same thing to me last year. And I'm sorry; I should have warned you about him."

"He was always talking about women, and I was terrified he'd drop me."

"Randy, Gene's a closet case. He casts you as the queer one so he doesn't have to admit the truth about himself. That's why he thinks he's got to get as many girls as possible—to 'prove his manhood.' Of course, then he treats them like shit, and they leave him. And that's the one thing he can't stand. I'm guessing you were the one who broke it off."

"Yes. I told him we were through right after that whole episode with Mitch."

"That explains everything. He wanted revenge."

"Revenge? What do you mean?"

"If somebody leaves Gene, it threatens his delusion of superiority and he has to face the truth about himself, so he goes out of his way to hurt them. Becky Worthingham broke up with him, and he went after her sister to spite her. When I broke up with him, he started spreading rumors about me, and that's when those seniors started picking on me—He told them I liked one of them. And that time he saw the two of us together, he must have assumed you and I were a couple. So he spotted me at the dance, followed me outside, and as soon as he got me alone, he started hitting me."

"Then it *was* my fault you got beat up."

"No. Listen, Randy, it was *definitely* not your fault. If he'd seen you with anyone after you rejected him, he'd have done the same thing. It was his way of trying to hurt you. The fact that he happened to see you with me was just a bonus for him. He could get back at you and beat me up for leaving him last year in the process. That's why he went out of his way to find that red paint. He wanted the message to be crystal clear to whoever found me."

"You've got to report him."

Jeremy shakes his head. "No. If I report him, he'll only claim I tried to suck him off or something, and that'll be the end of that. And he might even try to bring your name into things. No, I'm not even going to bother. It wouldn't do any good."

"So you're just going to let him get away with it?"

"Right now nobody gives a damn if you're gay and being bullied. Maybe there'll come a day when people will listen and do something about bullies like him, but not here, not today."

"It's not right. How do you stand it?"

"When nobody will help you, you've just got to keep telling yourself you're better than that, and you've got to believe you *will* get through it. It helps if you can find a friend, but even if you can't, the important thing is to never give in. Don't buy into the crap they want you to believe about yourself. Don't give them the satisfaction. And listen, sooner or later, people like that always get what's coming to them. It's just a matter of time."

It's the most I've ever heard Jeremy say at one time, and I'm stunned at how smart he is.

"Come on," he says, standing up. "Why are we wasting time? We've got more important things to do than talk about Gene Murphy. We've got to get you and Kerry back together."

BUT DESPITE EVERYBODY'S best efforts, as the next week progresses, it becomes clear no amount of urging or persuasion will convince Kerry to even give me a hearing. Things reach a breaking point on Tuesday afternoon in study hall. Blake tries yet again to convince Kerry to give me a second chance only to have him explode, "I just can't do it! Will you please just leave me alone?" After that, even Annie has to admit it's hopeless.

I screwed up my one chance with that special someone I'd dreamed about for so long, and now I'm suffering the consequences. To say I've been an emotional mess is like saying World War II was a minor disagreement.

Thank God I've got *South Pacific* to help take my mind off things.

Thursday night is the dress rehearsal. And it's a nightmare. The guy playing Emile can't remember his lines, the girl playing Nellie is tripping over the easiest moves in what passes for a dance routine, and Blake's singing is so off-key that I've been expecting the windows to shatter any minute.

And that's just on stage.

Off stage, two of the stagehands collide so hard they almost knock each other out, one of the props falls over and nearly kills the girl playing Bloody Mary, and, to cap it all off, the orchestra sounds like this is the first time they've ever even seen the music. During "Some Enchanted Evening," I'm tempted to ask if it might not be better to hire the Sex Pistols.

We take a break after the first act. We don't deserve it, but we sure do need it. Really, the first act has been a disaster of Godzilla proportions.

Mitch, Blake, and I wearily step into the chilly night air. The light flurry that was falling earlier has gone and taken its clouds with it. Shame. A blizzard would have been a great excuse to cancel the show. But no, now that it's finally cold enough for snow to stick, we're treated to a starry sky.

"Damn it!" Blake exclaims. "Why can't I stay on key tonight?"

"Well, it would help if the orchestra could stay in tune," Mitch grumbles. "At the rate the string section's going, by Monday there won't be any cats left around here."

"It's not our fault," counters a female voice, and Marilyn comes walking up to us. "They left the heat off until sometime this evening. That's bad for everything. The temperature affects the tuning, and the humidity's not good for the instruments. And—" she turns to Blake "—it's probably why your poor voice has had it so hard tonight."

"And I felt so bad when your string popped in the middle of Bali-Ha'i," Blake says with all the sympathy of a mourner at a funeral.

"You knew it was me?" she says and tilts her head. Meanwhile, Mitch rolls his eyes and begins a slow retreat.

"I always hear your violin," Blake replies soothingly. "You've got the most sensitive tone in the whole string section."

After three and a half more minutes of the would-be lovebirds chirping compliments back and forth, I'm tempted to sneak off like Mitch did. It's Thanksgiving all over again. They're in their own little world and have completely forgotten I'm even standing here.

And God! The way they dance around the whole concept of liking each other is ridiculous. It's so obvious they're into each other. I just don't understand why they're so afraid of admitting it to themselves.

They should be more honest about how they feel.

A lump suddenly forms in my throat. *Damn it! If I'd been more honest with Kerry from the start, we might still be together. I lost him precisely because I was afraid to be open and honest with him. Well, I'm not going to let that happen to Blake, damn it, not this time.*

"You know," I announce, "you two have so much in common, I'm surprised you aren't dating."

Blake's face pales. I've actually brought up the dreaded "*D*" word around a female—the very one he absolutely adores. Marilyn, on the other hand, smiles like a kid in a candy store. It's all the confirmation I need to know what I'm about to do is for Blake's own good, and that he'll thank me later—that is, if he doesn't have a stroke and die right now.

"Speaking of dates," I barrel on, giving Blake a grin, "have you asked Marilyn if she'll join the gang and us for our end-of-the-semester night on the town like you were planning to?"

Marilyn is all eyes, and every one of them is glued on Blake. She's doing everything but holding up a sign that says, *Go on and just ask me out, stupid!*

"I...uh...would have—"

I turn to Marilyn. "We're hitting The District on the nineteenth—first free night of the break."

"That sounds like so much fun," she says.

"You really think so?" Blake's eyes are searching hers.

"Of course! It sounds like a blast."

The wheels in Blake's head finally make a full rotation. "And you wouldn't mind going out with me—I mean us?"

"Sure, Blake." She latches on to the closest thing she'll ever get to him having the nerve to ask her out. "We could even go out sometime just the two of us, if you'd like."

"Yeah, okay," he says with an air of dreaminess that almost cracks me up.

"Great. So it's a *date* then." I seal the deal before Blake can screw it up. "Blake will call you and arrange to pick you up, and the two of you can meet the rest of us."

One of the violinists pokes his head out the door and calls Marilyn inside.

"Well, got to go." Her eyes are glowing at Blake. "Call me!"

"Yeah, okay," he manages to say as she gives his arm an affectionate squeeze and runs off, practically dancing like a ballerina.

Blake sways like he might pass out. "She's really going out with me!"

This time, I do laugh out loud before leading him to the steps and sitting him down.

"A...a real date," he stammers. "But w...what if she—"

"Shut up, Blake. The girl likes you. You've got nothing to worry about. Trust me."

"A date... " He whispers the word like it's an incantation, and I leave him to bask in the glow of realizing that Marilyn really *is* going out with him. For once, I've got something I can tell others about. I've actually scooped the Chadham High King of Gossip.

The second act is marginally better than the first, and Blake and I are silent as he drives us away from Chadham High. I'm sure his mind is filled with mixed emotions. His fears for the show are nearly outweighed by the miracle that he's really going to go out with Marilyn. A new world is opening up for him, and I couldn't be happier.

Or more jealous.

After turning out my bedside light, I stare into the darkness that is both my room and my life. Like every night since we broke up, I fall asleep to dreams filled with Kerry and a life I threw away.

FRIDAY MORNING. PREMIER Day for the Chadham High production of *South Pacific*. The bus pulls to a stop in front of the school, and I heave a sigh of relief. In a scant thirty-nine and a half hours, at least one of my nightmares will finally be over!

Blake is still all starry-eyed about Marilyn, and it's a good thing because it takes the edge off his opening-night nerves, which otherwise would grow to atomic bomb proportions by this evening. Exactly four seconds after the bus comes to a stop, Marilyn greets him, and he abandons me to spend the time before homeroom with her. The two of them slip off, already sharing the kind of "us" moment Kerry and I so briefly enjoyed.

As I approach Mrs. Beach's room, I can see Kerry at his desk. That he hasn't moved to a different seat in any of our classes is a measure of his determination to put the past—our past—behind him.

The bell rings, and Mrs. Beach takes roll, followed by the usual dull morning announcements, including a reminder about *South Pacific* tonight.

"Good luck on the show," Kerry whispers.

"Thanks, but you're not supposed to wish somebody good luck on opening night."

"Oh, okay. Well, have a rotten show then, I guess."

"I hope you'll come to see it."

"Maybe."

The bell rings, ending our conversation, and we go back to that terrible isolation in which for half the day, I'm separated from him by invisible walls, and for the other, I'm condemned to a bitter exile without him.

When I get home that afternoon, I find a small package waiting for me—a gift I'd ordered for Kerry. I had completely forgotten about it, and it's pointless now, but I take it upstairs and gift wrap it anyway.

It's a dreidel—something used in a game they play during Hanukkah. After finding the card I bought a few weeks ago and signing it, I write Kerry's name on the envelope and ask Mom to use the car. When I get to the Sawyer house, it looks like no one is home, so I leave the box and card on the doorstep. Then I go home to get ready for tonight's performance.

THE PREMIER OF *South Pacific* is a resounding success, but for me it's still a disaster. I so wanted to find Kerry waiting for me after the show that when he isn't there it feels like I've been punched in the stomach. It was crazy to think he'd come, but you know how it is: you cling to hope all the more when the odds are against you. I do my best to be sociable at the official cast party, but all I want is to go home, curl up, and die.

Saturday. The whole day is one long misery of moping and thinking about Kerry until Blake shows up and drags me back for the final performance. Everyone rushes to get into costume, and then we wait for what seems like forever until showtime. Finally, the house lights dim, the orchestra begins playing, and the curtain opens.

The first act seems to pass in the blink of an eye, and we break for intermission. Mitch and Hunter push the backstage door open, and a frigid burst of cold air hits us. While they chat together, I stroll around, killing time and waiting to be called back for act two.

The chill quiet is pierced by the squealing grunt of a laugh. "Randy! What a great show!" Annie runs up and hugs me.

"Yeah, it's fantastic," Mike says, giving me a pat on the back.

Jeremy nods.

They were all here last night, and here they are again. And the way they carry on, you'd think I was the reason the show is so good.

Suddenly, Annie stops talking in mid-sentence. Jeremy and Mike stare behind me. I turn around and freeze.

There he is, as beautiful as ever—Kerry Sawyer.

"Hi," is all he has to say, and that lump that's been threatening to choke me ever since we broke up, grips my throat.

"Hi."

"I got the dreidel. Thank you."

"You're welcome."

"It's a good show," he says after a second.

"Annie Brock!"

Out of nowhere Marilyn appears. "You've *got* to come to my party tonight! You all do. Please, promise me you'll come."

Mike glances at Annie for confirmation. She's already saying yes, while Jeremy nods.

"Great! See ya later," Marilyn says, before bouncing off to interrupt Mitch and Hunter.

We all just stand there. Kerry and I are facing each other, but he's looking down. Annie pulls at a strand of hair. Mike shifts and puts his hands in his jacket pockets.

Jeremy clears his throat loudly.

"It's cold. I'm going in." He turns and marches off to the front of the building with Mike and Annie hurrying after him.

"I'm glad you came."

"Like I said, it's a good show. You're doing a great job."

"Thanks."

Kerry sighs. "Listen, Owen was the first and only guy I was ever with before you. I was in love with him and dreamed about us being together forever. Then just before we moved, I found out he'd been seeing another guy the whole time. And he said it was all my fault and that nobody could ever want to be with me. It just about killed me, and I thought I'd never get over it. But then I came here and met you, and you were so nice, and the more I got to know you, the more I was attracted to you. I fell in love with you, and I thought I could trust you."

I take a breath and swallow. "Kerry, I'm pretty new to all of this. It's only been a couple of months since I even admitted to myself I was gay. The thing with Gene started before I met you. He wanted sex, and I thought it meant he loved me. But he didn't, he just used me. And then I met you and fell in love with you. You've been the only one I've wanted since the first second I laid eyes on you. But I thought you were straight, so I tried to make myself want Mitch, but I didn't, and I never could. You're the only one I ever really wanted."

"What about Jamie Becker?"

For the first time tonight, our eyes meet.

"Kerry, I'm not perfect, and I know I'm not good enough for you. The only reason the thing with Jamie happened in the first place was because I just couldn't believe someone as wonderful as you could really want me—much less love me. And I knew it was a mistake as soon as it happened. I lied about it because I thought if you knew, it would just prove to you how worthless I am. But I should have told you the truth. I should have told you how I felt from the beginning. I'm in love with you, Kerry. I'm in love with you, and I promise I won't ever lie to you again. Please give me another chance to prove it."

"I want to, Randy, I really do. It's just...I'm...afraid."

"I'm afraid too. I don't want to get hurt any more than you do. Look, I've had sex without love, and I never want to be part of something like that again. That's the truth. Can't we put the past behind us?"

"I don't know. Can we?"

"I want to try. Do you?"

"Time, folks!" Mr. Szinhely's voice rings out. "Come on, come on, everybody; we're running late!"

Hunter grabs me by the arm and starts pulling me away. Kerry's still standing there as Mitch throws open the backstage door and pushes me inside.

Chapter 22: Dancing in the Moonlight

IT'S TEN-FOURTEEN. After the pressure of last night's premier, and more than a few ridiculous but forgivable, goof-ups in the second act tonight, *South Pacific* is finally over. Mr. Szinhely and Mr. Harmon are ecstatic; both nights' performances were sold out and received standing ovations.

The curtain calls seem to go on forever. No doubt about it, the audience loved the show. They're as generous with their applause as you could expect, given that everyone involved in the production is somebody's son, daughter, or grandchild. Blake's never looked happier, especially when he receives his own separate standing ovation. It starts in the orchestra section led by Marilyn—much to Mary Beth's annoyance.

When the curtain finally closes for the last time, I bolt for the dressing room to get my makeup off and change. I keep peeking in the mirror hoping to see Kerry walking in behind me. But by the time I'm back in my own clothes, I'm crestfallen. There's been no sign of him.

Blake and I emerge to a nearly empty auditorium. Kerry is nowhere in sight. The closer we get to the lobby the more I want to run, but a push of the door reveals only a few students, a couple of teachers, and the janitor, who looks more than a little impatient to lock up.

We step outside to a chilly cloudless sky and a nearly empty parking lot. My eyes dart this way and that, hoping to see Kerry standing there waiting for me.

He's got to be here. He can't have gone home.

But by the time we get to the car, I have to face it; he's not here. He's decided he doesn't want to chance it with me.

It's really over.

I ask Blake to drop me off at home, but he insists attending the party will do me good. The drive to Marilyn's house is, for me, as mournful as the drive home from a cemetery. City glow fades into a rural darkness punctuated only by stars and a bright lunar crescent.

Blake pulls over to the shoulder and parks behind six other cars. More vehicles crowd the driveway and the other side of the road. The sound of music—the Buzzcocks—blasts from inside the Romer house and roars through the cold air like a low-flying jet.

As we approach the door, "One Step Beyond" begins pounding through the walls, and I wonder if anyone will even hear us ring the bell. But before Blake can reach out his hand, the door swings open and a wave of loud music and warm air nearly knocks us over. Marilyn greets us with a smile that's as dazzling as the country sky above us. She gives me a quick hug before turning her full attention back to Blake. I leave them blushing and chattering to each other about the show.

Some twenty people crowd an otherwise roomy den, and I can see more in the next room. Those who aren't dancing are in dense little groups talking. Almost everyone holds plastic cups, and a few are smoking. The air is thick and acrid.

Once I've worked my way around to the refreshment table, I'm surprised—but not displeased—to find several bottles of alcohol and a cooler that includes nearly as many beers as sodas. Being the responsible teenager that I am, I don't hesitate to make a mature and sensible decision—I'm going to get drunk.

I pop the top on a beer can, take a huge swig, and decide that keeping close to the supply source for my intended intoxication is as good a place as any to hang out. Various members of the cast and crew come and go in search of their own refreshments. I exchange congratulations and polite compliments with them.

Joe Christopher breaks free of a group he's chatting with and comes my way.

"You did good out there tonight," he says in a beery voice.

"Thanks. None of it could have happened without you guys though."

"True," he says with a grin, swaying slightly as he guzzles down another large slug from his bottle, "but us techies love to make other people look good."

Mary Beth sidles up next to him and takes his arm. Having lost the battle for Blake's heart, she must have set her sights on Joe. She could do worse; he's not bad-looking.

"Hey, Joe. Wasn't tonight wonderful?" She sounds like she's already had a couple tonight herself. She smiles seductively at him, her eyes alight with *Americanus femalius* predatory fire.

For the next couple of minutes, she and Joe engage in their own version of a Blake and Marilyn Mutual Admiration Society style dialogue. I'm ready to sneak off and leave them to their alcohol-logged libidos when Blake and Marilyn join us.

The instant Mary Beth sees them, her arm locks Joe in a sidelong embrace, and the fire in her eyes turns murderous. She may have replaced Blake with Joe, but she's still holding a grudge. In fact, right now, she's holding Joe's arm like she's ready to snap it off and beat Marilyn over the head with it.

Now I'm definitely ready to quietly slip away.

On the surface, the conversation is polite, if forced. It's mostly between the two girls, with Blake throwing in a comment every now and then. He's floating on his own little cloud of Marilyn worship. And Joe? I can't tell whether he's happy to have a girl like Mary Beth clinging to him, or just grateful for her support to keep him from falling over. But the funny thing is, he and Blake are totally oblivious to the death rays the two females keep shooting at each other. Neither of them realizes that just below the surface, the subterranean warfare is becoming more fierce by the second. (Or is it "fiercer"? Whatever.)

I look around for an escape route.

And then I see them.

Mitch and Hunter, lost in a romantic moment all their own, are dancing together to a slow number by Heart. Suddenly, the room feels hot and stuffy. I take a gulp of my beer as the full weight of Kerry's absence bears down on me like a mountain. My face feels clammy and my eyes sting. All I want is to get away.

Mary Beth glances at me and notices the look on my face. She follows my gaze until her eyes land on the two dancers just as Hunter reaches up to kiss Mitch. Her face contorts into the very personification of horrified outrage.

"Oh my God! What are they doing?" she exclaims like she's come across two zombies snacking on brain sandwiches. "Ooo! That is so sick! They're faggots! Marilyn, are you just going to stand there and let them do that in your house?"

She's loud and almost spitting out her words. All conversation in the room comes to a stop. Every eye bounces between Mary Beth and the two now very embarrassed boys. A couple of people wear expressions that say they probably share her opinion, but most just look uncomfortable with the awkward scene unfolding before them.

"What's the problem?" Marilyn asks innocently. "They were just dancing."

"Just dancing?" Mary Beth says as Joe untangles his arm from her grasp. "Marilyn, they were kissing!"

"So they were kissing," Blake says. "So what? They weren't doing anything to you."

Joe nods in agreement.

Mary Beth stares at them like she's worried they've been stung by the homo-bug and might start necking with each other any second.

She turns back to Marilyn. "You've got to kick them out. They're boys. Boys aren't supposed to kiss and dance with other boys. It's unnatural."

"Mary Beth," Blake says, "what do you think *South Pacific* was all about?"

"What's that got to do with anything?"

"A lot," Marilyn responds.

The room is dead quiet; someone's taken the record off.

"South Pacific is about prejudice," she continues. "It's about people falling in love and being hated for it because of who they are. You've been going on and on about how great it was when Blake sang "You've Got to be Carefully Taught" but did you ever listen to the words? Did you ever even think about what it's about? It's about how wrong it is to hate someone for something they can't help—like the color of their skin."

"But that's different!"

"Is it?" Marilyn says. "Do you really think people can help who they fall in love with? Or who they're attracted to?"

"The Bible says it's a sin."

"The Bible also says God is no respecter of persons," Blake says.

"So?"

"So if God *is* love, that means love is no respecter of persons either. And Jesus did say to love one another."

"Well, I'm not staying in the same room with sicko fags."

"Well, you don't have to," Marilyn counters with cool politeness.

Mary Beth flushes with rage and begins marching for the door.

"You just wait till people hear about this," she declares. "Those two are sinners. They should know better than to behave like that. It's disgusting and it's a sin."

"Oh, Mary Beth?" Marilyn says. "Before you go, I just want you to know one thing. If you start running your mouth about Mitch and

Hunter to anyone, I'll have a few things to let people know about you. Things I can back up with details and witnesses. Things you won't like people knowing—like a certain incident behind the bleachers with Jake Wilson."

Mary Beth's face is a hydrogen-bomb explosion of rage as she turns on her heels, flings the door open, and slams it to behind her.

"I'm sorry for that everyone," Marilyn says, resuming her role as the consummate hostess. "I hope we can all go back to enjoying ourselves now. But if any of you have a problem with any of the other people here, either don't look at them or feel free to say good night."

The buzz of several conversations erupts all at once, and somebody puts the music back on. Marilyn gives my arm a squeeze and walks over to Mitch and Hunter. Joe finishes off his beer, grabs another one, and goes in search of another girl to hang out with. Blake smiles at me before following after Marilyn. I wander into the kitchen, set my unfinished beer on a counter, and open the back door.

The air has that cleanness only a cold winter night can bring. It's crisp and fragrant with the aroma of a smoking chimney somewhere nearby. The country sky is dotted with millions of stars, and the still darkness is a sharp contrast to the light and noise inside. Out here, even the slightest rustle brought on by an occasional breeze is like the delicate plucking of some mystical harp. In comparison, the sounds inside the house seem harsh, graceless, and rowdy. It only adds to my melancholy feeling.

Then I hear an unmistakable vacuum cleaner laugh rise above the music. Annie, Mike, and Jeremy have arrived.

I guess everybody's here. Everybody but Kerry.

An image of Mitch and Hunter dancing together floats across my mind. *Will there ever be a day when gay people can just go to a club and dance together like a straight couple?*

I sigh and think of Kerry. I see us walking along the boardwalk at the park holding hands, or sitting on a bench kissing. People pass us and smile. An elderly woman says what a nice couple we make, and we blush. It's a dream world where we don't have to hide who we are or how we feel about each other.

A shooting star captures my attention. I watch its trail fade in the night sky.

"Did you make a wish?"

I swing around. Kerry stands before me like a vision, his face aglow with a bashful smile. Even in the soft darkness, his eyes shine in a beautiful display of shifting yellows and greens.

"You... You're here."

"Sorry I didn't get to see you after the show. I needed to run an errand. These are for you." He holds out a small bouquet of flowers. "Before I left the house tonight, I spun the dreidel. It came up gimmel, which means the player wins it all. But after we talked, I realized that the only way I could have everything I want was to have you."

I fall into his arms, crushing the flowers, tears in my eyes. "I thought I'd lost you forever. Oh Kerry, I promise I'll never lie to you again."

"I promise I'll never give you reason to doubt me."

"I love you."

"I love you too."

Inside the house, a bouncy new-wave number gives way to the old King Harvest song "Dancing in the Moonlight." Out here, I kiss the boy I love and thank the heavens for granting my wish. In the darkness, we begin to sway to the music.

Kerry was wrong about one thing though. He's a wonderful dancer.

IT'S A MOONLESS night. The rush-hour traffic has thinned out, and there aren't too many people on the street. The only light comes from streetlamps and shops. It's really cold, and I reflexively wrap my arm around Kerry's and lean in closer.

A voice from a passing car shouts, "Faggots!"

Embarrassed, I let go of his arm and move away a little, not wanting to make us targets. But Kerry looks over and smiles at me.

"I am so in love with you."

"And I love you so much."

We're the first ones to arrive at Tino's Pizza Nook. The restaurant is warm and inviting, and the smell of pizza ignites our appetites. It doesn't take long for Annie and Mike to arrive with Jeremy. Blake and Marilyn aren't far behind them.

Our table is in a section somewhat closed off from the rest of the dining room. With this bit of privacy, we all relax a little and celebrate. Mike's elephant came in first place in the competition, I took second, and Annie and Jeremy tied for third. But the best part is some rich dude actually did buy all four pieces for his office in the Brewster Building downtown. Tonight, the four of us are using our prize money to split the cost of the meal.

The waitress, a woman in her twenties, comes to greet us. On one side of the table, she finds Kerry and me holding hands. Across from us, Annie is in the middle of planting a sloppy kiss on Mike.

The waitress doesn't even blink. If anything, her smile widens.

"Do you need a few more minutes?"

"I think we're ready to order," Blake says, letting go of Marilyn's hand.

After taking our order to the cooks, the waitress returns to distribute glasses and pitchers of soda and iced tea.

"Where's your date tonight, handsome?" she asks when she comes to Jeremy.

"I'm in between at the moment."

She gives him a wink. "If you want, I could send one of our younger girls over. We've got a couple who would really go for a cute one like you."

"Thanks," he replies without batting an eye. "But unless you've got a good-looking guy to send over, it wouldn't work out."

"Oh, okay," she says and smiles. "Tell you what. I'll keep my eyes open, and if a hot young hunk comes in, I'll send him your way."

Jeremy nods as Annie snorts out a fit of laughter, and we all join in.

"Maybe there's hope in this world for you guys yet," Blake says.

And so things go. Unlike our last night out together, not only is the food delicious but the service is perfect. Marilyn fits in well with our gang, and Annie is delighted to have yet one more person at the table to bask in the light of her artistic glow. Everyone is in good spirits, and I'm so happy to be with all my friends.

And to have Kerry.

That morning back in September when I looked in the mirror and discovered I was gay seems like ages ago. So much has happened since then, and I've come to realize a lot of things. Like, I never appreciated how much damage prejudice causes. It makes people hate somebody simply because of who they are. It's cruel, and it can be violent. But even when it's not, it's still wrong. And bullying doesn't always involve being hit; words can be just as hurtful. But even if somebody puts you down, you don't have to accept what they say about you. Being different doesn't mean you're defective, and you don't have to buy into the hateful things people say about you. Believe in yourself, and you'll find friends where you least expect them.

The most important thing I've learned is that finding your special someone is about a lot more than who turns you on physically. It's about finding someone you can share *you* with—who you really are— That's what matters. Falling in love requires time, a lot of work, and above all, honesty. But it's so worth it. It's sort of a spiritual thing, you know? Like two people becoming conjoined at the soul.

Or is it "joined"?

Whatever.

At the end of the evening, we leave a big tip and all say our goodbyes. Kerry and I walk back to the car, this time hand in hand the whole way. Of the few people that pass by, most pretend not to notice, and one person scowls, but another gives us an encouraging smile.

We get to the car and share a passionate kiss before heading home. Tonight, I sit close to Kerry and hold his hand. We don't say much; we don't need to. We've got each other and the certainty of our love. Besides, we've got the rest of the holiday to talk and plan out next semester. I don't know what the New Year will bring, but I'm definitely looking forward to it.

About the Author

Who is Huston Piner?

Huston Piner always wanted to be a writer but realized from an early age that learning to read would have to take precedence. A voracious reader, he loves nothing more than a well-told story, a glass of red, and music playing in the background. His writings focus on ordinary gay teenagers and young adults struggling with their orientation in the face of cultural prejudice and the evolving influence of LGBTQA+ rights on society. He and his partner live in a house ruled by three domineering cats in the mid-Atlantic region.

Email: hustonpiner@comcast.net

Website: www.HustonPiner.com

Facebook: www.facebook.com/Huston-Piner-409082522533786/

Twitter: @HustonPiner

Other books by this author

Seasons of Chadham High Series

My Life as a Myth

Coming Soon from

Breaths We Take

Seasons of Chadham High, Book Three

Excerpt

There are certain days when everything just seems to come together. Then there are those days when things all fly apart. Well, there's also the kind when things begin to change. For me, a sunny day at the start of my junior year was such a day. It began like any other, but before it was over, my life had taken a turn, and soon, everything—from my relationships with friends and family to what I thought I knew about love—would be changed forever.

So there we were, at one of the tables outside the lunchroom, just back from Labor Day weekend. Doris and I were sitting across from Hope and Ted, all of us soaking up the sunshine. The wind was a little gusty, but nobody was complaining. At least it drove the stench off. (Only Chadham High would put the dumpsters right around the corner from the school's one outdoor eating area.)

"Hey Ben, pass the salt."

I cut Ted a reproachful glance. The only shaker was two tables away.

"Why am I always the one who has to get the salt?"

"Don't be such a whiner. It's like social contract theory. You do little things for us, and we all do little things for you."

"Such as...?"

Hope flicked sandy-brown bangs out of her face. "Such as making sure you find the right guy to hook up with."

"The right guy?" I said, depositing the shaker just out of Ted's reach. "What do you mean the right guy?"

"Oh come on, Ben. You know when the right guy comes along we'll all chip in to help you get him."

"Yeah, yeah, like that's ever going to happen. Here. At Chadham High. In this lifetime."

Doris nudged me in the side. "You've just got to be patient."

"Patient? My high school career's already halfway over, and I've got nothing to show for it. 'The right guy.' At this point, I'd be happy to have *any* guy show even a hint of interest in me."

I had barely finished speaking when Grant Framingham shuffled past us. Doris raised a sarcastic eyebrow and snickered, watching me grimace at his weasel-like nose and mousy brown hair.

"Really? *Any* guy?"

"Uh, no. On second thought, I'll wait for the right guy."

"You mean Colby Ryder," Hope said in a playful, mocking tone.

As if on cue, Colby emerged from the lunchroom, that luxurious ebony hair of his floating in the breeze, those dark-chocolate eyes gleaming in the sunlight. My heartbeat quickened, and my skin tingled at the very sight of him. He was so hot you could get burned just by touching him—not that I've had that opportunity, mind you, or am ever likely to.

I watched him pass us, my shoulders slumping, while various fantasy images danced through my head.

"Oh God, what I could do to that boy. Why oh why, couldn't he be gay?"

"Benjie," Doris chirped in a singsong voice. "Whining."

"It's just not fair," I said peevishly. "And I'm *not* a whiner."

They all laughed.

Okay. The truth is, maybe I *did* whine a bit—every now and then. But put yourself in my shoes. Whining just comes with the territory when you're seventeen years old, gay, and devilishly handsome, *and* you've got about as much chance of finding a boyfriend as you do winning the lottery.

My problem was a question of demographics. Chadham High was one of those places where everybody fit into neat little boxes. We had the snotty *I'm Involved in Everything and All the Teachers Love Me* association. Then there was the *I'm a Jock and I'll Punch Your Face if I Want To* crew. We had the obligatory *I'm Smart and You're Not* guild, the *My Religion Says You're Going to Hell* congregation, and any number of the *I'm a (*fill in the demographic group of choice*) and I'm Better Than You* societies. And of course, what self-respecting high school would be complete without the *Dude, Pass that Doobie* tribe? As for the rest, they all fell into the *Please God, Just Let Me Live Long Enough to Get Out of Here* nation. That's the box Ted, Doris, Hope, and I were all in.

But what we *didn't* seem to have at good old Chadham High, at least as far as I'd been able to tell over the past two years, was more than the one lone gay student—me. Now, they say statistically, at least five percent of any given population will be homosexual. That means there should have been about a hundred or so young gay people running around, and therefore, at least a few of them should have been healthy gay males. But if there were any other queers at Chadham High besides me, I'd long since come to the conclusion they were masters of disguise. I mean, sheesh. Talk about keeping a low profile.

I plopped my elbow on the table, my chin cupped in my hand. "Why can't any of the beautiful guys around here be gay?"

"Well," Ted said, "good looks are God's compensation for not giving us straight guys a good sense of fashion."

Doris leaned back in her chair and stared at him with a startled expression.

"Oh Ted, I'm so sorry, and you lost out on *both*."

She burst into a fit of laughter, and Hope and I snickered.

Ted ignored her, stretched for the shaker, and sighed when he had to half stand to reach it. Then he unceremoniously dumped an ungodly large mountain of salt on his food.

Doris scowled.

"Ted, I swear you're going to give yourself a coronary."

He raised a sodium-laden fork to his mouth. "It's the only way I can stand to eat this crap."

She shook her head as Hope picked up the shaker and poured a liberal mound of salt onto her own plate.

"You know, you *could* just get an apple or an orange."

"Even the fruit here stinks," he said through a mouthful of whatever it was he was eating.

He was right. I glanced down at the orange peel lying in my tray. There's sour, and then there's sour, but the sour in that orange had been just plain off.

Doris twiddled a strand of wavy black hair. "Has anybody had any luck finding something for their community service project?"

"I was hoping to do the Y," Hope said, "but they told me all their volunteer openings were already filled weeks ago, and they've got a waiting list a mile long."

"Yeah," Ted said. "I got the same answer when I called the city park service Friday afternoon. Apparently, the school board didn't take into consideration that there are only so many volunteer positions available in Chadham County. Adding juniors and seniors to the number of underclassmen already required to do CS was an idea bound to fail."

"Well," Doris said with a grin, "I've got *my* community service project all set and ready. I talked with my priest, and she said I could help out preparing the Saturday meals-on-wheels plates."

"Hey," Hope said, "do you think I could help out there too?"

"I can ask. I don't know how much help they need though. She told me they've got a pretty large group of people working it. But yeah, I'm sure they'll let you. And even if they don't, if I drive you there Saturday, they've at least got to give you credit for the time you're there with me."

Hope smiled. "Cool. What about you, Ben? Are you having any luck?"

I folded my arms and sighed. "Oh yeah, I'm having great luck—all of it bad. Last week, I went to city hall, and they said no to everything, even the neighborhood beautification program. Apparently, just pulling up weeds around here requires some kind of advanced degree in agriculture. And Saturday, I even checked out the library. Nothing."

"Well," Doris said, "you'd better come up with something. A hundred hours is a lot of time to fill, especially if you've got to limit it to weekends and after school."

"Don't rub it in," Ted said.

Hope patted him on the wrist. "Aw, I'm sure you'll both find something."

I scoffed. "Tell me something, Hope. Your middle name wouldn't be 'Springs eternal' by any chance, would it?

Also Available from NineStar Press

Connect with NineStar Press

www.ninestarpress.com

www.facebook.com/ninestarpress

www.facebook.com/groups/NineStarNiche

www.twitter.com/ninestarpress

www.tumblr.com/blog/ninestarpress

www.ingramcontent.com/pod-product-compliance
Lightning Source LLC
Chambersburg PA
CBHW060549190726
48283CB00003B/931
9781948608039